BEFORE THERE WERE SKELETONS

A MARKETVILLE MYSTERY

LARGE PRINT

JUDY PENZ SHELUK

Superior Shores Press

PRAISE FOR BEFORE THERE WERE SKELETONS

"Calamity (Callie) Barnstable is a character that you know you'd love to meet in real life. Smart, endearingly human, she tackles her latest complex case with energy and determination."—*Maureen Jennings, author of the Murdoch Mysteries.*

"An absorbing tale centered around Calamity Barnstable's investigation into the cold cases of three missing women."—*Brenda Chapman, author of* BLIND DATE

"A daughter just looking for answers about her mother's disappearance sets Callie Barnstable on a journey uncovering curious connections, personal insights, and an engaging mystery." —*Kathleen Costa, KINGS RIVER LIFE MAGAZINE.*

"Calamity's back! And while she investigates the cold-case disappearance of three seemingly-unrelated young women, she grapples with ghosts from her own—and her mother's—past."—*Winona Kent, author of the Jason Davey mystery series*

"A cleverly plotted, intricately woven story."—Allison Dore, host of The Breakdown, Sirius XM

PRAISE FOR THE MARKETVILLE MYSTERIES

Skeletons in the Attic (#1)

"A smartly constructed mystery in the good old-fashioned and highly readable sense." — *Jack Batten, The Toronto Star*

"A thought-provoking, haunting tale of decades-old deception." —*Annette Dashofy, author of the Zoe Chambers mystery series*

Past & Present (#2)

"A tense, emotionally gripping, multifaceted mystery that serves both as a perfect continuation of Callie's life story and as a fine stand-alone read for newcomers." — *Midwest Book Review*

"A well-crafted story that keeps readers engaged as history blends into the present." — *Debra H. Goldstein, author of the Sarah Blair mystery series*

A Fool's Journey (#3)

"A compelling page-turning mystery you won't want to miss." – *Rick Mofina, author of The Lying House*

"A well-crafted mystery with fabulous characters and a series of twists and turns that keep you hooked until the end." — *Mike Martin, author of the Sgt. Windflower mystery series*

PRAISE FOR THE GLASS DOLPHIN MYSTERIES

The Hanged Man's Noose (#1)

"A small town with a dark past, its inhabitants full of secrets, a ruthless developer, and an intrepid reporter with secrets of her own come together to create a can't-put-down-read."—*Vicki Delany, author of the Sherlock Holmes Bookshop mystery series*

A Hole in One (#2)

"A twisty tale chock full of clues and red herrings, antiques and secrets, and relationships that aren't what they seem." —*Jane K. Cleland, author of the Josie Prescott Antiques mysteries and MASTERING PLOT TWISTS*

Where There's A Will (#3)

"An intriguing and unputdownable tale of reality TV, real estate, and long-simmering grudges that will leave cozy mystery fans completely satisfied." —*Lois Winston, author of the Anastasia Pollack Crafting mysteries*

ALSO BY JUDY PENZ SHELUK

NOVELS

GLASS DOLPHIN MYSTERIES

THE HANGED MAN'S NOOSE (#1)

A HOLE IN ONE (#2)

WHERE THERE'S A WILL (#3)

MARKETVILLE MYSTERIES

SKELETONS IN THE ATTIC (#1)

PAST & PRESENT (#2)

A FOOL'S JOURNEY (#3)

BEFORE THERE WERE SKELETONS (#4)

BOX SETS

THE GLASS DOLPHIN MYSTERY SERIES: BOOKS 1 - 3

THE MARKETVILLE MYSTERY SERIES, BOOKS 1 - 3

SHORT STORY COLLECTIONS

THE BEST LAID PLANS: 21 STORIES OF MYSTERY & SUSPENSE (EDITOR)

HEARTBREAKS & HALF-TRUTHS: 22 STORIES OF

Before There Were Skeletons: A Marketville Mystery #4

Edited by Ti Locke

Proofread by to Catherine Bianco

Cover Design by Hunter Martin

Published by Superior Shores Press

ISBN Trade Paperback: 978-1-989495-45-2

ISBN e-book: 978-1-989495-46-9

ISBN Large Print: 978-1-989495-49-0

First Edition: October 2022

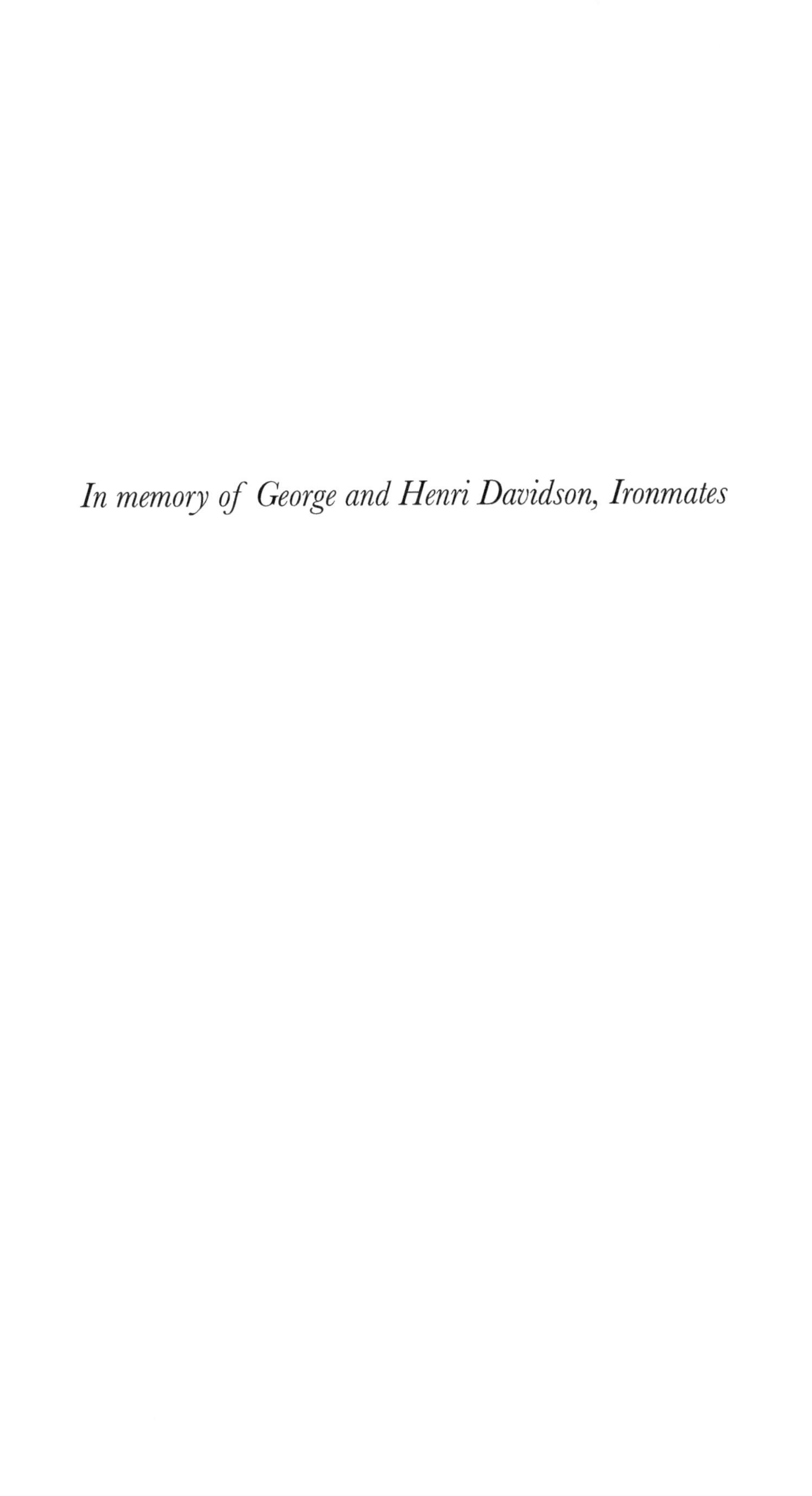

In memory of George and Henri Davidson, Ironmates

1

I'VE READ that our dreams are the mind's way of processing our emotions. I'm not sure if that's true, but for the first time in a very long while, I dreamt of my mother.

I was about five, standing on a footstool in our sunshine-yellow kitchen, my mom baking a white cake and letting me lick the bowl. She was young, early twenties, her long blonde hair pulled back in a ponytail, a few tendrils wisping around her heart-shaped face. I was laughing at something she said when her eyes changed from blue to brown, her hair to short, curly, and iron gray, and I knew I'd been tricked, that the woman I'd been baking with wasn't my mother but my grandmother. And then my grandmother morphed back into my mother again, only this time I was crying, huge, racking sobs, and the cake was sitting on the counter, burned black beyond recognition.

I woke up, my face wet with tears, my body slick with perspiration, and tapped my phone. 5:55. Earlier than I usually got up, but I couldn't imagine trying to fall back asleep. The 5:55 was also disconcerting. I'm not a superstitious person, but it seemed that I was seeing a lot of 5-5-5 lately. I'd noticed it on license plates, house numbers, things I didn't usually pay attention to.

Misty Rivers, a self-proclaimed psychic, would know. She'd helped me at Past & Present Investigations with several cases, most notably the Brandon Colbeck investigation, where her knowledge of tarot had been instrumental in finding the truth. She would know what to make of 5-5-5 and maybe my dream. But Misty had moved to Vancouver Island, happily married to a man she'd met on a blind date. It had been months since we'd texted or emailed, let alone talked.

But that didn't mean I couldn't email her now. I made myself a cup of tea, sat down at my desktop, opened my email, entered *Question for You* in the Subject line, and started typing.

Hey Misty, it's been too long, hope all is well with you and Alan.

I stopped. For the life of me I couldn't remember if his name was spelled Allen, Alan, or

Allan. I backtracked, deleted Alan, entered *your hubby* and then got to the purpose of the message.

I've been seeing the numbers 5-5-5 everywhere. I glance at the clock on the stove, 5:55. Notice the license plate of the car parked in front of me at the mall, ending in 555. Got a flyer for a new all-day breakfast diner at 555 Poplar. Eggstravaganza. Catchy, if you enjoy a good pun, though they'll need good food and better prices to last.
But back to the point. This morning, after waking from a very strange dream about my mother, my grandmother, and a burned cake, I checked my phone and the time was 5:55. I seem to recall you telling me that seeing number sequences had some meaning, but I can't remember what or why. I suppose I could google it, but I don't trust any of those sites. How do I know they're legit? Or that they won't plant spyware or something worse in my computer? It's the kind of thing Ben was always warning me about when I'm researching a case.
Of course, it could all be attributed to coincidence, but…anyway, I'd love your opinion on it. Am I reading too much into this whole 5-5-5 business? Tell me yes and I'll forget any of it ever happened.
Best,
Callie

I read it over, went back and changed *Ben was* to *Ben is*, and not just because it was grammatically correct. I wasn't ready to tell anyone that Ben and I had parted ways and knowing Misty, she'd read between the lines and start asking questions of her own. On a whim, I added a description of my odd burned-cake dream to the email, hit send, slipped into the shower and scrubbed until my skin felt raw. And then I kept on scrubbing.

2

———————

RULE NUMBER ONE. Don't ask a question if you don't want an honest answer.

I asked Ben anyway. "I take it we're still fighting?"

"We'd have to be in a relationship to be fighting."

And there you had it. Ben Benedetti was the man I thought I might have a future with, at least until now. It would appear the Barnstable Valentine's Day curse was alive and well.

At least he didn't kiss me on the forehead on his way out.

I hated when men did that.

VALENTINE'S DAY and I have a long history, none of it happy. My mother disappeared on Valentine's Day and nothing good has happened to me on February 14 since. Abandonment issues? Yeah, pretty obvious why I can't, or maybe won't, stay in a relationship, right? Loser radar, I used to call it, though Ben isn't a loser. We just want different things. Or maybe we want the same things at different times.

Perhaps there's a chance for us yet. The thought gives me hope, and I'm surprised at how much I want to grasp at it. I shook my head to clear it of the notion. The reality is I'm alone in more ways than one, and I have love to thank for it.

I WAS STARING into my cabinets, wondering what to have for breakfast, when my landline rang. I perked up. Clients called the landline and business has been slow. I get robocalls on the line too, but I didn't glance at the call display. I might not have answered if I had.

It was my grandmother, Yvette Osgoode. I hadn't seen her since the summer of 2019, a tension-filled meeting in the Toronto law office of Leith Hampton for the reading of my great-grandmother, Olivia Osgoode's, will. I remembered my grandfather's face, bright as a bowl of borscht, my grandmother, spine ramrod straight, her eyes averted, unable to face his wrath, my pain. Avoidance at its finest.

"Calamity," she said, "It's been too long."

Too long was a matter of opinion. Why was she calling me now?

I'd accepted that neither set of grandparents wanted anything to do with me, their only grandchild. Part of the reason was my late father's stubbornness. He'd never forgiven the Barnstables or the Osgoodes for turning their backs on a pair of teenagers with a baby on the way. It wasn't until after he'd died in an "unfortunate workplace accident" that I discovered I had grandparents who were not only alive, but quite well and thriving.

The discovery hasn't brought us any closer. It seems I have the same stubborn streak as James David Barnstable. Daddy would be proud.

3

—————

I took a deep breath. "Yvette," I said, "to what do I owe the pleasure?"

If my grandmother detected the note of sarcasm in my voice, she chose to ignore it. Yvette was a master when it came to ignoring anyone or anything she deemed remotely unpleasant.

"Your grandfather and I are selling our house in Moore Gate Manor," she said. "Downsizing, the real estate agents call it."

Moore Gate Manor was in the nosebleed rich section of Lakeside, a former resort community bordering Lake Miakoda. It had been steadfastly developing over the past two decades, though the last three years had seen unprecedented growth. If there was a square foot of land remaining that hadn't been built on, or up, there were plans to develop it, and the more density the builder could pack in, the better. The Osgoode McMansion, however, was in a gated enclave featuring manicured gardens, interlocking brick driveways, six-car garages, and the occasional moat. Okay, there weren't any moats. But there would be if Teslas needed further security. I wondered if the inevitable explosion of strip malls, dollar stores, and gridlocked traffic outside the enclave had prompted my grandparents' desire to move.

"Downsizing," I said, instead, and waited for Yvette to elaborate. Not that I wasn't curious about the where, when, and why, but the Barnstable in me was too stubborn to ask.

"Your grandfather felt it was the right time to leave Lakeside."

Her tone told me she wasn't convinced, and I wondered how long they'd argued over the decision. My grandmother had an occasional flash of steely resolve, but Corbin Osgoode was a man used to getting his own way. It was what had made him a millionaire many times over. That and his ruthless disregard for anyone but himself.

"What about Osgoode Construction?" I asked, before I could stop myself.

"We're in the process of selling it as well. Your grandfather and I are still on the green side of eighty, but not by much, and it's not as if we have anyone to leave it to."

I bit back a response. Was Yvette unaware that she'd just dismissed her only grandchild as being unworthy to inherit? I wasn't going to be the one to remind her. And if it was an intentional slight, I wasn't going to let her know just how much it stung. Not that I wanted their money, any more than my parents had. They'd both gone to their graves without giving in. I planned to follow their lead.

"What about the employees?"

I could almost hear Yvette's shrug at the question. "I'm sure they'll find other jobs. And they'll get severance packages."

Spoken like someone who's never had to work a day in her life, never felt the pressure of diminishing prospects and past-due rent. Never had to work at a dead-end call center job at a bank so wealthy, one day's losses wouldn't put a dent in its bottom line. She continued before I had a chance to offer an opinion.

"As you can imagine, there's a lot involved. Legalities and whatnot."

"I'm sure Leith Hampton will take care of the fine print."

A long pause, then, "We're not using Hampton & Associates. Corbin felt it would be better to have a local law firm handle the matter."

Which meant my grandfather still wasn't over the terms of my great-grandmother's will. I felt a perverse sense of satisfaction in knowing that despite his best efforts, Olivia Osgoode's wishes had been respected, and I'd remained the main beneficiary.

I wondered how much money Corbin had squandered in legal fees before conceding he had no case. My guess was more than the estate had been worth, maybe by a wide margin. But Corbin's fight had never been about the money. If every dime had gone to her caretakers at the Cedar County Retirement Residence, or some obscure, and possibly illicit, charity, that he could have accepted. Anyone but the child of the man who'd impregnated his daughter. The fact that my father had raised me on his own after my mother disappeared had done nothing to soften his position.

Which brought me back to my original question. Why, after all this time, was my grandmother calling? And what, if anything, did selling the house in Moore Gate Manor have to do with me?

4

Everyone tells a story in their own way, and, with rare exceptions, no one starts at the beginning. That's the one thing I've learned from working at a call center and running Past & Present Investigations these past five years. I waited. Silence is a powerful tool.

I didn't have to wait long.

"The thing about downsizing," my grandmother said, "is that you're forced to go through every closet and cupboard, and this house has plenty of both. We've been here since 1979, you can imagine the things we've accumulated."

I looked around my pared-down surroundings and bit back a snort. I live and work from a narrow two-story, two-bedroom Victorian on the dodgy end of Edward Street in Marketville's business section. My real estate agent, Poppy Spencer, had assured me that closets of any size in a house with this much character—realtor speak for "old and tiny"—were a bonus. I'd be hard-pressed to spend more than fifteen minutes clearing either one. Even so, I knew all about digging through belongings and dredging up the past. Sixteen Snapdragon Circle, the house I'd inherited from my father, the one that had brought me from Toronto to Marketville, had been filled with my parents' secrets, including an actual skeleton in the attic.

"I can imagine," I said, pushing aside the memories. "Have you hired someone to help you declutter?"

That garnered me a dry chuckle. "You'd think so, wouldn't you, and if Corbin had his way, that's the route we'd be taking. But I can't bring myself to let a stranger go through our things. Besides, I'm finding it quite cathartic, rummaging through the T-shirts and trinkets. I've been making three piles: keep, donate, and trash. That's what all the experts recommend. And I find we have surprisingly little trash. There are so many places to donate these days. I suppose there are so many in need, though your grandfather would call them handouts." She sighed. "I'm not sure that I disagree."

Patience has never been one of my virtues and I was beginning to lose what little I had. "Not everyone is born to a life of privilege," I said, not quite biting back the snark. *And not everyone wants it*, I could have added, but didn't. Yvette knew that as well as anyone. After all, it was her daughter who'd run away from it.

Another dry chuckle, then, "I'm well aware, and I'm not calling to debate you on it."

My last vestige of patience dissipated. "Then why are you calling, Yvette? Because I can't imagine you'd find me trustworthy enough to clean your closets."

"Don't be tiresome, Calamity. I've never once intimated you weren't trustworthy."

"I believe your husband might disagree with you on that one."

"This isn't about your grandfather. It's about your mother."

"What about her?"

"We've kept her bedroom like a bit of a shrine, complete with the frilly mauve bedspread and posters of Andy Gibb and Shaun Cassidy."

Who? A few taps on my cell revealed old photos of young men with feathered hair and toothy smiles. I was born in 1980, my teen crushes were Tom Cruise and the Backstreet Boys, especially Nick Carter, and I had a whole wall of my room dedicated to the Spice Girls and Girl Power.

I couldn't imagine my activist mother in a frilly bedroom. But people change, she was twenty-three and I was six when she disappeared. When I investigated her disappearance thirty years later, I didn't realize how much the truth would hurt me. I'd found myself unequal to acceptance or forgiveness. The truth, it would seem, does not always set you free.

"I'm still not sure how any of this impacts me."

"I'd like you to come here and help me sort through her things. I thought you might find something to give you closure."

I remembered what I'd been told when working on Brandon Colbeck's very cold case. "Closure is a television term that doesn't exist in real life. There are always loose ends and unanswered questions, and both come with heartache. I've already had more than my fair share of heartache."

"Then perhaps there will be a memento or two that you'd like to keep."

A memento or two? I couldn't imagine anything I wanted less.

I found myself telling Yvette I'd think about it.

I was still thinking about it when I decided to check out Eggstravaganza for breakfast. I got dressed and headed out the door.

5

EGGSTRAVAGANZA WAS the sort of restaurant that tried so hard, it was doomed to fail. A dozen types of coffee. Laminated menus the size of movie posters. Cutesy names like Over Eggstra and The Sunny Side of Poplar Street, a dizzying array of omelets and crepes featuring dozens of cheeses, veggie, and meat add-ins, sides ranging from hash browns and home fries to Salsa Verde and deep-fried dills, a dozen kinds of bread. How were they going to keep everything fresh and in stock?

I gave them six months. A year tops. I wished it were otherwise, but you can't please everyone and trying to do so is a recipe for disaster.

I ordered Columbian coffee, a spinach with feta omelet, home fries, and buttered pumpernickel toast. The tired-looking twenty-something waitress wore skinny black jeans, a bright orange t-shirt with matching baseball cap, and an apron embroidered with clucking chickens. No matter how bad the food was, or how slow the service, I promised myself I'd give her a decent tip. No one should have to dress like that for a minimum wage job.

The food and the service were both within the margin of decent, and I took my time eating, in no mad rush to face a day without a client or purpose. My mind drifted to Ben. We'd met during the Colbeck case and hung out at Unwired, his wi-fi free pub where all electronics, including cell phones and tablets, were checked at the door. It had seemed like an odd business for a guy who'd once been a white hat hacker, but he said he wanted nothing to do with his old life. We'd been good for a while. Better than good. But both of us had, in turn, been reluctant to commit to something more permanent. It was ironic, really. When I thought I might be ready for the next step, he hadn't been. And now that he was…

My thoughts wandered to my grandmother, and by association, my mother. The dream with the burned cake. Was it a subliminal message, my subconscious warning me of what was to come? What good could come of me digging through my mother's past—her teenaged past, no less.

And yet, I found myself wanting to do it. Not for a memento, but for some sense of understanding who my mother, Abigail Doris Osgoode, was before I entered her life.

I tabled the thought for another time, gestured for the bill, and did a quick check of my phone for messages, heartened to find a lengthy email from Misty. I could imagine her typing away on her tablet, her fingernails painted midnight blue, silver sparkles on the tips, a tacky French manicure that only she could carry off. I was slipping my phone into my purse when the waitress set the bill on the table, with *"Thank you, come again, Denim"* written underneath the amount due. She was holding a credit/debit machine.

"Denim," I said. "That's an unusual first name."

She smiled, her dark eyes crinkling around the corners. "I've got an older brother. Half-brother, actually. Levi. I guess you could say my mama liked the blues."

"There are worse names," I said, pulling out my wallet. I was doing cash only since I'd run up a credit card debt that needed some knocking down. "I'm Calamity."

The smile broadened. "Calamity. As in Calamity Barnstable? The woman behind Past & Present Investigations?"

"One and the same."

"I thought I recognized you from a photo in the *Marketville Post*. They ran an article about you a while back. I was going to contact you, but I lost my nerve."

An article I'd paid for, I thought, but didn't say, not that the advert had led to plethora of cases. Or any cases, really. If it hadn't been for my inheritance and rehoming lost dogs and cats the past two years, I might have had to reconsider nine-to-five options of employment. The thought made me shudder. "They did indeed. Why did you lose your nerve? Do you have something that needs investigating?"

"No, I was going to ask if you were hiring. I've got some investigative experience." She pulled a pen from behind her ear, picked up the bill, and scribbled something down. "Here's my number. I'm not really cut out to be a waitress, but you do what you've got to do to make ends meet, am I right? Anyway, no pressure."

She darted off to serve another table before I could respond, as if she'd once again lost her nerve. It was just as well because I didn't know what I would have answered. True, most of my team at P&P had disbursed, Misty to Allen/Allan/Alan in British Columbia, and my best friend and former partner, Chantelle Marchand, back to Ottawa for a fresh start with her ex-husband, formerly known as Lance the Loser. Only Shirley Harrington, a retired archives librarian, remained, and she spent as much time in Florida as she did in Marketville.

But I needed a case before I could hire anyone, and those had been few and far between. I tucked the bill inside my wallet and tossed a twenty on the table, more than enough to cover the meal with a too-generous tip. It was only after I got home that I looked at Denim's phone number.

Wouldn't you know it? Her phone number ended in 555.

6

———————

I GRABBED a glass of water and went straight to Misty's email, feeling a bit ridiculous in my eagerness to do so. When I'd moved to Marketville in 2016, I thought Misty was a charlatan. But I'd come to know her and like her, and even if I hadn't entirely bought into her beliefs, or her psychic persona, I'd learned to trust her. I began reading.

> *Hey Callie,*
> *OMG it's so wonderful to hear from you and can*
> *you believe it, I was planning on sending you an*
> *email this week. Great minds. Thanks for asking*
> *about Alan, he's doing well, and we are loving*
> *Beautiful British Columbia.*

I smiled at the Alan, wondering if Misty had

realized I'd forgotten how to spell his name. I made a mental note to remember and read on.

> *We've bought an RV—an RV, can you believe it!—and have been exploring the province. There's so much more to British Columbia than Vancouver, Victoria, and Whistler (though they are all lovely places). If you are ever out this way, you'll always have a place to stay with us. We left Vancouver Island and settled in Kelowna, bought a small condo overlooking Okanagan Lake, and there's a den that doubles as a guest room. But you didn't write looking for an invite! I can almost hear you saying, "C'mon, Misty, get on with it."*

I smiled again, knowing she was right, and I missed her even more. Misty had a conversational way of writing that made you feel as if you were in the room with her and not thousands of miles apart. I kept reading.

> *Okay, so, you asked about seeing repeating number sequences. That could be 1-1-1 or 2-2-2, or any series of numbers, really. In your case it's 5-5-5. In numerology, every number, from our date of birth to our house number, has a unique meaning and holds significance in our everyday lives. And because numbers are everywhere, our spirit guides use them to communicate with us, which is why they are referred to as angel numbers.*

Of course, not everyone believes in spirit guides, and skeptics have been known to call numerology a pseudoscience, a practice or belief that claims to be factual, but is incompatible with scientific method. They will tell you that angel numbers are nonsense, or that your repeated sightings of 5-5-5 are nothing more than coincidence created by confirmation bias. In other words, you are looking for, and therefore noticing, incidents of 5-5-5 in the same way you might be noticing white Honda Civics after buying one. That there were always plenty of white Honda Civics, but you just didn't pay attention because there had been no reason to do so before you owned one.

I sat back, reminded of Past & Present's first official case, the 1956 murder of Anneliese Prei, and how confirmation bias had impacted the investigation. Was that all this was? A white Honda Civic syndrome? Part of me was relieved to think that was it, because the thought of spirit guides and angel numbers was hard to fathom. A bigger part of me wanted something more tangible.

And that was the very definition of confirmation bias. I shook my head and turned my attention back to the email.

Just as in Tarot, there can be many interpretations for the same sequence of numbers. In the case of 5-5-5, however, the most likely message is that significant changes are coming your way. The spirit guides are also asking you to let go of any fear that may be holding you back and to view new opportunities presented as a means towards growth and understanding.

Remember that change is inevitable and that without it our lives would be stagnant. Trust that your spirit guides have only your best interests at heart. Facing change and new opportunities with an open mind will allow you to view things from a different perspective.

You mentioned a dream, though you'd have to take the other aspects of the dream into account. Dreaming about your mother signifies happiness in love or personal affairs, whereas grandparents represent protection and security. Unlike your personal situation, most people are comforted when dreaming about their mother or grandparents. In that, the cake is equally enigmatic. Dreaming of a cake foretells satisfaction in social and business affairs, but in your case the cake was burnt, which may be indicative of another meaning. Quite the paradox.

I hope some of this helps, Callie. I am only a phone call away if you want to talk.
Best,
Misty

I reread the email twice more, with a wry grin at her interpretation of my dream. Then I called my grandmother. I wasn't ready for a family reunion, but we might be able to reach a compromise.

Maybe it *was* time to view things from a different perspective.

7

WE STRUCK A DEAL. My grandmother would de-shrine my mother's room, rid it of posters and clothes long out of style (though who knew, a vintage shop might love them). If, and only if, there was something she felt I should have, then I would come to collect it.

I'd no sooner ended the call when the ringtone on my cell chimed the opening chords to *Small Town* by John Mellencamp, one of my late father's favorite songs. This time I looked at the call display and was pleased to see the name Lucy Daneluk on the screen. Pleased, but more than a little unnerved, because I'd been thinking about the Brandon Colbeck case, and Lucy had been instrumental in helping to solve it. Misty would say my spirit guides were preparing me for what was next.

It was good to hear Lucy's voice again. As the

founder of the Ontario Registry of Missing and Unidentified Adults, Lucy's business entailed compiling a database of Ontario's missing and unidentified adults. But though we liked and respected one another, our connection could best be described as "business friends," and it had been at least two years since we'd last talked. Unlike the call from my grandmother, however, it really had been too long. I said as much.

"Phone rings both ways," she said, laughing.

"It does, indeed," I said, "not that I've had much to report. What about you? Are you still running the Registry?"

"I am, though I'll admit it's wearing me down. There aren't enough happy endings. Lately I've been concentrating on the unidentified, trying to cross reference them to the missing adults in my database and others, like the RCMP's website Canada's Missing."

"Surely the police have the resources to do that?"

"They do, but there's always a new case. An unidentified body discovered in the 1970s isn't going to be a top priority, so I made it mine. I've never heard of an instance where the family of an unidentified person doesn't care what became of their loved one. Which brings me to why I called."

"You're looking for help?"

"Yes, but not with that. I had a young woman

contact me yesterday. She lives in Miakoda Falls, which, I believe, is close to Marketville."

"Forty minutes, give or take. What did this young woman want?"

"Information on a cold case, beyond what was listed on the website. I told her to contact the Cedar Country Police. She's done that, to no avail, and asked if I knew of a good investigator, someone with experience in cold cases. I thought of you immediately."

Could this be a paying gig? "That's very kind of you."

"Kindness has nothing to do with it. You live in the vicinity, and you're good at what you do because you care. It's not just a job to you."

"I appreciate you saying so. What's the young woman's name?"

"All in good time. First, I have to know if you're interested."

"I'd have to read the details before committing, but if you're interested, I'm interested."

"I hoped you would be. I'll text you the case number on the Registry. Read the details. If you're still interested, I can fill you in on the rest. Sound like a plan?"

I wanted to know more. Everything. But I also knew this wasn't going to work that way. "It does. And Lucy?"

"Yes?"

"Thank you."

"You may not thank me after you're read the details of the case."

"Now you've piqued my curiosity. Are they that horrific?"

"Not horrific, no, more like similar to…" Lucy's voice trailed off, then, "Let's talk tomorrow."

She hung up before I could ask her anything else.

8

Lucy's text arrived moments later. I made myself a cup of cinnamon rooibos tea and pulled a pen and new notebook from my considerable stash. This one had a swirl of pinks, blues, and greens, with the word **BELIEVE** embossed in gold on the front cover. Perfect.

That done, I sat down at my computer and went to the Ontario Registry of Missing and Unidentified Adults website.

The basic structure remained the same as I remembered it. Two distinct search sections, one for Unidentified Adults and one for Missing Adults. A third section offered Publications. Beneath the headings was a listing of new and updated cases. As of February 1, three missing person updates had been added, along with a dozen cases dating back to 2003. A footnote advised, "All services provided by the Ontario Registry of Missing and Unidentified Adults are done without cost to families. Cases appearing on the website are approved by family members and/or police prior to posting. Families who contact this Registry for information are not obligated to add their loved one to the website."

I clicked on a recent listing, saddened to find only the sparsest of details. A Black female, 39, last seen in Toronto, the exact location unspecified. Her weight, hair, and eye color were all listed as Unknown. There was a solitary blurred photograph of a dark-skinned woman wearing a blue striped knit toque and a multi-colored sweater or jacket, her eyes downcast, her face in shadow. I assumed the picture had been taken by a street webcam or security video, possibly one from a convenience store, but either way, it wasn't much help. How was it that someone could go missing, and there wasn't a single soul who knew the color of her hair and eyes? I said a silent prayer for the woman and entered the case number Lucy had texted me.

VERONICA CELESTE GOODMAN

SUMMARY
Date of Disappearance: February 14, 1995
Location of Disappearance: Miakoda Falls, Ontario
Age at Disappearance: 18 years

Height (estimate): 5'4"
Weight (estimate): 115 lbs.
Hair Color: Dark blonde
Eye Colour: Blue
Gender: Female
Race: Caucasian
Aliases: None known

DETAILS
Dental Information: Unknown
Medical Information: Unknown
Notable Identifiers: Tattoo of blue dragonfly on left ankle
Complexion: Fair
Build: Slender
Clothing/Jewelry:
Jacket: Brown suede, fringed
Shirt: Red silk
Pants: Black jeans
Footwear: White running shoes, make unknown
Jewelry: Last seen wearing a silver bracelet and heart-shaped pendant

ADDITIONAL INFORMATION
Veronica (known as "Nicki" to her friends and "Roni" to her family) worked as a server at The Miakoda Bar & Grille that was located at the corner of Queen and Water Streets, within a ten-minute walk from her

basement apartment, and a popular spot for teachers and staff at Miakoda High. The restaurant closed at 10 p.m. At approximately 10:10 p.m., the owner noticed Veronica speaking with a dark-haired man of medium height and build outside the bar. He did not recognize the man as a patron and assumed that Veronica had arranged to meet a boyfriend after work.

Veronica was last seen walking towards the parking lot behind the bar, the man beside her. They appeared to be having a friendly conversation. When she did not return home by midnight, her older sister, who had been babysitting Veronica's one-year-old daughter, phoned the police, explaining that Veronica was never home later than 10:30. The following day, another server found a pendant, later identified as Veronica's, in the parking lot. There was no sign of her bracelet.

The police investigation established that Veronica was a devoted single mother. She had signed a new lease on her basement apartment ten days before her disappearance, and there was $850 cash in the apartment. The police concluded that it was unlikely that Veronica's disappearance was voluntary.

Source File: Cedar Country Tri-Community Policing Center, Case CCPD02141995-VCG. Contact: Detective Sheridan Merryfield.

A photograph depicted a pretty, petite blonde with full lips, a pert nose, and oval face, her hair tied back into a ponytail, wearing a black tank top, Toronto Blue Jays baseball cap, and diamond stud earrings. There were no age progressed photos.

I sat back, mulling over what I'd read. Wrote down five things under Veronica Celeste Goodman in my BELIEVE notebook: Disappeared Valentine's Day. Heart-shaped necklace. Bracelet. Daughter. Pregnant at seventeen.

Then I called Lucy Daneluk.

I DIDN'T WASTE time on niceties. "I see the similarities between my mom's disappearance and this case. Pregnant at seventeen. Disappearing on Valentine's Day. The jewelry."

"Precisely," Lucy said.

"The woman who contacted you about this case. How old is she?"

"Twenty-eight."

I did some mental math. She would have been a year old in 1995. "Is she the daughter? The infant left behind on Valentine's Day?"

"Yes. Any other questions?"

"Age progressed photos. There aren't any. Why?" And even as I said it, I knew the answer. "The police don't believe she's alive, do they?"

"I can't speak for what the police may or not believe," Lucy said, in a tone that brooked no argument.

I wasn't sure if I'd hit a nerve or crossed an invisible line. Either way, I wasn't going there. I looked at the notes jotted down in my BELIEVE notebook. *I was ready for this*, I told myself, *and the Valentine's Day/missing mother connection is nothing more than coincidence.*

"I'd like to try to find her," I said. "Or at least, find out what happened to her."

I could almost hear Lucy's smile over the phone. "The client's name is Kathleen Goodman. I'll send you her contact information, tell her you'll be in touch." A pause, then, "But before you do, I have two more missing women you should read about first. The case files I have don't connect them, but they may be related."

She hung up before I could ask her more, my phone pinging thirty seconds later. I poured myself another cup of tea, clicked on the first link, and started reading.

9

———————

THERE'S something about a cold case file that can break the hardest of hearts. It doesn't matter if you've never known the missing person, their friends, or their family, or even if they might be intentionally missing for reasons known only to them. As I read, and reread, the cases of Kelly Anne Acquolina and Wanetta Bulmer, I was once again reminded of one thing: I didn't know how Lucy Daneluk did it, day after day, week after week. I didn't know how I'd done it before. And yet, here I was, ready to delve into the past once again.

KELLY ANNE ACQUOLINA

SUMMARY

Date of Disappearance: January 31, 1995

Location of Disappearance: Miakoda Falls, Ontario
Age at Disappearance: 20 years
Height (estimate): 5'5"
Weight (estimate): 110 lbs.
Hair Color: Light brown, with blonde streaks at time of disappearance
Eye Colour: Blue
Gender: Female
Race: Caucasian
Aliases: Unknown

DETAILS
Dental Information: Unknown
Medical Information: Unknown
Notable Identifiers: Silver stud in the left nostril
Complexion: Fair
Build: Very slender
Clothing/Jewelry:
Jacket: Black hip-length parka with a fur-lined hood
Pants: Blue jeans
Footwear: Black Dr. (Doc) Martens
Ring: Sterling silver ring with heart and crown, worn on middle finger, right hand

ADDITIONAL INFORMATION
Kelly was last seen at approximately 7 p.m. outside of Fiona's Fish & Chips on Bayview

Road in Miakoda Falls, where she had just finished her shift as a waitress. She was approaching a black sedan, possibly a Toyota Corolla, parked at the side of the road. There appeared to be just one person, the driver, inside.

At the time of her disappearance, Kelly was scheduled to testify against an ex-boyfriend who had been charged with assaulting her. Without her testimony, the charges were withdrawn.

The subsequent police investigation could not rule out that Kelly, worried about her upcoming court appearance, may have decided to run away. However, her family believes that if this were true, she would have eventually made contact.

In 2005, Kelly's former high school teacher came forward and reported seeing her at Canada's Wonderland. The sighting was never confirmed.

SOURCE FILE: Cedar Country Tri-Community Policing Center, Case CCPD02011995-KKA. Contact: Detective Sheridan Merryfield.

The photographs of Kelly, one in color, one in black and white, showed an attractive young woman with shoulder-length brown hair, thick brows and lush eyelashes, full lips painted coral pink, and a round face with a soft chin. In the black and white photo, she was seated and wearing a graduation gown, her expression solemn, hands folded demurely on her lap. There was a hint of a smile in the color photo, as if she were harboring a secret. There was no evidence of a nose ring in either, though it was possible the tiny hole couldn't be seen in a grainy photograph.

I studied the picture, assessing. Based on the trace of adolescent acne scarring her skin and the graduation gown, the photos might have been taken a couple of years before she'd been pierced. The ring was too small to make out clearly and the image pixelated when I tried to zoom in, but my gut told me that the ring was important.

I jotted down her name and added four more things in my BELIEVE notebook: Ex-boyfriend. High school. Family. Fiona's Fish & Chips. Silver ring with heart and crown. Nose piercing. Then I clicked the link to the third case.

WANETTA GEORGINA BULMER

SUMMARY
Date of Disappearance: January 17, 1995
Location of Disappearance: Miakoda Falls, Ontario
Age at Disappearance: 20 years
Height (estimate): 5'3"

Weight (estimate): 100 lbs.
Hair Color: Dark brown, platinum blonde streaks at the time of her disappearance
Eye Colour: Brown
Gender: Female
Race:
Aliases: Unknown

DETAILS
Dental Information: Unknown
Medical Information: Unknown
Notable Identifiers: Pierced ears, mole on upper lip
Complexion: Pale to medium
Build: Slim
Clothing/Jewelry:
Jacket: Brown, corduroy, bomber style
Pants: Brown corduroy
Footwear: Brown knee-high leather boots
Jewelry: Silver earrings with feather design

ADDITIONAL INFORMATION
On the morning of her disappearance, Wanetta deposited a paycheck at the TD Bank on the corner of Queen and Victoria. She was scheduled to work the noon-to-nine shift at Blue Goose Grocery but called her boss at approximately 10 a.m. to say that she could not come in as she had an exam that evening. Just before 6 p.m., a teacher saw

her running across the school grounds. Wanetta did not write the exam, and no one saw her enter or leave the school.

Wanetta was reported missing four days after her disappearance when she didn't come to work or class. Her landlady said Wanetta had only recently moved into the boarding house, but that she was a quiet girl who kept to herself. Wanetta's purse had been left behind.

At the time of her disappearance, Wanetta was completing two high school credits at night school, working part-time at the grocery, and volunteering with the elderly at a local retirement home. She had plans to attend college for a degree in nursing. Wanetta appeared to be a newcomer to Miakoda Falls and the Cedar County Police were unable to locate any next-of-kin. However, following their investigation, the police determined that Wanetta's life was stable and that there was no reason to suspect that she had run away.

SOURCE FILE: Cedar Country Tri-Community Policing Center, Case CCPD02381995-KRB. Contact: Detective Sheridan Merryfield.

Once again, there were no age-progressed

pictures, though the photograph of Wanetta appeared to be of professional quality, with the blurred blue background you often saw in studio headshots. She was smiling, her face tilted towards the camera as if saying, "You caught me."

Wanetta was a pretty girl with a delicate face, thin, straight nose, dimpled chin, and brown bangs sweeping her forehead. Her hair fell soft and loose on bare, slightly stooped shoulders, one side tucked behind her ear, revealing a hook-style earring with two etched silver feathers, one small, one long and dangling.

I tried to envision her with platinum blonde streaks. Would they have softened or hardened her appearance, and what would she look like today as a woman in her mid-forties?

I turned the page in my BELIEVE notebook. This time I wrote: Wanetta Georgina Bulmer. Paycheck. Purse. Wallet? ID? Silver feather earrings. Blue Goose Grocery. Retirement home. Professional photo? Family?

Then I began comparing notes.

10

I BECAME proficient with Excel when I logged fraud complaints at the bank's call center. There's something clinical and detached about recording data on a spreadsheet, and both are necessary qualities when delving into cold cases. For this application, I wouldn't need the mathematical aspects of Excel, but as an organizational tool, it was tough to beat.

The grid established, I began filling in the blanks. I could always add additional columns or rows, if necessary, though for the time being I planned to write any observations down in my notebook.

DATE OF DISAPPEARANCE
Veronica: February 14, 1995

Kelly: January 31, 1995
Wanetta: January 17, 1995

DETAILS OF DISAPPEARANCE
Veronica: 10:10 pm., talking to a man outside bar, friendly?
Kelly: 7 p.m., approaching black sedan, Toyota Corolla?
Wanetta: 6 p.m. teacher saw running across school grounds, skipped night school exam.

HEIGHT
Veronica: 5'4"
Kelly: 5'5"
Wanetta: 5'3"

WEIGHT (LBS.)
Veronica: 115
Kelly: 110
Wanetta: 100

BUILD
Veronica: slender
Kelly: very slender
Wanetta: slim

AGE
Veronica: 18
Kelly: 20
Wanetta: 20

HAIR
Veronica: dark blonde, long
Kelly: light brown with blonde streaks, long
Wanetta: dark brown with platinum streaks, long

EYES
Veronica: blue
Kelly: blue
Wanetta: brown

COMPLEXION
Veronica: fair
Kelly: fair
Wanetta: pale to medium

RACE
Veronica: Caucasian
Kelly: Caucasian
Wanetta: blank

JEWELRY
Veronica: silver link bracelet
Kelly: silver stud, left nostril, silver ring with heart
Wanetta: silver feather earrings

EMPLOYER
Veronica: Miakoda Bar & Grille (server)
Kelly: Fiona's Fish & Chips (server)

Wanetta: Blue Goose Grocery (cashier), volunteer, retirement home

OTHER
Veronica: single mom (1-year-old)
Kelly: ex-boyfriend (assault), possible sighting 2005
Wanetta: night school, newcomer to MF, boarding house, family?

I reviewed the list, then started with the Date of Disappearance, googling "Calendar, 1995." That brought up several images. I selected one and noted that all three disappearances had taken place on a Tuesday, exactly two weeks apart, Wanetta, Kelly, then Veronica. They'd all disappeared in the evening.

Height, weight, and build came next. The similarities were striking. True, there was a difference in height from the shortest, Wanetta, to the tallest, Kelly, but two inches wasn't enough to be considered significant, and based on their weight, all three women could be described as petite.

The ages also differed, but not by much. A twenty-year-old can pass for eighteen, and vice versa.

Wanetta stood out, relatively new to Miakoda Falls, no family found. Brown eyes instead of blue, the race left blank. What did that mean? That the police didn't know? Or hadn't taken the time to write it down in the report? I made a note to ask Lucy.

But all three women wore silver jewelry, had long hair, one was blonde, two with blonde highlights. All three would have appeared fair-haired. Their complexions varied, but they were all probably pale in January and February.

If, as Lucy suspected, the cases were connected, and *if* all three women had been abducted, whoever was responsible was attracted to a definite type. Since all three worked with the public, Veronica and Kelly as servers, and Wanetta as a cashier, they may well have known their abductor beforehand, or at least by sight. Even so, there didn't appear to be any direct correlation between the three, though it was too early to rule out the possibility. Unlike Cedar County's burgeoning tri-communities of Lakeside and Lount's Landing, Miakoda Fall's population had decreased since the closure of the mill in 1997. It would still have been a small town, and it was possible the women knew each other, or had at least crossed paths. Had they dated the same man?

Three cases, one potential client. I wasn't sure I could do it alone. But what choice did I have? Misty was traveling in B.C. and Shirley was in Tampa until May. True, she could do online research from there, but the last time we spoke she'd been immersed in her condo community, with daily golf, evening mahjong, and potluck dinners. I couldn't in good conscience drag her away from her well-earned retirement. As for Chantelle, she was in Ottawa, making a new life with Lance.

I called Chantelle anyway. Faint hope is better than none.

"How's Lance?" I asked, omitting "the loser" reference.

"We're good," Chantelle said, and it sounded as if she meant it. "We've started a business researching family trees called 'Genetically Speaking.' So far, it's doing well."

"I'm glad," I said, and I was. I wanted Chantelle to be happy. Wanted her to be happy with Lance.

"How's Ben?" she asked, and I wished she hadn't.

"Not so good. I mean, I'm sure he's good, but us as a couple, not so much."

"Maybe you shouldn't have flirted with that guy at Luke and Emily's wedding. The author of those medieval mysteries? Hudson?"

"Hudson Tanaka, and I wasn't flirting, I was being hospitable. Besides, the wedding was months ago, and Ben couldn't make it so…it's not like he would have seen any flirting, if there was any flirting to be seen."

"So, you're not seeing Hudson Tanaka?"

I sighed. I'd forgotten how obsessed Chantelle was with romance. "No, I'm not seeing Hudson Tanaka. Haven't seen him since the wedding." Which wasn't entirely true, but it wasn't like we'd been on a date, more like a "what had we been thinking and had alcohol been involved" moment at a Marketville diner. There was no chance that Ben would have seen us and even if he had…I let the thought trail off, unwilling to go there.

Chantelle seemed to get it. Or pretended she did.

"So, you're still seeing Ben, it's just that things are a bit rocky?"

"A little more than rocky. We're taking a break, a long story for a different day. Now, can we get to the reason I'm calling?"

"Far be it for me to stop you," she said, and as I told her about Veronica, Kelly, and Wanetta I could imagine her hunched over the phone, charcoal gray eyes serious, as she listened to me blather on. Almost certain she'd say, "I can help you with that, Callie."

She didn't.

"Let me know if you need help building a family tree," she said, instead. Her way of saying she was out, not in.

I hung up, discouraged and devoid of all hope.

And then I thought of Denim. She said she had investigative experience. Not that I could afford to hire her without a client.

I riffled through my wallet, found the receipt with her phone number. But first, I needed to meet Kathleen Goodman.

11

Kathleen was delighted to hear from me, always a good sign, though I've come to learn that nothing is ever guaranteed until both parties sign on the dotted line. We agreed to meet the following morning to sort out the details, which left me the afternoon to tidy up the main floor. I may work from home, but I pride myself on having a professional setup. I've transformed the main level into a combined living/office space, with a six-foot long mission oak table and eight wooden chairs. The table weighed a ton, and it had cost more than I'd wanted to spend, but it had plenty of drawers, allowing it to work as conference table, dining table, and desk. I'd also created a small, but intimate, seating area underneath the kitchen pass-through, with two reproduction mission oak recliners upholstered in an abstract fabric of hunter green, gold, and burgundy. Those I'd found on Craigslist for a song, and the extra-wide wooden arms meant I didn't need end tables, which was just as well, given the lack of space.

I finished putting things in order, dug the receipt out of my wallet from Eggstravaganza, and contemplated my options. The common sense part of me said I should wait until I had a signed contract in hand. But I knew, just as Lucy had known when she'd sent me the links, that I'd be digging into the disappearances of Veronica, Kelly, and Wanetta, even if I had to do it on my own time and on my own dime. Besides, being able to tell Kathleen I had an assistant had to count for something. And Denim, as a server herself, might have insights that I wouldn't.

I made the call.

DENIM PROMISED to come over as soon as her shift ended at three. She arrived at three forty-five, on a day when we were experiencing the sort of deep-freeze cold you got in Marketville in mid-February, where if your eyes water, the tears froze on your cheeks, and your nostrils feel as if they're plugged with ice.

She wore a knee-length red parka with faux-fur lined hood, brown salt-stained Uggs—salt stains unavoidable by this point of the winter—and a

"Raising the Roof" toque. Proceeds from the sale of the toques funded long-term solutions for homelessness in Canada, and I liked that Denim supported the initiative.

I took her jacket and hat and noted that she'd swapped the orange tee for a blue long-sleeved shirt with silky fringes that reached mid-thigh, the words "Free Spirit" written in navy across the front. Her hair, which had been tied back and invisible under her ball cap at the diner, hung loose and full, with dark roots to match her eyes and a mass of bleached blonde curls that spiraled past her shoulders. Only the skinny black jeans remained, a faint reminder of her server self.

If she was nervous, it wasn't evident, another mark in her favor. I needed someone with confidence, someone who could command a room when the occupants didn't want to be commanded. I asked her to take a seat at the table, then offered her tea, coffee, or water. She declined all three and asked if we could get down to the interview. I wasn't sure if she needed to be somewhere else or just wasn't one for small talk, but either way, I respected the request. I wasn't in the market for a new best friend. What I needed was an affordable apprentice, emphasis on the affordable.

I took my seat across from her and got started. "Full name?"

"I go by Denim. You know, like Lizzo or Pink."

She looked at me, assessing, then, "Or like Cher or Madonna."

I suppressed a smile. I was forty-two, soon to be forty-three, probably old enough to be her mother. I expect she thought I'd never heard of Lizzo or Pink. "Be that as it may, *Denim*," I said, emphasizing her name, "if I hire you, you'll want to be paid for your work as an independent contractor, which means I need your last name. Did you bring a CV?"

She nodded and pulled an envelope from her purse, took out a one-page document, smoothed out the folds, and slid it towards me. Denim Hopkins. Graduated from Marketville High six years ago, making her twenty-four or thereabouts. *Definitely old enough to be her mother*, I thought, feeling ancient.

I read her resume. There was a five-year stint at a firm in Toronto, where her duties were listed as "reception, data entry, accounts payable and receivable." There was a four-month gap in employment, followed by her job as a server at Eggstravaganza. I glanced at her address: 555 Poplar, Unit B, Marketville, which meant she was living above the diner. I wondered if the rent was part of her compensation package.

"This morning you mentioned you had investigative experience," I said. "I don't see that mentioned here."

"I do, just not the paying kind."

"What other kind is there?"

"The kind where you search for your deadbeat ex after he takes off like a thief in the night, drains your joint bank account, and lets the rent check bounce."

"Did you find him?"

Denim pursed her lips. "Last I heard he was living in Port Credit off the proceeds of my hard-earned cash, with my former best female friend keeping him company. By the time I'd got there, they were gone. I'm still digging."

"Ahh."

"Yeah, ahh. Don't worry, I get even, not mad."

Something about the way she said it made me believe her. "And you returned to Marketville because?"

"Because living alone in Toronto on a crappy office job salary is impossible. Because Toronto was always too busy for me, everyone going nowhere in a hurry. Because my single mother mom, God rest her soul, wanted me to have a relationship with my stepbrother Levi after she passed, even though he's a judgmental SOB who never had so much as five minutes for me or my ex, though it turns out he *was* right about my ex. But mostly because Levi owns the restaurant and the building that houses Eggstravaganza. He's letting me live there rent free in exchange for four shifts a week. It's like I told you. You do what you've got to do to make ends meet. But I'm seriously not cut out to be a waitress."

I appreciated her honesty. "I thought you were okay. As a waitress, I mean."

"Being capable of doing a job and being cut out for it are two different things."

She was right. I had been good at my call center job. Employee-of-the-Year good. Didn't mean I hadn't hated every minute of it. And there was something about Denim that made me think she was, if not experienced, at least trainable.

"What sort of money are you looking for?"

"I'm not as worried about the money as the training and experience. I want to learn to do what you do. Maybe become a partner down the road."

She had ambition, I had to give her that. "Five dollars an hour over minimum wage, and I can teach you what I know."

"Thank you."

"Don't thank me yet. I'm going to meet with a potential client tomorrow. If she hires me, you've got the gig."

"And if she doesn't?"

"Then you're going to be serving eggs for a little while longer."

12

Kathleen Goodman arrived promptly at ten
a.m. Wednesday morning. The photograph of her
mother on the Registry had been small and taken
when Veronica would have been ten years younger
than the attractive woman standing before me, but
the familial resemblance was strong: a petite blonde
with full lips and inky blue eyes in a delicate, oval
face. Only the nose was different, similar, to be sure,
but narrower overall. She was carrying a small
navy-blue duffel bag with a dragonfly design. I
remembered that Veronica had a blue dragonfly
tattoo on her left ankle and wondered if the bag's
pattern was coincidental.

"I'll be *so* glad when winter is over," she said
shrugging out of her boots, parka, hat, and mittens.

"It's not my favorite season either. I keep
thinking I should take up some sort of activity, like

skiing or snowshoeing, maybe curling, but I haven't gone beyond the thinking about it stage." I smiled. "Calamity Barnstable. I go by Callie."

She returned the smile. "Kathleen Goodman, and I go by Kate."

"Can I get you anything? Coffee, tea, cocoa, water?"

"Coffee would be great. Black, one sugar."

"I'll get a pot on. Grab a chair and if you have anything to show-and-tell in that duffle bag of yours, you may as well get it on the table."

By the time I returned from the kitchen, holding two mugs of coffee, Kate had set a green velvet jewelry box on the table. She was chewing her bottom lip and checking her phone. She put the phone down as soon as I entered.

"Sorry," she said. "I hate it when people check their phones at the table."

"It's okay. I wasn't in the room, and it's not as if we're eating. But I know what you mean. It's one of my pet peeves, too." I placed the coffee in front of her. "Do you have any questions before we get started?

Kate nodded. "Lucy Daneluk told me that you investigate cold cases. My mother disappeared in 1995 and the police have gotten nowhere. How do I know you'll do any better?"

"You don't. And, in all honesty, I might not." I paused for a moment, then, "The reality is, no matter what the outcome is, you're almost certain to be disappointed."

A frown creased Kate's face. "I don't understand."

I know you don't, I thought, *but I do*. "Option A. I spend however many hours you contract for, with nothing to show for it beyond a report detailing where, what, when, and how those billable hours were spent."

"That *would* be disappointing." Said with an eye roll.

I ignored the sarcasm. "Option B. Your mother has dissociative amnesia, the result of a traumatic experience. It's a condition where a person can't remember important information about their life. But dissociative amnesia is rare, affecting only 1 percent of men and 2.6 percent of women in the general population. Of that small percentage, an even smaller percentage will experience what is known as dissociative fugue, where the individual may forget all or most of their personal information, such as their name, personal history, friends, and family. Though memory usually returns, sometimes slowly and sometimes suddenly, in some cases the person is never able to fully recover the lost memories."

"Meaning I might find my mother, but she'd have no recollection of giving birth to me."

I nodded.

"What's Option C?"

"Your mother is dead, though whether that occurred in 1995 or yesterday is another question. That brings us to Option D. Your mother is alive and well and amnesia-free, living somewhere, without the slightest inclination to think about her past or care about your welfare." I gestured to the dragonfly pattern on the duffel bag. "She may not even like dragonflies any longer."

Kate leaned forward. "Or Option E, she's alive and well and knows where I am and how I'm doing and for some reason, can't or won't contact me." She blushed, "OK, that's unrealistic, sounds like the plot of a movie. But why do this for a living, trying to solve cold cases, if the outcomes are as disappointing as you say? Is there never a happy ending?"

I thought about that for a moment. I hadn't seen one, personally, at least not in the fairy tale sort of way, but that didn't mean such a thing didn't exist. "Maybe it's enough to just know the answer. To be able to move forward."

"Past the dragonflies."

"I was going to say skeletons, but yeah. Past the dragonflies."

Kate seemed to consider that, then, "Did you know dragonflies only live seven months?"

"No, I didn't."

"I wonder, sometimes, if my mother knew that.

If she decided to fly away before her time was up." She paused, then, "Can I ask you one more question? Before we get to the nuts and bolts of the contract? Why cold cases?"

"You mean, what's a nice girl like me doing in a job like this?"

"Something like that."

"My mother disappeared when I was six. Left me and my father to fend for ourselves."

"Oh."

"On Valentine's Day."

That netted me another "oh," the similarities between the two cases becoming apparent, and then… "Your mom?"

When I didn't answer right away, she said, "I'm sorry, none of my business, right?"

"You're here for answers, and I'm here to try to get them for you, as long as you understand that there are no guarantees."

"I understand."

"In that case, let's get started."

13

———

WE AGREED to fifty hours at my usual flat rate per hour, plus expenses. Kate e-transferred a fifty percent deposit into my bank account, the remaining half and any expenses incurred due at the twenty-five-hour mark, should the investigation merit continuation. If there wasn't a single lead by the halfway point, it was a fair bet none would be forthcoming. There was also an option to extend the number of hours in mutually agreed upon increments. I used to be somewhat lax with my paperwork and deposit collecting, but I've learned that getting paid after the fact can be almost as difficult as solving a case.

The contract signed, it was time to hear Kate's story. We started with her upbringing.

"I was raised by my Aunt Lindsay," she began. "Lindsay Doucette. She's my mother's sister, fifteen years her senior, and divorced long before I arrived on the scene. Aunt Lindsay said my mom was a menopause baby and a surprise to their parents.

I did some mental calculations. "Your mom was born in 1978, which would mean she'd be forty-four now. So, your aunt would be close to sixty, is that right?"

"Yes, though she looks and acts younger. Runs marathons, passionate about golf, swims like a fish." Kate smiled. "Aunt Lindsay says she owes her youthful good looks and lust for life to the fact she never remarried after she divorced my uncle."

"What does she think about you hiring someone to find your mother?"

Kate's smile faded. "Let's just say she's a reluctant participant."

"Meaning?"

"She's willing to fund some of the investigation if you appear to be making progress. Mostly, she's worried I'll get hurt."

"In other words, she loves you."

"I suppose."

"And your father?"

"No idea who he is. I sent my DNA to Ancestry.ca but there were no close matches. Aunt Lindsay claims not to know. If she does, she isn't saying."

"What about your uncle? Her ex-husband? What's his take on all of this?"

"Never met him."

"What about your grandparents? Are they still alive?"

"That would be another no. But we weren't close. I saw them twice a year, at Christmas and my birthday, though seldom on the exact date, more like when it was convenient for them."

I was once again reminded of the similarities in our lives. Our mothers disappearing on Valentine's Day. Teen pregnancy. And now, a lack of grandparental involvement. There was a story behind the story there, and one that might best be told by Aunt Lindsay. I let it drop.

"Anything else you can tell me? To share?"

"I found a website dedicated to finding Veronica Goodman, really old school, on Angelfire. It's been archived, a screen shot, but nothing more there than I've told you." Kate gestured to the green velvet box. "I have my mother's necklace, the one found in the parking lot behind The Miakoda Bar & Grille. The officer in charge gave it to me in 2015, twenty years after her disappearance." A sad smile. "I took that to mean they had given up all hope of finding her."

I opened the box and removed a silver chain holding a three-dimensional heart-shaped scrollwork pendant, a shiny black stone in the center. I turned it over. A hallmark of 925, indicating it was sterling silver. The chain was a good weight and featured a spring ring closure, made more secure by a safety chain from hook to eye. Even if the spring had opened, the safety chain should have prevented it from falling off Veronica's neck. I was about to mention it when Kate spoke again.

"I googled to find similar necklaces. I found one on Etsy that is close. The listing said it was vintage 1990s, sterling silver, and the stone was onyx." She dug into the dragonfly bag and pulled out a printout of the online listing. It was being offered at $60, though I knew to Kate her mother's necklace was priceless.

"Has either the closure or the chain been repaired?"

Kate shook her head, puzzled. "No, why?"

"The necklace was found in the back parking lot of the restaurant. I'd assumed someone had torn it off in a struggle, but if it's unbroken, it could mean any number of things."

"Such as?"

"She may not have worn it while working, if so, she may have kept the necklace tucked inside her purse or jacket pocket. It could have fallen out during a struggle, though there's no report of finding any other personal belongings. She could also have offered it as a payment for her freedom, though that scenario is unlikely. It's pretty, but of nominal value. I also don't think her abductor, if she was abducted, would have left it lying in plain sight. She could have dropped it deliberately, like leaving a trail of breadcrumbs. In that case, she knew she was in trouble. Or she may have been trying to send a message pointing to the person who gave it to her."

"I thought that it might have been a Valentine's Day gift, or a gift from her lover," Kate said, "but the chain not broken, that never crossed my mind."

"That's why you've hired me. What else have you got?"

Kate riffled through the dragonfly bag again, this time retrieving a photograph housed in an 8" by 10" stained glass frame.

"This is the only thing I inherited from my grandparents, unless you count a small trust fund that kicks in when I'm thirty," she said, sliding it toward me. "She's standing outside Aunt Lindsay's house on Trillium Way. My aunt still lives there."

It was a picture of a very pregnant Veronica standing outside a brown brick bungalow. She was wearing jeans, white running shoes, a turquoise maternity top, and an openwork silver panel bracelet with a vintage vibe. There was no sign of the heart-shaped pendant.

I pointed to Veronica's wrist. "The bracelet mentioned in the missing person report. Is this it?"

Kate nodded. "It was my grandmother's bracelet, so it must be an antique, right? She gave it to my mom when she turned sixteen. It's quite beautiful, with the floral and foliage decoration on the links. The workmanship is so intricate. You should see it under a magnifying glass."

I could imagine Kate doing just that, hour after hour, and knew I'd be doing much the same thing, not that I harbored any hope that it would provide a clue to Veronica's disappearance. I wrote a duplicate receipt for the necklace and photograph and handed the originals to Kate. "I'll return both when the investigation is over."

Kate tucked the receipts inside the duffel, then looked me straight in the eye, her gaze unflinching. "Do you think I'm crazy, trying to find out what happened all these years later? It's not like I've led an unhappy life. Aunt Lindsay has never let me want for a thing. And when I look at what little you have to go on, it seems impossible."

"One, it's not just me. I have an assistant who will help me." *Not true right this minute, but I knew Denim would leap at the chance.* "Two, I don't think you're crazy. And three, I may have more to go on than you think."

"Do tell," she said, and leaned forward, the look of wide-eyed anticipation on Kate's face enough to break my heart.

I just hoped, in trying to help her, that I wouldn't be breaking hers.

14

———————

I HAD PRINTED off the case files of the three missing women from the Ontario Registry of Missing and Unidentified Adults. "You've read the case listing on your mother," I said, "but there are two other cases that may be related." I slid the documents detailing the disappearance of Kelly Anne Acquolina and Wanetta Georgina Bulmer across the table.

Kate's blue eyes stared at me. *The same shade of inky blue as her mother's*, I thought, and realized I needed to distance myself, to think of that woman as Veronica Celeste Goodman. Only then would I be able to view whatever I discovered objectively. I couldn't force the pieces of the puzzle to fit together. They had to fit of their own accord. Period.

"Two other women," she said, without so much as a glance at the paperwork in front of her. "Are you going to look into those cases and invoice me for those as well?"

It had never occurred to me that Kate might suspect me of padding her bill. The thought angered and saddened me. Had someone taken advantage of her before? Was I overreacting? I took a deep breath before responding. There was no need to get into an unnecessary confrontation.

"I won't bill you for any hours that don't impact the investigation of Veronica's disappearance. That said, it would be irresponsible not to do at least some digging into the other two cases since there are a number of similarities. However, if you suspect I'm trying to scam you in some way..." I made a move to take back the papers. Kate put her hand over them, her face flushed, whether with embarrassment or anger, I wasn't sure.

"It's just that Aunt Lindsay has been duped in the past."

One more thing to ask Lindsay Doucette about. In the meantime, I needed to know that Kate was on board. Or off it. What I couldn't deal with was the second-guessing. "I'm sorry if that's what has happened in the past, but if this investigation is going to work, you have to trust me. Do you think you can do that?"

Kate bit her lower lip, then nodded. "Yes."

"Okay then. There are two cases that bear similarities to Veronica's. I'd like you to read them and let me know your first impression of each."

I'd used the reference of Veronica versus "your mother" in the hopes Kate would distance herself enough to review the cases of Kelly and Wanetta without prejudice. If she noticed the distinction, she made no comment. Instead, she took a few minutes to read the reports while I sat by, biding my time.

"I can see why you think they might be related," she said. "Their general appearance. The places they worked. Their disappearances were unexplained, unexpected, around the same time, and in the same small town. What I don't understand is how investigating the disappearances of Kelly Acquolina or Wanetta Bulmer will lead you to my mother."

"I don't know if it will," I admitted. "I just know that I have to explore every avenue."

"Why haven't the police connected the cases?"

"My guess is if they have, they aren't making the information public. Of course, I'll have to check with them first, hope they're in a sharing frame of mind."

Kate shook her head. "I haven't found the officer in charge to be much on sharing."

"Do you remember his name?"

"Detective Sheridan Merryfield. Cedar Country Tri-Community Policing Center, Miakoda Falls. Always kind but not much on providing details."

Detective Sheridan Merryfield, the same contact who was listed in the missing person case listings. I patted Kate's hand. "Maybe that's because he doesn't have any details to share. Let me take it from here."

"Do you think you'll be successful?" Hopeful. Frightened. Skeptical. All of the above.

"I'm going to do my best."

That seemed to placate her, at least for the moment, though I worried that Kate might be a problematic client, one I might regret taking on. As if I were in any position to turn down a client, problematic or not.

I called Denim the minute Kate left the house.

"You've got the gig," I said without preamble. "How soon can you get here?"

15

I WAS MAPPING out a strategy in my head while waiting for Denim to arrive when my landline rang. I almost hoped it was a duct cleaning service or one of those annoying political polls where you could determine who was funding the initiative based on the way the questions were slanted.

No such luck. Yvette's voice came through loud and clear.

"Calamity," she said. "I've cleaned out Abigail's bedroom. It was quite liberating."

"I'm delighted to hear it. I suppose that means you won't be needing me to come by."

"On the contrary. Your mother left her high school yearbooks behind. There are five, though of course your mother was long gone by the time the last one was printed. I doubt Abigail even saw the 1978-79 yearbook. Nonetheless, one makes a commitment to purchase these at the beginning of the year, and I've never been one to shirk a commitment. I thought they might be of interest. Give you an insight of who she was before…" her words trailed off and I could imagine her biting her tongue.

Before I was born, I thought, but didn't say. Because what would be the point of saying it? Unless I wanted to make a point. *Like maybe her daughter would have stayed in school if her parents had supported her, hadn't turned her out for getting pregnant.*

Yvette spoke before I could voice my opinion. "I was hoping you could come by tomorrow morning to collect them. Say around nine?"

The woman knew how to make a request sound like an order. I felt my spine stiffen.

"Tomorrow morning? I'm sorry, but that won't work for me."

"If you're concerned about meeting your grandfather, you needn't be. He has a meeting in Toronto. He'll be catching the early GO train and won't be back until late afternoon."

"It has nothing to do with him," I said, though that was part of it.

"Then I don't see the problem."

You wouldn't. "I've been hired to work on a case. I have a meeting in a few minutes with my assistant to formulate an action plan. Perhaps you could mail the yearbooks or send them by courier."

"I wouldn't dream of entrusting them to the

post office or some random courier. Besides, if you have an assistant, then he or she should be capable of handling things for a couple of hours tomorrow morning."

"Even so, the drive to Lakeside and back will take ninety minutes alone. At the beginning of a case—"

"I understand," Yvette interrupted. "You're busy. That's fine. If you'd rather me come to you, save you some time, I can do that. My driver would welcome the opportunity. In fact, why don't I spare you the commute? I can leave within the hour."

Come here? I shuddered at the thought. At least if I drove to Lakeside, I could manage the timeline. I wouldn't even have to enter the house. Just pick up the yearbooks I didn't want and couldn't possibly need and scurry out of Moore Gate Manor. "It's better if I come there."

"Fine by me."

Of course it was fine by her. She was getting exactly what she asked for in the first place. "It will have to be earlier than nine, say eight-thirty," I said, determined to prove that I was in control.

"In that case, how about eight?" Yvette asked, and I swear I could hear a hint of amusement in her voice.

Sometimes, it's easier to concede. I was going to be getting up at the crack of dawn and I had no one to blame but myself. "I'll see you then."

"I'm looking forward to it. And Calamity?"

"Yes?"

"I'll expect you to stay for breakfast, so don't bother eating beforehand. It's the least I can do, getting you up so early."

She hung up before I could refuse. A woman used to getting her own way. No wonder my mother had been such a disappointment to her. Or perhaps the very reason my mother had found the ultimate way to disappoint.

16

My doorbell chimed moments later and left me no time to process the conversation with Yvette. It was just as well. When it came to my mother, my imagination generally led me to dark places I'd rather not revisit. Don't even get me started on my grandparents.

I'm not an envious person by nature, but inviting Denim inside, taking note of her flushed exuberance, platinum pigtails poking out of her Raising the Roof toque, struck a chord inside me. At what age did pigtails stop looking cute and start looking like a desperate attempt to look young, or worse, thinking you were still young enough to carry off them off? I wasn't sure, but I thought I might be past that best before date, and for a second or two I felt…well…envy. Not for her youth, but her open, eager face, a face that said everything would be alright in the end. I hoped, at least in the case of Veronica Celeste Goodman, that she was right. I also knew that no matter the outcome, there was no guarantee of a happy ending. I was paying Denim —and billing Kate— by the hour, however, which meant getting to the point and getting there fast.

I'd never missed Chantelle, Misty, and Shirley more. We'd been a team, not just employer/employee. Hours, minutes, days, none of it had factored into the work as we divvied up whatever small amount of money was left after expenses at the end of an investigation. I knew that expecting the same level of commitment from Denim wasn't realistic, or even fair, but it didn't mean I couldn't be nostalgic. I shook the feelings off and handed her a pen, a blue spiral-bound notebook, BE A GOAL GETTER embossed in gold on the cover, a black binder, the typed version of the three possibly linked cases inside and recapped my meeting with Kate Goodman. To her credit, Denim didn't interrupt, nor did she begin flipping through the pages as I gave the run-through. There was something reassuring about someone who gave me their undivided attention. Not to suck up, but because they were sincerely interested in what I had to say. At least that was my read on it, though I'll admit to being biased. Who doesn't want to believe they are endlessly fascinating?

After the recap, I asked her to review the case

reports and offer any first impressions. She nodded and began reading. I was encouraged to see her making notes, though I found the frequency with which she checked her cell phone irksome.

"You wanted my first impressions," Denim said, after the better part of an hour had passed. During that time, I'd brought out a plate of oatmeal raisin cookies and made us each a cup of tea, Earl Grey for her, cinnamon rooibos for me. I'd resisted the urge to pace, though it hadn't been easy. Frankly, the whole phone checking thing had ticked me off. This case had to be more important than a text message.

I bit back my annoyance and attempted a reassuring smile. "I would."

Denim smiled back, oblivious to any angst on my part. "I agree that the cases could be linked," she began. "The women all lived and worked in Miakoda Falls, had jobs that would bring them in contact with the public, *and* they were around the same age with physical similarities. More importantly, the dates of disappearance are exactly two weeks apart, always on a Tuesday."

"I wondered if you'd catch that. The Tuesday connection. How'd you figure it out?"

"I googled 1995 calendars on my phone," Denim said, as if the answer should be obvious. "And I wonder why there isn't any sort of cross-reference notation on these files. Will we be contacting the Cedar County Police?"

"*I* will be doing that, but it's a faint hope that whoever the detective in charge is will tell me anything beyond that it's still an ongoing investigation and whatever is on the registry."

"Not like TV then."

"Not even close. What else did you spot?"

"The necklace found behind The Miakoda Bar & Grille, the one that had belonged to Veronica. According to Kate, the chain had not been broken. You offer two possibilities. That it was accidentally dropped, having fallen out of her coat pocket or purse, or left as a clue."

"That's right."

"Isn't it also possible that the necklace was a Valentine's Day gift? Perhaps one that she didn't want to accept? It was a heart, after all."

"Kate wondered that too, but then, how would it have been identified as Veronica's?"

"Maybe whoever found it was the one who gave it to her. Or knew who gave it to her."

I smiled. *This was what brainstorming was all about.* "It's certainly another possibility. Whatever the answer, I need to ask the sister, Lindsay Doucette, about the necklace. How long Veronica had owned it, was it a gift or did she buy it herself, did she wear it every day, or did she only wear it on special occasions."

I saw a look of disappointment cross Denim's face and realized why. "I know you'd like to be there with me, and under normal circumstances I'd agree, but Lindsay will be a reluctant participant at best. The last thing we need is her to feel as if she's being interrogated by two people."

"I hadn't thought of that," Denim said. "I guess I have a lot to learn."

"And you will. Now, what else? Do you agree with the police that this wasn't a voluntary disappearance?"

"Veronica signed a new lease *and* left $850 behind. I checked an online inflation calculator. That's the equivalent of almost $1,450 today. As a single mom working as a waitress, trying to save that much up, plus first and last month's rent, couldn't have been easy. I don't see her walking away from that. Unless…"

"Unless?"

"Unless she came into money, won the lottery, or had a better offer, in which case her disappearance might have been planned in advance. But that's a big leap and even so, I can't believe she'd leave her daughter behind."

I hadn't thought of the lottery/better offer angle. As for leaving her daughter behind, I was firsthand proof that some mothers were capable of doing just that. They might even believe the act was selfless, that leaving was in the best interest of their child. I said as much to Denim, leaving my personal drama out of it, and began tossing out ideas, ranging from fear of putting Kate in some sort of danger if Veronica stayed, to the possibility that Veronica was battling drug or alcohol addiction.

"But surely if there was any hint of addiction, the case file would have mentioned it," Denim said.

I shook my head, recalling a conversation with Lucy Daneluk. "Police do not always publicly reveal whether the missing person had any addiction issues. They might withhold the information at the request of the family, so as not to embarrass the missing person. Others don't want it posted because of the perception that if the missing is seen as an 'addict,' people are less likely to take it seriously. But for our purposes here, let's assume there was no addiction. Where does that leave us?"

Denim considered that for a moment, then, "Veronica wanting to protect Kate, or abduction by person or persons unknown."

In short, we were no further ahead. Unless…

"Another unless," I said. "It's possible that Veronica was putting on an act, tired of being a single teen mom, and planning to bolt, maybe with the help of the man in the black car."

"Who might have been a new boyfriend," Denim said.

"It's also possible that her sister covered for her," I said. "Are there any other avenues you think we should explore?"

"I checked and The Miakoda Bar & Grille no longer exists, or if it does, it doesn't have any social media presence, no website, Facebook page, or

Instagram account. I find that unlikely, though anything is possible. The other option is that it still exists at the same location under a different name, and almost certainly, different ownership. The only way to know for sure is to go to Miakoda Falls and ask around. I could do that under the guise of looking for work as a server." She grinned. "No offense, but I fit that bill better than you do."

"None taken."

"While I'm there, I can check out the town's one and only tattoo parlor. It's only been in business since 2015, so it's doubtful that whoever inked the dragonfly on Veronica's ankle works there, but it's important to follow up every lead, no matter how slim."

I immediately thought of Sam Sanchez, owner of Trust Few Tattoo, and how she'd been instrumental in solving the Brandon Colbeck case. "No need," I said. "I have a friend who owns a tattoo parlor. Let me start with her, see if she's got anything to share."

But I was also thinking of Denim's words: *Follow up every lead, no matter how slim.* A born investigator? Or a woman after my own heart?

17

We decided to go over Kelly Anne Acquolina's missing person report next.

"The good news is there's still a Fiona's Fish & Chips and it's still on Bayview," Denim said, referring to her notes. "The bad news is Fiona, last name Ferguson, sold it to a woman named Gloria Moroziuk in November 2021. Gloria used to own the Sunrise Café in Lount's Landing. She sold it in 2015 to a guy named Nigel Watters, two t's, and moved to Miakoda Falls, where she worked at Fiona's as a short order cook. She returned to Lount's Landing in late 2020 and purchased Sydney's Smoothie Bar from Sydney Van Fraassen, but Gloria couldn't make a go of it. Sydney's the star of that CKHTV series, *Newlywed Wish List*. She's also an Executive Producer on *Barn Stars*."

"How do you know all this?"

"I watch a lot of CKHTV, and I always read the closing credits."

"I meant the restaurant stuff."

"There's a website some restaurant and bar workers use to scope out prospective employers in Cedar County. Not exactly mainstream, more of a dark web kind of thing. Lots of info on there."

It would also explain the frequent checks of her phone, though to get all that information in an hour... Despite my earlier annoyance, I was impressed.

"Right. Do you know who's behind it?"

"Rumor has it it's some old guy who used to be a white hat hacker and now owns a bar on Edward Street."

Ben Benedetti, I thought, and found it funny that Denim thought him old at forty-five.

"Anyway, it doesn't matter who's behind it, does it?" Denim said, platinum pigtails bobbing. "All of the people who were in the restaurant biz in Miakoda Falls in 1995 will need to be interviewed if we can find them. I'd be happy to do it."

I wondered if I should call Ben, ask him if he could dig deeper into the past, but I wasn't sure if I could face the possibility of more rejection.

I took Denim up on her offer.

"I THINK the photograph of Kelly on the Missing Adult website was taken at least a year before her disappearance," Denim said. "She's got acne and her nose doesn't look pierced. I think the first one is a grad photo and the other a yearbook pic."

"I thought the same thing. Not sure how we'd get an old yearbook, though." *Unless it was one of my mother's, ha, ha, and ha.*

"We could ask on social media? Not many people my age are on Facebook, but someone in their forties probably is. Or maybe the high school keeps copies. Maybe Instagram? I don't see it as a TikTok or Twitter kinda thing."

Social media stuff was the sort of work I found tedious, though it would need to be followed up. I felt my shoulders sag at the thought.

"I can follow the social angle up if you'd like," Denim said.

I shot her a grateful smile. "That would be great."

"What about the Claddagh ring? Should we try to follow that up?"

"The Claddagh ring?"

"The ring she's wearing on her right hand. It's a traditional Irish ring where the center heart represents love, the crown stands for loyalty, and two clasped hands symbolize friendship. I snapped a photo of it with my phone."

Denim found the photo, tapped the screen, and

spread her fingers to enlarge it. Why hadn't I thought of that?

"I've seen these before," I said. "I just never put a name to it. I wonder, was it a gift from a friend, or a lover? It's on her right hand, which leads me to think it was a gift from a friend. Then again, it could also have been gift from her ex-boyfriend. Maybe wearing it on her right hand signified that she still cared for him."

"We need to find the ex-boyfriend," Denim said.

If only things were that simple. "That might be a challenge. The charges were dropped when she disappeared. Even if there were any records, surely they would have been expunged by now."

Denim shook her head. "Not necessarily. I had a friend…long story but when he tried to cross the border into the U.S., he discovered the dropped charges were still on his record. Seems that in the case of dropped or dismissed charges, records are not wiped completely clean as if nothing happened, at least not on their own. If you've been charged with a criminal offense like assault, then your fingerprints are shared on the CPIC, the Canadian Police Information Centre system. It's managed by the RCMP."

I knew about CPIC, of course, but I didn't want to make Denim feel foolish. "You said, 'at least not on their own.' What did your friend do?"

"He put in a formal request to have all trace of

his criminal record destroyed. In his case, he was successful, but that doesn't mean Kelly's ex did that."

"Whether he did or didn't is irrelevant. We don't have any legal standing to dig into those records."

I knew I sounded defeatist, even as I said it, but Denim, bless her naïve heart, wasn't about to let it go. "Kelly must have had family, right? Friends? They would know his name."

I nodded, though considering all the long shots and wild theories we've come up with today, finding Kelly's ex today may have been the longest and the wildest. Denim, however, was far from finished.

"What about the possible sighting at Canada's Wonderland by a former high school teacher? Should we not talk to him or her?"

She was full of ideas and enthusiasm, I had to give her that, even if I found it all a bit exhausting. I added finding the ex-boyfriend and teacher to our to-do list.

That left us with one more case. Wanetta Georgina Bulmer, the first of the three women to go missing. Did she hold the key to the other two? And if so, how were we going to connect the missing dots?

18

———

DENIM and I started by reviewing the obvious similarities: age, height, weight, general appearance. I'd also made note of the paycheck, purse, and Blue Goose Grocery, though to me the most important points were the paycheck and the purse. But before I revealed my hand, I wanted to know what Denim thought first, and why.

"Okay," she said, "the case listing states that she had deposited a paycheck the morning she left. But she left her purse in her room. Would she not have put her paycheck in her purse? Which leads me to believe that she may have returned home at some point that day, but her landlord wasn't aware of it."

I'd had the same thoughts. Even so, I wouldn't be doing my job as mentor if I didn't play Devil's advocate now and again. "She could have put the check in her pocket. Only used her purse for going out at night or what-have-you."

"Possible," Denim said, "but I don't buy it. Here's a twenty-year-old woman with a job, taking night school courses to get into nursing school, and volunteering at a retirement home. She's not some flake that stuffs a paycheck in her back pocket and hopes it won't pop out the first time she sits down. She's the kind of person who carries a purse for day-to-day stuff."

"Maybe she had more than one purse?"

"Oh. Yeah. Maybe. Or she left her purse behind but not her wallet. There's no mention of a wallet, which means she may have had her ID. Besides, I checked on my phone and in 1995 the wallet purse wasn't even a thing. So…" She let the sentence dangle, waggling her eyebrows.

I really needed to get better at googling on my phone. "What about the Blue Goose Grocery? Did you check to see if it was still open? And the retirement homes?"

"Yup on the Blue Goose. Even has the same owner. Nathaniel Spracklen. There were two retirement homes operating in 1995. Both are still in operation, though one has been converted to a hospice."

I sat back, surprised, and dare I admit it, more than a little impressed by this bleached blonde, pigtailed, dynamo. Even so, I owed it to her to be honest.

"Even if we find out the name of the retirement home, the odds of anyone who is still working there twenty-six years later are slim, and there's no chance they would have kept volunteer records going that far back, even if they were willing to share them."

"What are you saying? We just give up?"

"Of course not. I'd like you to go to Miakoda Falls, check out the Blue Goose Grocery, Fiona's Fish & Chips, and whatever might have replaced the Miakoda Bar & Grille. It's a long shot but sometimes those pay off."

"I'd love to but…" Denim shifted in her seat, "there's just one problem."

A problem this early on. That wasn't a good sign. I attempted a sympathetic look.

"What's that?"

"I have one more shift at Eggstravaganza. Tomorrow. I can't start until the Friday."

"Just one more?"

Denim nodded. "Yeah. I told Levi I had a real job beginning the day after next. I do, don't I?" Said with a look of, what was that expression on her face? Pleading? Hope? Desperation? All of the above, but more importantly, an overarching layer of pride. I realized for the first time just how much this job meant to her, and it solidified my decision even more.

I didn't answer her right away. Instead, I went to the kitchen, returning with a bottle of ice-cold San

Pellegrino and two champagne flutes. "It might be too early in the day for alcohol, but there are some rituals that need to be done right, even if it is only with sparkling water."

Denim's eyes brimmed with unshed tears as we clinked glasses, her toast heartfelt and impassioned.

"To finding the truth."

I couldn't have said it better myself.

19

I woke up to find that it had snowed during the night, more of a dusting than a dumping, but enough to make the roads greasy. I decided to take the slower, more familiar route to Lakeside instead of the new highway extension.

It was quickly apparent that the drive from Marketville to Lakeside had changed substantially since the first time I'd made the trek with Chantelle in 2016. Back then I hadn't yet met my maternal grandparents, and the pie-eyed optimist in me had envisioned a "happily ever after" reunion. Maybe not that day, but one day, perhaps, in the future.

It wasn't to be, any more than the familiarity of the route, now a thing of the past. Row upon row of super-skinny three-story townhomes flourished where fields of corn and bales of hay had once claimed the land.

The first evidence of this was Vito's Fine Foods. What was once a neighborhood grocer, specializing in farm-to-table produce, grain-fed poultry, and locally sourced baked goods, had morphed into a sprawling superstore that probably put profits before people.

I knew that I was being unfair, too judgmental, that it was possible those same local touches would still be there, albeit with an enhanced selection. *I would check it out on the way back*, I promised myself, remembering the perfection of Vito's Own brand of spicy-sweet tomato sauce, the takeout salad of mixed greens, cherry tomatoes, and bocconcini drizzled with store-made balsamic vinaigrette.

But this trip wasn't about a visit to Vito's, it was about collecting five yearbooks that had once belonged to my mother, choking down breakfast with my grandmother, and getting out of Moore Gate Manor unscathed, though I wasn't optimistic about the latter. Yvette Osgoode had a way of getting under my skin the way no one else could. Well, except for my grandfather, but then again, he was in a class by himself.

THE "WELCOME TO LAKESIDE" sign featured a stylized green pine over cerulean blue water. The sign hadn't changed since the last time I was there, nor had Winding Lake Drive, which was still a narrow, two-lane road, likely because there was no room to widen it, the now-frozen lake on one side and homes overlooking the water on the other. The homes themselves were a different story. There was little evidence of the small, seasonal cottages that had once lined the street, most replaced by multi-level mansions with floor-to-ceiling windows and glass block towers, the sort of house you might find on the cover of *Architectural Digest*. I grimaced, then grinned at the over-the-top opulence. Compared to these places, Moore Gate Manor could almost be considered the "poor side of town." No wonder Corbin thought it was time to move. He never could stand to be one-upped.

I drove past Ben's Convenience and couldn't help but notice that it, too, had been the beneficiary of a facelift. Gone was the asphalt shingled roof and white clapboard exterior, replaced with cedar shakes and dove gray board-and-batten siding trimmed in ivory. I checked the time. Twelve minutes ahead of schedule. I pulled into a parking spot adjacent to the store, turned off the car, and hopped out, curious to see if the interior had been equally spruced up.

I'd been expecting to find Ben behind the counter. A grizzled man with bushy white hair, a permanent suntan, and a perpetual scowl, each summer he'd be out front selling overpriced bottles of water and grilling hot dogs, sausages, and burgers—beef or veggie—the price of each going up or down, depending on the temperature and the number of tourists and triathletes. Except Ben wasn't there. In his place was an attractive, brown-skinned woman with an athletic build, jet black eyes and hair, and an engaging smile. I pegged her to be mid-thirties, though she could have been a couple of years on either side. My eyes scanned the space. Beyond the packs of cigarettes hidden behind the counter in white-paneled cupboards, there remained the usual convenience store basics: tinned food, bread, milk, and processed cheese slices, along with soda, chips, chocolate, chewing gum, candy and, catering to the year-round running crowd and avid three- (and occasionally four-) season cyclists that frequented Winding Lake Drive, an impressive variety of energy bars and sports drinks. Even so, everything, from the polished wooden shelves to the wall of built-in freezers and glass-paneled refrigeration units, had been elevated to the next level, as though any trace of Ben's decades in this store required complete and utter obliteration. Only the flooring, a thick, industrial, speckled rubber compound—the kind you might find inside a gym or hockey arena—seemed vaguely reminiscent of the man from the past, though even as I thought it, I recalled nondescript linoleum, stained, scuffed, and scarred by years of dropped food, cycling shoes, and snowmobiler's boots.

Which meant that there was nothing left in Ben's Convenience that bore a trace of Ben, and while I'd never really known him, or, truth be told, even particularly liked him, the realization made me a little bit sad.

"We get a lot of cyclists in here during the season," the woman said, catching my look and pointing to the floor. "The cleats on their shoes are murder on most floors."

I knew where she was coming from. I'd dated a guy one summer, a triathlete with a fantastic body but not much else to offer. We'd spent more than a few days at that beach while he faithfully practiced open water swimming and I admired his form. Unfortunately, I was far from his only admirer, and the only thing he was faithful to was training.

"I used to come here a few years back," I said. "Dated a guy training for Ironman Canada. I remember the way the old linoleum looked." *The way the old store looked.*

The woman smiled. "Ah, that would have been when Ben owned the place. I'm Manjit. I bought it from him when he retired three years ago, invested in some much-needed renovations. Hence the new name. Lakeside Convenience. Not exactly inspired but it gets the point across."

"I didn't even notice the new name," I said, feeling foolish. "I was on my way to…to an appointment and I thought I'd pop in and say hello to Ben." I picked up a pack of spearmint gum and a local newspaper and slid them across the counter past a glass display case filled with scratch-and-win lottery tickets. "I'll take these, and a Crossword scratch ticket. The top one will be fine."

Manjit opened the case, pulled out the ticket, and rang up my purchases, studying me with unabashed curiosity. "You must be Yvette Osgoode's granddaughter. Calamity, isn't it?"

My surprise must have been evident because she proceeded to enlighten me.

"You look just like her. Younger, of course, and her eyes are much darker than yours. I understand you investigate cold cases. That must be exciting."

I wasn't sure from her tone if she was being sincere or sarcastic. Either way, I felt as if I'd been beamed down from another planet. "It has its moments," I said, working hard to keep my expression neutral. I glanced around the store. It was nicer now than when it was Ben's, but I couldn't imagine Yvette shopping here and chatting about her granddaughter's choice of employment.

"I'm the Chair of the Lakeside Cares Committee," Manjit said, sensing my confusion. "We organize fundraising initiatives for several local charities and non-profits. Unlike some of the other society women who volunteer at LCC because it looks good, Yvette is a tireless worker, and we are lucky to have her. Not only does she come up with good ideas, she follows them to fruition. From what I understand, your mother was the same, started the Marketville Food Bank back in the eighties."

Had Yvette been proud? Or had she tried to

take ownership of her daughter's accomplishments? I didn't know. I also didn't know how my name had come up. As much as I wanted to ask, I couldn't bring myself to say the words, though I wasn't sure why. Instead, I said, "Ah, of course," as if the answer was evident, and scurried out the door.

"Good luck on the scratch ticket," Manjit called after me. "Those Crossword ones are my favorite."

20

THE STOP at Lakeside Convenience had cost me a few minutes. Even so, I found myself driving below the posted speed limit as I turned into Moore Gate Estates. There wasn't a locked gate, per se, but it felt as if there should be, as though you weren't welcome unless you belonged, preferably from birth.

The main thoroughfare was Moore Gate Manor, which wound its way through a maze of McMansions that had once dwarfed anything on Winding Lake Drive.

The Osgoode home was located at the end of a cul-de-sac with a lakefront view. Number 127 was by far the largest on the block and reminded me of a medieval fairy tale castle, with fieldstone façade, turrets, and two-story towers. I wondered, not for the first time, if my teenaged mother had felt trapped inside those walls, a modern-day Rapunzel, if Jimmy Barnstable had seemed like the prince who would rescue her. I pulled into the driveway—heated from the looks of its snow-free surface—and sat there.

You can do this. I took a deep breath, resisted the urge to leave, and got out of the car.

The front door opened before I had an opportunity to knock.

"You're five minutes late," my grandmother said, looking at her watch.

"You've painted the door," I replied, refusing to be drawn in. "As I recall it used to be black."

"Our realtor felt that Musical Merlot—that's the name of the color—would look richer with the brass hardware and gray brick." Yvette favored me with a thin-lipped smile. "You're observant. I suppose that comes in handy in your profession."

She said "your profession" as though in quotation marks, the barely concealed contempt all too evident. I imagined the stories she'd told Manjit and the rest of the Lakeshore Cares volunteers and managed a thin-lipped smile of my own. "I think under the circumstances we can skip the pretense of having breakfast together and go straight to the purpose of my visit."

"If you insist," she said, lips pursed, though I couldn't help but notice the relief wash over her face. It would seem she'd had second thoughts since the invite. Why, then, did she feel compelled to hand over five yearbooks once belonging to my mother? I wasn't buying her story about giving me closure.

"I'll wait on the porch while you get them," I said, the idea of shivering in the cold preferable to going inside where the atmosphere would sure to be frostier.

"Don't be ridiculous. I wanted you to see your mother's room. Besides, it's freezing outside, and we don't need people gawking and talking because you're standing on the porch."

I suspected Yvette was far more concerned about neighborhood gossip than my need to see my mother's room or my wellbeing, but I entered the house, relinquished my coat and removed my boots.

I'd never been inside before. The first thing that struck me was the marble-tiled foyer, the color of clotted cream, streaked with ribbons of platinum. It occurred to me that I could fit the entire main floor of my house in the foyer. There was a library to the left, the walls stacked floor-to-ceiling with leather-bound books, a small ladder for access to the upper shelves discreetly tucked away to one side. I wondered if anyone had ever read the books, or if they were merely for show. A tan suede recliner had been placed in the corner next to the bay window, a poinsettia-patterned stained glass torchiere lamp behind it. Almost certainly Tiffany, I decided, confident in my decision. No knockoffs for the Osgoodes.

To my right was a brightly lit gourmet kitchen with gleaming granite countertops and cabinetry that mirrored the marble tiled foyer, state-of-the-art stainless-steel appliances, and dark cherry wood floors, complemented by pearl gray walls. A large, granite-topped island provided barstool seating and another food prep area, complete with sink and storage. I was almost sorry that I wasn't staying for breakfast. The opportunity to dine in such luxurious digs rarely came my way.

"Follow me," Yvette said, leading the way up a Scarlett O'Hara staircase to the second floor, then past a spacious landing to the end of a thickly carpeted hallway. "Abigail's quarters are…were in the tower. 'A room fit for a princess,' Corbin had said when we bought the house." Yvette's expression darkened as she opened the door. "I'm not sure Abigail felt the same way."

The bedroom had been stripped bare of furniture and posters, the lilac-hued walls patched and ready to be painted. A bank of floor-to-ceiling windows offered a view of Lake Miakoda, which was breathtaking, even on a dreary winter day.

The walk-in closet doors were open, revealing a dozen black silk padded hangers, though the clothing had been removed. It was as if Abigail Osgoode had never lived here.

All except for a single cardboard box, which I assumed contained the yearbooks.

"The stager is going to furnish the room once it's been painted," Yvette said.

"Have you looked through them?" I pointed to the box.

"No. What would be the point?"

"I don't know. What would be the point of me looking through them?"

Yvette gave me a sad smile. "Why do you think?"

"I've already told you I don't believe in closure."

"I wasn't talking about closure. I was talking about acceptance."

Acceptance. That was rich, coming from her. "What about Corbin?"

"He doesn't know Abigail left them behind. I'm not sure he would care, to be honest. As far as he was concerned, the day Abigail Osgoode left this house, she ceased to exist."

I nodded, her callous candor rendering me speechless.

"He might have been able to come to terms with her pregnancy. But marrying your father at City Hall, not telling us, giving up her dreams of university, he couldn't forgive that."

Her dreams or his? I shrugged and picked up the box.

We made our way out of the room and back down the spiral staircase to the foyer.

"What about you?" my grandmother asked as I put on my boots and coat.

"What about me?"

"Are you going to look through them?"

I stood up and looked at her for a long minute, then shook my head. "I don't know."

21

———————

I HEADED BACK to Marketville and skipped the planned stop at Vito's Fine Foods, even though Vito's Own Sauce and bocconcini salad beckoned. All I wanted to do was get home, where a hot bath and a cold chardonnay awaited me. Granted, not quite so early in the day, but later, absolutely. In the meantime, I had some serious thinking to do, and it had nothing to do with my mother's yearbooks stashed inside my trunk, the past waiting. I'd been hired by Kate Goodman to find out what happened to her mother. That had to be my top priority.

I'D BEEN fifteen when Veronica, Kelly, and Wanetta had disappeared, living in Toronto and oblivious to anything happening outside of my social circle.

News from a small town two hours north of the city would have been off my radar, though I vaguely recalled a span of a few weeks that winter when my father had insisted on picking me up after my evening shifts at Sunnydale Food Market. With true adolescent absorption, I hadn't thought of *why* he was suddenly willing to do so, only that it would save me from waiting for the bus or trudging through the snow on the three-mile walk home. It hadn't been long before I'd quit that job for greener pastures: sales associate at a trendy clothing store in the Scarborough Town Center, weekends only, with the perk of a staff discount on any purchases.

There were bound to be newspaper reports of all three disappearances, reports I would look for in local library archives, but first-hand knowledge was better. If I was lucky, Arabella Carpenter would be able to help me. We'd been friends since our high school days in Toronto, but she'd been living and working in Lount's Landing for the better part of the last fifteen years, the last seven as the owner of the Glass Dolphin antiques shop. A lot of her clientele lived in Miakoda Falls and she might know Gloria Moroziuk, and by extension, Fiona Ferguson.

Arabella answered on the first ring. "Glass Dolphin Antiques. Our old is your gold."

The slogan was new, and I wasn't sure it worked, but far be it for me to criticize. "It's Callie," I said.

"Callie, where have you been? I haven't seen you since Emily's baby shower and Glenis is almost a year old."

"Yeah, well. You know. Covid."

"Don't remind me." Arabella sighed. "It's been brutal on small business, and let's face it, antiques are far from essential. For a while there, we were closed more than we were open. On the upside, Emily had an extended maternity leave, and thanks to her efforts we have a great website, and Caitie has been terrific about managing it. Even so, online shopping and curbside delivery are a pale substitute for in-store browsing and impulse buys, and while folks are starting to come back, sales aren't where they used to be. But I can't complain. Lots of others have had it worse."

"Speaking of for better or worse, how are you and Levon? I'm still waiting for my invite to your wedding."

"We set the date twice but…"

"Yeah, I know. Covid."

"Yeah. And then we decided that just knowing we were both willing to commit was enough, at least for now. Levon sold his house, I got out of my rental, and we bought a century home within walking distance of the shop, in the same neighborhood as Luke and Emily. It needs a ton of renovations, and it's been designated as a historic site, which complicates the process, but we're enjoying the challenge."

"It all sounds great," I said, and meant it. Arabella and Levon had divorced years ago, but anyone who knew them also knew they were soulmates. The only question in anyone's mind had been when they were going to get back together. It had taken a few false starts and Luke and Emily's wedding for it to happen.

"Enough about me," Arabella said, interrupting my thoughts. "Are you still with Ben?"

"Ben and I are taking a break."

"I'm sorry, Callie."

"No need."

"What about Past & Present? Are you still running around with a fingerprint kit and magnifying glass?"

I smiled at the image, grateful that Arabella had dropped the inquiry into Ben. I'm not sure I would have had the answers. "It's not quite like that, but it is the reason for my call. I have a new case."

"How did I know this wasn't just a social call?" Arabella said, laughing. "How can I help?"

I filled her in on Kate Goodman's search for her mother, and how that led me to two other young women who went missing in Miakoda Falls around the same time and briefly summarized the cases. "The profiles are on the Ontario Registry of Missing and Unidentified Adults. They don't specifically link the cases, but Lucy Daneluk suspects they might be related. I think so, too, and I expect the police do as well."

"Do you have a name or names of the detectives in charge?"

"I do and it's the same on all three. Detective Sheridan Merryfield, Cedar Country Tri-Community Policing Center. Do you know him?"

A long pause, then, "We've met on a few occasions."

"What's he like?"

"Handsome. Intelligent. Hard working. Fair. But…"

"But?"

"He's not big on amateur sleuths."

The last comment rankled. "I'm an investigator with my own company and a winning track record. I'm not playing Jessica Fletcher here."

"I'm not convinced Merryfield will see the distinction. Even if he does, it would be best if you didn't mention that you know me or Emily. He's still getting over our involvement in the hole in one case, even if it was four years ago."

"Thanks for the heads up. Does that mean you won't help me?"

"Not won't. I'm just not sure *how* I can help. In the past, when I've been able to assist, there's been an antiques angle. I'm not getting that here."

"Veronica's necklace has a vintage vibe, though I'm pretty sure it was new in 1995, made to look retro. But that's not the reason I called you. I know you have clients in Miakoda Falls and thought you might know someone. Or even someone who knows someone. For example, Fiona's Fish & Chips was owned by a Fiona Ferguson at the time, but it's since been purchased by Gloria Moroziuk, who I understand owned a couple of food establishments in Lount's Landing."

"She did, and I do know Gloria, but last I heard, she'd moved out of province. We were never close, and we definitely haven't kept in touch, so I'm no help there."

"That's okay. I've hired an assistant, a young woman named Denim Hopkins. She's keen to start work, and Gloria is on her list. I suppose I'll start with Merryfield and see where that takes me."

"Hold on a ticky. I may not be any help when it comes to Gloria, but I can think of three people who might be of assistance, emphasis on the might."

I felt a small surge of optimism. "I can live with might. Who are they?"

"The first one would be Poppy Spencer. I don't think she was in real estate that far back, but she knows a lot of people."

"I can't believe I didn't think of her, but you're right. I'll give her a call. Who else?"

"Betsy Ehrlich. She's been living in Lount's Landing for ages, but she was born and raised in Miakoda Falls. She's around the same age as your three missing women."

I'd enjoyed more than a few meals at Betsy's

pub, The Hanged Man's Noose, and I liked her as a person. "How have things been for Betsy?"

"She survived, barely. She set up an outdoor patio, which was popular when the weather cooperated, and it helped that the government allowed the sale of alcohol with take-out and delivery, but it hasn't been easy. Fortunately, now that things have opened back up, people seem keen to go back for a pint and a meal. I'll give her your number."

"Thank you. Not to sound ungrateful, but who's the third person?"

"That would be Levon."

"Levon? I know he's lived in Lount's Landing forever, but I thought he grew up in Toronto. In 1995, he would have been, what? Sixteen? Surely he was still in Toronto at the time."

"Seventeen, and yes, he grew up in the city. But in 1995, he also spent a few months in Miakoda Falls. He moved to Lount's Landing when he was eighteen." Arabella paused. "I've written down the names of all three women. It's Levon's story to tell, but I'm sure he'd be willing to share it with you if he knows anything that might help. I'll talk to him tonight, have him get back to you one way or another."

"Thanks Arabella," I said, my curiosity piqued. "I knew I could count on you."

"I just hope you solve the case. Or should I say cases?"

"Cases," I said, "and so do I."

It was only after we hung up that I remembered my mother's yearbooks in the trunk of my car. *That, I decided, was a deliberate slip, my subconscious trying to protect me.* I willed myself to leave them there a while longer and couldn't bring myself to do it. The likelihood of someone breaking into my vehicle was remote, but with my luck tonight was the night it would happen. I slipped on a pair of boots and a jacket, then retrieved the box and put it in the spare bedroom. Out of sight, if not completely out of mind.

It wasn't a great solution, but it was *a* solution, and right about now, that was enough.

22

WITH MY MOTHER'S yearbooks safely stashed in the spare room, and time out for tea, scrambled eggs, and toast, I was ready to get back at it. In addition to Betsy, Poppy, and Levon, I needed to talk to Detective Sheridan Merryfield, Kate's aunt, Lindsay Doucette, and Ben. I steeled myself to call Merryfield, Arabella's warning that he was unlikely to be receptive fresh in my mind. But Denim was planning to go to Miakoda Falls tomorrow, and if he got wind of an investigation in his patch without his knowledge, I expected he'd be even less receptive to our presence.

I dialed, hoping for voicemail.

He answered on the first ring, a rich baritone voice, and I envisioned a tall man of generous proportions.

"Merryfield."

"Detective Merryfield. My name is Calamity Barnstable. I'm the owner of Past & Present Investigations. I specialize in—"

"Cold cases. Lucy Daneluk told me you'd be calling. I'll be honest with you. I don't usually have a lot of time for investigators, amateur or otherwise. But Lucy Daneluk speaks highly of you, and I respect both her and her opinion."

"Lucy is a wonderful advocate for the missing and unidentified. I've been fortunate to work with her in the past."

"The Brandon Colbeck case. I remember reading about it. You did good work there."

"Thank you."

"Lucy tells me that you've been hired to look into the 1995 disappearance of Veronica Celeste Goodman by her daughter, Kathleen."

"Yes, that's correct. Lucy felt two other disappearances might be related. Kelly Anne Acquolina and Wanetta Bulmer. After reading the case listings on the registry, I'm in agreement, though there's nothing in them that links them directly."

"We never made it public, a perhaps misguided effort to keep the residents of Miakoda Falls from panicking, but we didn't fool anyone. Three women, all roughly the same age with similar physical attributes, all working in the service industry, disappearing two weeks apart. It didn't take a detective to connect the dots. Not that I was a detective at the time. I'd only been on the force a few weeks when the women disappeared."

"Your superior was?"

"Detective Martin Renner, Marty to his friends. Died in 2005, complications from COPD. Smoked like a fiend, though lots of people did back then. Ontario might have banned smoking in public places and workplaces in the '90s, but that didn't stop Martin from spending a good amount of time outside puffing away, regardless of the weather."

Martin, I thought, not *Marty*. Not friends, then, more superior to subordinate.

"Martin was the lead on all three cases," Merryfield continued. "I'll admit as a rookie, I hadn't expected anything of that nature. Toronto or Ottawa, yes, but not in Cedar County. Not a week goes by when I don't think of those women. But we have a small force, without the time or resources to go digging into the past. Maybe one day, when I retire. But I digress. I'm assuming you called in the hope that I could provide more details than those included on the Registry."

"That was the hope, yes, sir."

There was a long silence and for a moment I wondered if we'd been disconnected. But then Merryfield spoke.

"I wish I could tell you there was a lot more to share. There isn't. And even if there was, I can't allow you to access our case files. That said, I am willing to have a discussion with you for whatever that might be worth. Can you come into the station tomorrow morning? Ten o'clock?"

"I can do that. Thank you, Detective."

"Thank Lucy Daneluk. If she hadn't sung your praises, this call would have ended at hello."

23

Buoyed by my unexpected success with Detective Merryfield, I decided to call Lindsay Doucette. According to Kate, her aunt would be a reluctant participant in this investigation, having been duped in the past. By what or who remained to be discovered. I added her number to my contacts and dialed.

"Hello?" Suspicious, as if the only people who called her were telemarketers, pollsters, and scammers. I could relate.

"May I speak to Lindsay Doucette please?"

"Speaking." The frost in her tone intensified. If she didn't recognize my voice, I was almost certainly up to no good.

"Ms. Doucette, my name is Calamity Barnstable. I'm—"

"The investigator my niece hired to find out what happened to Roni. Kate has spoken of nothing else since yesterday." Not quite suspicious any longer, but far from welcoming.

"I appreciate her confidence in me."

"I'm not sure what she expects you to find that the police couldn't."

"I expect she wants to learn the truth."

"Does she? Want the truth? Or is she hoping for a fairy tale ending, to be reunited with her mother after all these years? In my opinion, no good can come from dredging up the past. I told Kate as much, not that she listened."

Dredging up the past. Had Lindsay Doucette been harboring a secret or secrets, or was she merely being protective of her niece? "Be that as it may, I'm hoping you and I can meet. It would be helpful if you could share your memories, not just of the night she went missing, but of Ver...Roni."

"Roni to her family. Nikki to her friends. You're neither."

"I apologize. I didn't mean to presume—"

"I'm sure you didn't. No one ever means to presume and yet, assumptions are always made."

"Perhaps we could avoid that by meeting," I said, determined not to get rattled. "In my experience, even the smallest details can prove helpful."

A sigh of resignation, then, "In that case, let's

get it over with. I'm on Trillium Way in Marketville, number 28. I trust you know where that is?"

"I used to live on Snapdragon Circle."

"Small world. We moved to Marketville when Kate was four. Too many bad memories in Miakoda Falls. I'm surprised Kate didn't tell you."

So was I. I wondered if there was anything else Kate hadn't told me, not because she was deliberately hiding something, that wouldn't make sense since she'd hired me, but because she didn't realize whatever she knew might be important.

"It didn't come up," I said. "When are you available?"

"Are you free now?"

"I have another call to make, but it can wait."

"Then I'll see you in thirty."

It would take me ten minutes to freshen up, less than fifteen to get to Trillium Way, even if there was traffic, something becoming more common as Marketville continued to grow, the infrastructure to support that growth poorly planned and slow in coming. I also knew that I should feel grateful for the quick meeting.

And yet I was certain there was more to Lindsay's rapid-fire pivot from "nothing to be gained from dredging up the past" to her desire to "get it over with." I'd had those gut feelings in the past, that sense of disquiet, and those feelings had yet to be proven wrong.

Maybe this time would be different. I hoped so. Because Kate Goodman deserved the truth, with or without a fairy tale ending. Lindsay Doucette had to understand that, and it was my job to make sure she did.

24

The short drive over to Lindsay Doucette's house brought back memories of my first day in Marketville and the house on Snapdragon Circle I'd inherited from my late father. A cul-de-sac of 1970s bungalows, split-levels, and semis, each road ran off the central artery of Trillium Way and branched out to symmetrical side streets named after provincial wildflowers: Day Lily Drive, Lady's Slipper Lane, and Coneflower Crescent. I hadn't been back since Chantelle had sold her house on Snapdragon and moved to Ottawa, but nothing had changed. I wondered if Royce Ashford, my former next-door-neighbor and one-time love interest, still lived there. Had he married Mercy Dellacorte, an actress best known for her Icelandic yogurt commercials?

Catty doesn't become you, I told myself, pulling into

the double driveway of 28 Trillium Way, a modest brown brick bungalow with a single detached garage. I parked, got out of my car, and walked to the door, my briefcase with pen, notebook, framed photograph, and heart-shaped pendant in tow, and knocked.

Lindsay Doucette was an attractive woman in her late fifties, but where Kate was blonde and petite, Lindsay was tall, with the wiry body of a distance runner, her hair chestnut brown and streaked with silver. She greeted me with a smile that didn't quite reach her eyes.

"Calamity, please come in. Let me take your coat and hat. Boots go into the tray. There are some hand-knitted slippers in a basket. Please put on a pair, the hardwood floors can be cold at this time of year. Don't worry, I wash them after every wear."

I did as she instructed and followed her to a compact living room with two minuscule glass and wrought iron end tables, a charcoal leather recliner and matching love seat, off white walls, and a contemporary gas fireplace with yellow flames flickering out of river rock. The only artwork was a pair of black-framed pen-and-ink sketches of San Francisco's Golden Gate Bridge and Ghirardelli Square. I settled into the love seat, grateful for my cable-knit sweater and the slippers. Despite the fireplace, the room was chilly, and the cool tones and pinched expression on Lindsay's face did nothing to warm it.

"Thank you for taking the time to see me," I said.

She nodded. "It's not that I don't want to help. It's that I've been down this road too many times, first with the police, and then with a private investigator who charged plenty and came up empty. I've even resorted to consulting with a psychic who came highly recommended by one of my running partners. That was about ten years ago."

A psychic. It couldn't be...could it? Good grief, that was all I needed, for Lindsay to feel as if she'd been duped by Misty Rivers. "Do you remember the psychic's name?"

"I do. It was Misty Rivers. Specializes in tarot readings. Why, do you know her?"

"We've worked together in the past. She was most helpful in another missing adult case. A young man by the name of Brandon Colbeck."

The pinched expression on Lindsay's face softened ever so slightly. "I liked Misty, she seemed to genuinely care, wouldn't take a penny. Unfortunately, she couldn't...or perhaps wouldn't... say whether Roni was alive or dead. I never told Kate, mostly because there was nothing to tell. I always thought Misty agreed to see me, not because she could help, but because she didn't want some charlatan taking advantage of me." A pause, then, "How is Misty?"

"Married to a man she met on a blind date and living happily ever after in British Columbia."

Lindsay smiled. "I'm glad, not that I believe in happily ever after. But I've already told you that. Now, how about we get started with the interview?"

25

———————

OUR COMMON CONNECTION of Misty Rivers had thawed Lindsay's attitude towards me. She wasn't exactly effusive, but she'd also made a very welcome pot of Earl Grey tea and put out a plate of store-bought chocolate chip cookies.

"Tell me about the day Veronica went missing," I began. "Was there anything different about the way she was acting?"

"We weren't living together, so I can't speak to her actions earlier in the day, but I know she'd just signed a one-year lease on her basement apartment. Before that, she'd been month-to-month, but the landlady wanted a firmer commitment."

Landlady, not landlord. A small distinction, but possibly an important one. "How did Veronica feel about that?"

"Excited. Grateful. The apartment wasn't huge,

but it was only a ten-minute walk to the Miakoda Bar & Grille where she worked, and it was affordable. The landlady was a widow, no kids of her own, but she was good with Kate, watched her sometimes when I couldn't."

"Do you remember the landlady's name?"

Lindsay nodded. "Edith Buckman. We stayed in touch until she passed away in 2010, when Kate was sixteen. She was always giving Kate money for birthdays and Christmas and often for no reason at all. She left a generous trust for Kate to go to university or college, covered her food, accommodation, books, and tuition."

"What about the rest of her estate?"

"I believe it went to her nephew, Isaac Buckman. I recall Edith saying he was a musician, and on the road a lot. I don't think they were close, but she didn't have any other family."

I wrote down "Isaac Buckman" and "musician" in my notebook. "Were you and Kate surprised at the trust?"

"I know Kate was, though I'd suspected Edith had been planning something along those lines, asking questions about tuition and the like. The trust allowed Kate to graduate from U of T without debt, but…" Lindsay's voice trailed off.

"But?"

"I couldn't help but wonder what prompted Edith to provide the trust."

"And did you come to any conclusion?"

"Nothing I could prove, though I've often wondered if Edith knew more about Roni's disappearance than she was willing to let on, that paying for Kate's post-secondary education would ease whatever guilt she might be feeling. Absolute conjecture on my part, and I've never told anyone this, before now. But why else would she leave Kate a trust?"

Why else indeed?

"You don't strike me as the sort of person who resorts to flights of fancy. There must have been something to make you feel that way. Something she said or did?"

Lindsay shook her head. "Nothing like that. But the bar was ten minutes from Edith's house, and from what Roni told me, Edith was a regular. Didn't like to cook and didn't like to drink alone, liked to join in on the conversations going on around her, gossip a little. That was how Roni found out about the basement apartment. She was telling one of the other servers about needing to find a place to live. Mrs. Buckman overheard and told her she had a basement apartment that was available."

I considered that for a moment. "If Edith Buckman overheard Veronica talk about needing a place to live, she might have overheard other things. Is that what you're thinking?"

"I think it's possible. But if she did overhear anything, then she took it to her grave."

In short, quite literally a dead end.

What can I say? Sometimes my sense of humor borders on the macabre.

26

When it was clear Lindsay had nothing else to add about the night of Veronica's disappearance, or the days leading up to it, "same as usual," was how she'd put it, it was time to move on to the next item on my agenda.

"Kate told me she has no idea who her father is, and that you don't know, or if you do, you aren't telling. Which is it? Don't know or aren't telling?"

"Roni kept her private life private. Besides, she may have been my sister, but there was a fifteen-year age gap between us. I tended to mother her. She tended to treat me like a parent, or at least like an adult viewed with a modicum of suspicion."

I smiled. "In other words, you were on a need-to-know basis, and she didn't think you needed to know."

Lindsay laughed, and the sound warmed the

room better than any fireplace could. "Exactly. I do know she'd been dating a boy by the name of Travis Acquolina, but they'd broken up six months before."

"Acquolina. That can't be a common last name in Miakoda Falls. Any relation to Kelly Anne Acquolina, the young woman who went missing two weeks before Veronica?"

"Travis was her younger brother. He and Roni were two years younger than Kelly. Travis was a bit of a hothead, got himself sent to a version of juvie, not that anyone in town blamed him."

"Let me guess. He went after Kelly's ex-boyfriend, the one who'd been charged with assaulting her."

"Right again."

"Was that before or after Kelly went missing?"

"A couple of months later. Without Kelly to testify, the assault charge was withdrawn. Travis might even have gotten away with it, his word against Jamie's, but he'd been boasting to anyone who would listen that he was going to make sure Jamie knew what it felt like to be assaulted."

"Does this Jamie have a last name?"

"Gardiner, like the Expressway in Toronto. First name is actually Jamieson, that's i-e-s-o-n."

I wrote his name underneath Isaac Buckman's. "Where is Travis Acquolina now, do you know?"

Lindsay shook her head. "I heard he was released early from juvie for good behavior, took off, and never looked back, no idea where he landed or where he is now. I do know the police grilled him for all three disappearances, but nothing stuck. Nothing but the assault on Jamie."

I made a note—both Travis and Kelly Acquolina had disappeared, first Kelly, then Travis. "And Jamie? Did he walk away and never look back, too?"

"You'd think he would have, but no, he still lives here, owns Plank-it Pilates, Yoga & Fitness on Pine Street. I expect the police told him not to leave town, at least in the beginning, but I have no first-hand knowledge of that."

"Were Veronica and Kelly close?"

"Not especially. I mean, they knew each other because of Travis, but they didn't hang out."

"What about Jamie?"

"That would be another no. Miakoda Falls is a small town now, and it was a small town then, but it was big enough that a seventeen-year-old high school student like Roni wouldn't be running with a guy who'd already graduated. Especially one with Jamie's reputation." Lindsay offered up a sad smile. "I'm sorry, I don't think I've been overly helpful."

"On the contrary, I know more now than when I came here. I do have one more question about her jewelry. The floral link bracelet. I understand from Kate it was a gift from your mother, given to Veronica on her sixteenth birthday."

Lindsay nodded. "That's right."

"Did Veronica wear it often?"

"Rarely took it off. Loved it beyond reason."

"And the heart-shaped pendant? Any idea who gave that to her?"

"That one is easy. Me."

It was the one answer I hadn't been expecting. "You?"

"I thought it went well with the bracelet, had the same sort of vintage look. I gave it to her that morning at breakfast, for Valentine's Day. For luck." Lindsay's eyes welled with tears. "Turned out not to be so lucky, did it?"

"Maybe it was lucky, in a way. At least the police knew she'd been in the parking lot before she disappeared."

"Fat lot of good it did them," Lindsay said.

The woman had a point.

27

Denim had found the name of the retirement home—Miakoda Place—that Wanetta had volunteered at before leaving, and while it was a slim lead, it left me with a whole lot to think about on the way home from Lindsay Doucette's. I couldn't help but feel like I'd missed something important, but there comes a time when you just need to decompress. I had a half-filled journal with names and notes. My mother's five yearbooks, stashed in my spare bedroom, as if that made them disappear. And I was meeting with Detective Merryfield in the morning with four names in my back pocket: Travis Acquolina, Jamieson "Jamie" Gardiner, and Edith and Isaac Buckman.

But how to decompress, that was the question. When Chantelle lived here, we would get together for pizza and wine, and when I'd been dating Ben, I could hang out at Unwired, but both options were currently off the table. I seldom missed Toronto, but right about now the thought of hanging out in a bar where no one knew me held a certain appeal. Unfortunately, such places didn't exist in Marketville. Just like in the TV show *Cheers*, everyone here knew your name, especially if you ran a business digging up old secrets. What did exist, however, was Trust Few Tattoo, and while I'm still tattoo hesitant, since working on the Brandon Colbeck case, I'd become friendly with the owner, Sam Sanchez.

I'd also had the opportunity to meet her ninety-three-year-old grandfather, Nestor Sanchez. An itinerant tattoo artist for much of Sam's life, often living in shelters, if not on the street, the bond between them had nevertheless been strong, and while he wasn't a traditional role model, he'd managed to raise a strong woman.

"He always tried to come back and stick around, but he just wasn't cut out for a conventional life," Sam had told me after I'd met him, her eyes glistening with tears. "He won't stay this time either. The difference is, this time, he's come back to die." He'd done just that a few days later. To honor her grandfather's wishes, Sam hadn't planned a funeral or a celebration of life. Instead, she'd had his body cremated, temporarily closed Trust Few Tattoo, and taken six weeks off to travel and spread his ashes, using his sketchbook of places he'd visited as a guide. "A cathartic experience," was how Sam described it to me on her return, and I imagined it would have been.

My thoughts were still with Nestor when I arrived at Poplar Street, a mixed bag of retail, commercial, and questionable residential. For the past four years, realtors had been suggesting that Poplar Street was a neighborhood in transition, a good place to invest in a fixer-upper and gain some sweat equity. From the looks of things, any such transition had been delayed or abandoned, but the way housing prices had been escalating and squeezing out first-time buyers, Poplar Street was bound to land on someone's radar. I hoped so. I'd invested a good chunk of the inheritance from my great-grandmother into a semi-detached rental property. In the meantime, the house was tenanted, and after utilities and property taxes, I was almost breaking even.

Trust Few was sandwiched between Triple P Pizza, Pasta & Panzerotti and, new since I'd been here last, The Curried Chef. The building itself was narrow, with a red brick façade and charcoal board and batten that framed a gilt-lettered window and canary yellow door. I wondered when Totally Tempting Thai had closed, and whether it had been another casualty of Covid.

I opened the door to the droning sound of a tattoo machine and the sickly-sweet smell of industrial strength hand sanitizer. Sam's assistant,

Tash, glanced up from her smartphone when I walked in and favored me with a gap-toothed grin.

"Hey Callie. Don't tell me you've finally decided to get a tattoo," she said, waving her heavily inked hands at me. I remembered she called the symbols on her fingers "finger-bangers." The ones on her hands were new. Hand-bangers? I had no idea.

"Maybe someday," I said, thinking *not gonna happen*. "I'm wondering if Sam's in?"

"Just finishing up with a client, her last of the day. Have a seat, I'll tell her you're here."

"In that case, ask her if she'd like to have dinner with me. How's The Curried Chef?"

"I practically live there, but Sam prefers Triple P. That woman would eat pizza three meals a day."

A woman after my own heart.

"What about you?" Tash asked. "Are you working another case?"

"I am, and I have a question for her. Mostly, though, I just wanted to catch up and chill out. It's been a while and I've had a long day." I managed a tired smile. "I could use a friend."

"Sam's day hasn't been sunshine and roses either. Started off with a newly engaged woman who brought her maid of honor and six giggling bridesmaids to select a tattoo. The idea was they would all get the same one to celebrate the bride's upcoming nuptials. Sam spent an hour sketching designs until the bride-to-be ran out of the shop in tears, her bickering entourage trailing behind her."

Tash rolled her eyes. "As if you're ever going to reach a consensus with eight twenty-somethings on what they want tattooed, let alone where."

I grinned. "Sounds like Sam could use a friend, too."

"And a drink. The adult beverage kind. Hang tight while I ask her."

SAM SAUNTERED into the reception area ten minutes later, peeling off her latex gloves. She smiled, her cornflower blue eyes crinkling at the corners, the tiny diamond in her eyetooth sparking under the fluorescent lighting. Her long dark hair was still shaved on one side, the name SANCHEZ visible beneath the stubble. I couldn't begin to imagine how much that must hurt, and I had no intention of ever finding out.

"Callie," Sam said. "It's good to see you. Tash tells me you're buying me dinner."

"Wine and pizza at Triple P, if that works."

"You had me at wine. The day I've had…" She sized me up, top to bottom. "Then again, I have a feeling your day wasn't much better. C'mon. Let's commiserate."

THE DINING AREA of Triple P Panzerotti and Pizza was exactly the cliché you expected it to be, with scenes from Italian landmarks lining the walls and the tables topped with red-and-white checked cloths and stainless-topped glass shakers of oregano, pepper flakes, garlic powder, and parmesan. We'd no sooner taken a seat under a poster of the Leaning Tower of Pisa when our server appeared, plastic menus in hand. We opted to share a large Margherita pizza and a half-liter of house white.

The order in, and our wine glasses filled, Sam started by regaling me with her version of the morning's bridezilla and her minions. She was a natural born storyteller, mimicking both voice and mannerisms, and I found myself laughing harder than I had in a very long time.

"So," she said, after our pizza arrived. "Enough about my day. Tash tells me you've got a new case. How can I help?"

I filled her in on the basics between bites. Three young women, all from Miakoda Falls, all missing in the winter of 1995. "The woman I've been hired to investigate, Veronica Goodman, had a tattoo of a blue dragonfly on her left ankle. I know it's a long shot, but I thought you might give me a lead on who owned a tattoo parlor there in 1995."

Sam shook her head. "I didn't apprentice until 1997, and that was here in Marketville. Miakoda Falls would have been like a foreign country to me. Even if I did know, the odds of the artist remembering Veronica, or her tattoo, are slim and none, and slim just left town. Everything about it is just too generic. Left ankle. Dragonfly. Might as well be a maple leaf or a butterfly."

I felt an irrational surge of disappointment. "I know you're right. But she was only eighteen."

"Which was, and is, the legal age to get a tattoo without parental consent."

"Yes, but she'd *just* turned eighteen."

"And you thought, because it was recent, it might have struck a chord with the tattoo artist who'd done it."

"Yeah."

"In which case, don't you think the police would have had the same thoughts? Have you been in touch with them yet?"

"I'm meeting with a Detective Merryfield tomorrow morning. I'm not sure how much information he'll give me."

"Likely not much, if I know the police. Okay, I'll do some calling around, but don't get your hopes up."

"I won't. Thank you."

Sam smiled, the diamond in her tooth catching the light. "Anything for a friend. Now, enough shop talk. How's Ben?"

"Ah," I said. "I was afraid you were going to ask me that."

28

I ARRIVED back home feeling energized and optimistic. Sometimes all you needed was pizza, wine, and a sympathetic ear, especially when it came to my on-again-off-again relationship with Ben. Sam's undivided attention didn't change the fact that my relationship with Ben was in the rearview mirror, but by the time we left the restaurant—both of us promising not to leave it so long until the next time—I realized I was more okay with that than not. It wasn't that I didn't care for him. I did. On some level I even loved him, just as I'd loved Royce and the cheating triathlete before him. But there was never that visceral connection like the one Levon and Arabella had, or like Emily had found in Luke. I've heard it said that lightning was more likely to strike than a single woman over forty finding her soulmate, but

I was willing to hold out on the chance. Better to die alone, than die being lonely with someone, right?

Morbid thoughts aside, I knew at some point in the investigation I might have to call Ben. At least now I could do it without feeling like I had the hidden agenda of getting back together. But first, I needed to transcribe my notes from my meeting with Lindsay Doucette while the interview was still fresh in my mind.

My father used to say, "A dull pencil is sharper than the sharpest mind," and that advice has never let me down. It's also led to my obsession with notebooks, but there are worse fixations, and the process of transcription from pen-and-paper to Word was a soothing ritual. It also served a dual purpose, providing the basis of what would be a report for my client, and revealing things I had missed in the moment.

Such was the case now, I thought as I highlighted two paragraphs.

Me (start of interview): On the day Veronica disappeared, was there anything different about the way she was acting?

L: We weren't living together, so I can't speak to her actions earlier in the day, but I know she'd just signed a one-year lease on her basement apartment.

Me (near end of interview): Do you know who gave Veronica the heart-shaped pendant?

L: Me. I gave it to her that morning at

breakfast, for Valentine's Day. For luck. Turned out not to be so lucky, did it?

And *that* was the important point I'd missed, the thing that had niggled at me when I'd left Lindsay Doucette's house. Because only one of those two statements could be true.

Which was the lie? That she hadn't seen Veronica that morning? Or that she'd given her the pendant? It was equally possible that both statements were lies. That she *had* seen Veronica that morning, but she *hadn't* been the one to give her the pendant.

Had there been any hesitation when she'd answered me about it? I didn't recall any, hadn't made a note of it. *"That one's easy,"* she'd said.

Unless it was a practiced lie, a fabrication she'd perfected to protect someone. But who and why? Because, if my theory was accurate, and I believed that it was, then Veronica had purposely left the pendant in the parking lot as a clue. Whether that was a clue *for* her sister, or a clue pointing *to* her sister, remained to be seen.

I reread my notes over and over, wondering if Lindsay could have been behind her sister's disappearance, and if so, why.

Misty Rivers might know something, though according to Lindsay she hadn't been able to tell if Veronica had been dead or alive. Still, it was a loose end that needed tying up, and it would be better to talk to her than do it by email. I checked the time, surprised to find it was almost one o'clock in the morning.

But not quite ten o'clock in British Columbia. Was it too late to call? I decided it was, and not just because I was being considerate. I had a big day ahead of me tomorrow. I shut off my cell and made my way to bed, bleary-eyed and none the wiser.

29

I woke up late, sleeping through my alarm and groggy from a restless night. I turned on the coffeemaker, grabbed a quick shower, threw on a pair of jeans and a sweater, took a couple of oatmeal raisin cookies from the cupboard, and poured myself a cup of coffee for the road, feeling anything but relaxed and ready for my meeting with Merryfield.

My hand was almost on the doorknob when my cell phone rang. I glanced at the call display. Poppy Spencer. As much as I wanted to talk to her, now was not the time. I needed to process my thoughts on the drive to Miakoda Falls and even a short conversation would make me late. I let it go to voicemail, feeling a modicum of guilt at the decision, but something told me Detective Merryfield wouldn't be the kind of man who appreciated tardiness. Besides, first impressions mattered, and I needed him a lot more than he needed me.

Much like the drive to Lakeside, the scenery on the way to Miakoda Falls had been considerably altered, with fields of forests razed to make way for big box stores and multi-family residential developments with names like Spruce Hills and Tree Meadows. *We have the extended GO train system to thank for that*, I thought, driving past a packed parking lot in the Cedar County GO lot. What was once a lengthy commute south to Toronto could now be managed in just over an hour. Even so, I didn't envy anyone who spent two-plus hours of their day on a train and was grateful I didn't have to do it.

I arrived in Miakoda Falls fifteen minutes ahead of schedule, thanks to light northbound traffic and a heavy foot. The Cedar County Tri-Community Policing Center was located inside what appeared to be the original train station. I knew that the Center had been opened at a time when Lount's Landing, Lakeside, and Miakoda Falls had been growing in leaps and bounds, fueled by a buoyant economy, high paying jobs at the mill, and rumors of an automotive plant coming to the area.

Since then, the mill had closed, the automaker had fallen upon recessionary times, and any plans for opening a new plant had been abandoned, which caused much of the tri-town's workforce to seek housing and employment opportunities elsewhere. But if the new subdivisions, "Smart" centers, and big box stores were any indication, things were back on the upswing. It always amused me how folks moved into rural communities to get away from it all, only to bring the "all" back to the community they'd escaped to. It would just be a matter of time before the police department outgrew its current digs, and possibly, its current Detective. I wondered if Merryfield cared. Maybe he was willing to see me because retirement, either encouraged or voluntary, was imminent.

I stopped speculating long enough to listen to the phone message left by Poppy. She'd invited me to her office if I had time later today. I loved it when things came together like that. A quick text, *IN TOWN, WILL CALL WHEN DONE*, and I was ready to face the formidable Detective Sheridan Merryfield.

30

THE MAN SITTING behind the desk across from me didn't look like he was going to retire any time soon. Detective Merryfield appeared to be in his late forties, a large man with even larger hands, warm brown eyes, skin the color of burnished copper, and a tortured smile hidden behind good teeth and better manners. In 1995, he would have been about the same age as the women who'd gone missing. I revised my earlier opinion of him. This wasn't an old cop looking to retire in a blaze of glory. This was a man who still wondered about the missing women and was willing to speak with me about them. Sleeping with the enemy. Metaphorically speaking, of course.

Did I mention I found him insanely attractive?

"As I told you on the phone," Merryfield began, "I don't usually discuss cases with anyone outside of the force, but Lucy Daneluk wouldn't recommend anyone who wasn't trustworthy. I've also taken the liberty of delving into your background, and you've had some success where traditional methods have failed. That said, before we begin, understand that I'm limited by what I can legally tell you, though I'll try to steer you away from dead ends."

I nodded, though my earlier optimism was beginning to wane.

"I must also have your absolute assurance that you will keep what I tell you confidential. In other words, you didn't hear it from me. Is that clear?"

"Anything else?"

"Yes. You must also keep me apprised of any new findings. And I do mean any, not any that you decide to select."

"Of course."

"I also need your assurance that you will call me, day or night, if you suspect you may be in any danger." Merryfield slid a business card across his desk.

The idea of putting myself or Denim into harm's way hadn't occurred to me, though I suppose it should have. Someone's secret had been safe since 1995. If we were successful, the secret or secrets would be exposed. I took the card.

"You have my assurance."

"Let's hope you're better at following the rules than Arabella Carpenter."

Arabella...how on earth? I shifted in my seat.

Merryfield grinned at my discomfort. "You thought I didn't know you were friends? I *am* a detective, after all. Contrary to what Arabella might believe, I admire her. She's honest, forthright, and loyal to a fault. I just wish she didn't get involved in active police investigations. Thankfully, things have been sleepy in Lount's Landing, at least where Arabella and Emily are concerned."

"I'll be sure to tell her of your admiration," I said, laying on the sarcasm.

Merryfield's grin broadened, and I found myself being drawn into his charm like a magnet to iron. *Stop it, Callie. You're just out of a relationship and the last thing you need is to get involved with a cop.*

"I'm sure you will," he said. "Now, as much as it pains me to admit it, we're no further ahead with our investigation into the disappearances of Veronica Goodman, Kelly Acquolina, and Wanetta Bulmer than we were in 1995. There's been a concerted effort by many police departments to try a variety of initiatives in the hope they will generate information on unsolved murders and missing person's cases. For instance, Special task forces, familial DNA, video vignettes, Facebook posts, utilizing dedicated websites like the Ontario Registry of Missing and Unidentified Adults. We've tried them all with various degrees of success, hence my relationship with Lucy Daneluk. Unfortunately, in the case of the three women in question, we haven't been successful."

"Why do you think that is?"

Merryfield shrugged. "We're a small force with limited resources, but it's more than that. At the time of these disappearances, even as recently as twenty years ago, it was civilians, not police, who compiled databases inviting the public to participate in the resolution of cold cases. The success of groups, such as the Doe Network and the Ontario Registry of Missing and Unidentified Adults, was the driving force behind police turning to the Internet, at least in Ontario. In some cases, online groups have an advantage, in that they can provide services for those who are not comfortable reaching out to police directly. All this is a long way of saying I'll tell you what I can, though it's precious little beyond what's listed on the Registry."

"I appreciate your honesty."

"Like I said before, Lucy Daneluk is one of the good guys. I suggest we review the cases chronologically, starting with Wanetta Georgina Bulmer."

I'd brought heavily annotated printouts of all three Registry listings to the meeting. I removed them from my briefcase, shuffled Wanetta Bulmer's to the top, the most salient points highlighted in yellow. "One thing that struck me as odd was Wanetta left her purse behind, yet she deposited her paycheck the morning she left home. Wouldn't she have put her paycheck in her purse?"

"A solid observation," Merryfield said, opening

a file on this desk. "Yes, she left her purse behind. It contained a pack of tissue, lip gloss, tampon holder, hairbrush, and her employee badge for Blue Goose Grocery. What it didn't contain was her wallet."

"I wondered about that. It means she had money and ID with her."

"That was our conclusion since no wallet was ever found. The contents could have included her school ID, ATM bank card, and Visa."

"Driver's license?"

"Unknown, but unlikely. She didn't own a car, and there was no record of a driver's license being issued to her."

"Social insurance number? She would have needed one to get a credit card."

Merryfield shook his head. "Most people believe that, but there is no legal obligation in Canada to provide a SIN on a credit card application."

"But surely there is, in order to be employed?"

"That would be another no. Employees were not legally obligated to provide their SIN to employers until 2013, at which time new Employment Insurance Regulations came into effect. Regardless, the owner of the Blue Goose Grocery admitted to hiring Wanetta and others under the table." Merryfield's mouth twisted at the memory. "The Blue Goose has since discontinued that practice."

"And the retirement home?"

"Strictly volunteer. No SIN required."

So, the Social Insurance Number was a dead end. But… "What about the bank card? Are there records of that?"

"The last time she used the bank card was the morning she deposited her paycheck. The Visa card was used a week before, for the purchase of a pair of silver earrings with a feather design, brown knee-high leather boots, a brown corduroy bomber jacket, and brown corduroy straight-leg pants."

"New clothes, as in maybe she had a date?"

"Speculation, but possible."

"But also, the same outfit that she wore the day she disappeared."

"Yes. The charge to her Visa card was never paid and neither the TD bank card nor Visa has been used since. But she also made one other purchase the day of her spending spree. A pair of scrubs, the kind recommended by the nursing program."

"She'd been accepted without completing her last two high school credits?"

Merryfield shook his head. "No, but no one doubted she'd get there, least of all Wanetta. Those scrubs were on the Final Sale Clearance rack, and one of the reasons the department concluded she didn't leave here voluntarily. This was a hard-working, ambitious young woman planning for her future, not a confused adolescent looking for a quick way out."

Everything Merryfield had told me made sense,

but outside of Wanetta's Visa purchases, I hadn't learned much beyond what had been reported on the Registry. Even so, something niggled. I thought about it as he studied me, his dark eyes watchful, his large hands clasped in front of him. *Damn, but he was good looking in a burly cop sort of way.*

I pushed aside the thought. "Here's what I'm struggling with. Wanetta was twenty and getting ready for what appeared to be a promising future. But she was also in night school getting two more credits. Which meant she needed two more courses to graduate, or her marks needed a serious leg up. Which was it?"

Merryfield nodded approvingly, as if I were a clever student. "Very astute. My guess is she'd dropped math and science in high school for courses that would have raised her overall grade point average, then realized both were required for nursing. My impression was she was on her way to getting honors in both classes."

"The teachers. Are they still teaching?"

Merryfield shook his head. "One retired, one dead. Cancer."

"And the one who saw her running across the school grounds?"

"Retired since 2014. Lives in a bungalow in Miakoda Hills."

He said it as if I should be familiar with Miakoda Hills. I wasn't and said so.

"It's a four-season, active adult lifestyle condo

community built around the Miakoda Falls Golf & Country Club."

"And the retired teacher's name?"

"Loretta Dartmoor, Miss, not Ms. You'd be wise to remember that should you decide to pay her a visit." Merryfield tried to suppress a smile and didn't quite manage. "Apparently the students used to call her Miss Dark Mood, although I daresay never to her face."

"Anything else I should know?"

"Miss Dartmoor is quite an avid golfer. Do you golf?"

"I've golfed. Charity tournaments, usually best ball. I wouldn't classify myself as a golfer."

"That's unfortunate, since you're probably a decade or more away from buying in the Hills." Merryfield must have caught my puzzled expression because he went on to clarify. "Miss Dartmoor also works Saturdays at the Miakoda Hills Sales Office. And yes, in answer to your unasked question, I've been keeping informal tabs on her. Not surveillance, I have no reason to believe she knows more than what she told us in 1995, but…"

Merryfield let the sentence dangle, the expression on his face inscrutable.

Today was Friday, which meant the earliest I'd be able to see her would be tomorrow. But Merryfield's cryptic comment had me wondering.

"Was she—"

"The same teacher who reported seeing Kelly

Anne Acquolina at Canada's Wonderland? That would be another yes, with one distinction. Miss Dartmoor was Kelly's high school teacher. Wanetta wasn't a student at Miakoda High, though her adult night classes were held there."

"Meaning, she would know Kelly well, but not necessarily Wanetta."

"It's something to consider. And since I have nothing more to add about Wanetta Bulmer, I'd suggest we review Kelly's case next."

My gut told me that I'd missed something important, a question I should have asked, but what? It would come to me, later, after I'd had time to process everything Merryfield had to tell me. I leaned back in my chair and nodded.

"Over to you, Detective Merryfield."

31

"KELLY ANNE ACQUOLINA," Merryfield began. "No disrespect to the mother of your client, but of all three cases, this is the one that got under my skin. A nineteen-year-old woman, willing to testify that she'd been assaulted, the charges dropped when she disappeared. Coincidence, maybe, but I don't believe in coincidence. Nevertheless, my former boss was convinced that she ran away because she was frightened about testifying against her ex-boyfriend, and in my opinion her disappearance wasn't investigated as thoroughly as it could have been. Even after Veronica Goodman disappeared, his position on Kelly didn't change. As far as Detective Martin Renner was concerned, Kelly was a runaway, end of story."

"According to the Registry, her family thought otherwise."

Merryfield sighed. "That's the thing that wasn't in the missing person report. Her parents did believe she'd run away, at least in the beginning. Kelly had grown increasingly nervous about going to court. She'd asked for the charges to be dropped and had recanted her earlier statement to police. It was only after months had passed without any word from her that her parents got worried."

"I don't understand. Wouldn't filing charges and going to court be her decision?"

"The short answer is no. The long answer is maybe, but not really. In Ontario, police are the ones who lay criminal charges. With most cases, we have some discretion as to whether or not those charges are laid. That's not the case with domestic violence, where the police have a zero-tolerance policy. We will always lay charges when it comes to a romantic relationship."

"And the charge against Kelly's ex was domestic assault?"

"It was. A neighbor called 911 when she heard a woman screaming for help at the apartment next door. When our officer arrived on the scene, Kelly was hysterical. She claimed that her boyfriend had threatened to kill her. The boyfriend was drunk, mouthy, and combative. Our officer on the scene had no alternative but to charge him with assault. Once the police lay charges, the decision to prosecute lies only with the prosecutor, though the charges can be withdrawn."

"Does that happen often?"

"Often enough. The prosecutor might believe the case isn't winnable or not in the public interest. In domestic assault cases, a common reason to withdraw charges is because the victim recants all or some of their earlier statement. But it's important to note that a prosecutor will not automatically withdraw charges because a victim recants, even if they do so in writing. In Kelly's case, the prosecutor had not yet withdrawn the domestic assault charge when she disappeared. Without her testimony, the case became unwinnable, and the charges were ultimately withdrawn."

I tried to process that and failed. "Shouldn't the charges automatically be withdrawn if the victim recants?"

Merryfield shook his head. "The system is designed to protect the victim. In general, prosecutors don't accept recant letters, preferring to refer the victim to the police. And then we investigate to make sure there is nothing suspicious about the letter. Accused people sometimes forge recant letters. Other times victims write them, but they are false or written under duress."

"Did Kelly recant in writing?"

"Yes, but there was some suspicion that she'd been coerced to do so."

"By the boyfriend?"

"By the boyfriend's father, an abusive brute of a man, not that we could ever prove it." Merryfield's eyes narrowed at the memory. "He would have been a prime suspect in Kelly's disappearance if he hadn't been sleeping off a DUI in our holding cell. He was stopped driving home from the ER, where he'd dropped off his son after beating him within an inch of his life. If there's a silver lining, it's that he gave his son an alibi for the night."

It was time to admit what I knew. "I spoke with Lindsay Doucette yesterday. She told me the boyfriend's name was Jamieson Gardiner, goes by Jamie. That he still lives in Miakoda Falls and owns a gym called Plank-It Pilates, Yoga & Fitness Center."

That netted me a raised eyebrow. "You *have* been busy. What she might not have told you is that after the assault charges were withdrawn, Jamie Gardiner checked himself into rehab, and he's been clean and sober ever since. He also runs a free, after-school fitness program for at-risk youth, among other things."

"And his father?"

"Died fifteen years ago. Jamie didn't go to the funeral."

"In other words, he's turned his life around."

"That he has, and the lives of many others. There are happy drunks and there are mean drunks. Like his father, Gardiner fell into the latter category, but he was smart enough to recognize it before it ruined his life."

Unfortunately, he didn't recognize it before it

ruined Kelly's. That is, if she was still alive. Changed man or not, I needed to pay Jamie Gardiner a visit, and sooner rather than later. Word traveled fast in a small town, and it wouldn't take long for folks to know that there was an investigator digging into the past. I had to see Jamie before that happened.

It was shaping up to be a very busy day.

32

IT WAS FINALLY time to talk about Veronica Goodman. I started by asking Merryfield about the dragonfly tattoo on her left ankle. "Veronica was eighteen at the time of her disappearance, the legal age to get a tattoo. I thought there might be something there."

"It's hard to believe, but there wasn't a single tattoo parlor in Cedar County, wasn't the demand then that there is today. According to her friends, Veronica got her tattoo in Toronto on her sixteenth birthday, which meant she either faked her ID or the necessary parental consent. She told her friends where she got the tattoo, and I did visit it, photograph in hand. None of the artists remembered her. It had been two years, after all, though if she'd gone for something a bit more unique…" Merryfield's voice trailed off.

Thanks to my conversation with Sam, I knew the tattoo was a long shot. Even so, I couldn't help but feel a sense of disappointment. I shook the feeling off and went to the next item on my agenda. "The heart-shaped pendant that was found in the parking lot behind the bar. Do you know who gave it to Veronica?"

"I expect you already know the answer."

I felt myself blush. "I wondered if Lindsay Doucette had told you the same thing. I don't know, there's something off about that. At first, she told me she hadn't seen Veronica that morning and at the end of our conversation, she said she'd given her the necklace that morning for luck. Only one of those things can be true. And the chain wasn't broken, it even had a safety catch on it. It's as if Veronica deliberately dropped it there. Maybe she was trying to tell us who was behind her abduction."

"*If* she was abducted," Merryfield said, "I can't imagine her sister was behind it. What possible motivation would she have had? By all accounts they were close, so close that Lindsay frequently looked after her niece while Veronica worked."

"*If* she was abducted? The Registry listing concluded it was unlikely that her disappearance was voluntary."

Merryfield sighed. "It *is* unlikely, especially since she'd signed a new lease and left money in her apartment, but that doesn't make it impossible.

According to the owner, Veronica appeared to be having a friendly conversation with a man outside the bar."

"What about the necklace? Do you believe that Veronica left it there on purpose?"

"I believe there's a strong probability, but that could just as easily be because she wanted us to know she'd been in the parking lot."

I wasn't about to give up so easily. "Then why the necklace? Why not the bracelet she never took off? How do we know that Lindsay isn't covering for someone else?"

"Lindsay had a receipt, a charge on her credit card, and we checked with the jewelry store." Merryfield gave me a look bordering on pity. "I wish I had more to tell you. The reality is our investigation into Veronica's disappearance yielded nothing beyond what you've already read on the Registry. It's as if she vanished into thin air."

But people don't disappear into thin air, I thought. Not unless they didn't want to be found. Or someone didn't want them found. Call it a hunch, call it anything you wanted. Lindsay was either lying or knew more than she was saying. And I was determined to find out why.

33

———

I LEFT Merryfield's office with yet another promise to keep him informed and texted Poppy to tell her I'd be there after lunch, then checked my map app for directions to Plank-It Pilates, Yoga & Fitness on Pine Street. First stop, Jamieson "Jamie" Gardiner.

I've been to my fair share of gyms over the years, and nothing about Plank-It was any different. The underlying aroma of disinfectant wipes and stale perspiration. The usual rows of treadmills, stationary bikes, circuit equipment, and rowing machines, lined up like soldiers waiting for battle, which, I supposed, they were in a way. There was also the obligatory wall of mirrors and stacks of weights, the buff and not-quite-buff-yet gym rats poised in front, lifting and ready for their selfies. At the end of the room there were three doors. Two were for the Men's and Women's Change Rooms.

The sign above the last door said Pilates & Yoga Studio.

A tattoo-sleeved, twenty-something woman with a bright white smile and neon pink hair greeted me at the reception desk. Pale complected and rail thin to the point of being gaunt, she gave me the urge to buy her a burger and milkshake, not that she was likely to consume either. Lining the wall behind her was an impressive display of Plank-It branded athletic wear, along with stainless steel water bottles, a variety of vegan protein powders, and what appeared to be a complete line of organic skin care products. Jamieson Gardiner was a man who took diversification seriously.

"Are you here for a tour?" she asked, batting a pair of mascara-spiked eyelashes that could slash a wrist.

I shook my head. "Actually, I was hoping to talk to Jamie."

"He's teaching a class now." She gestured towards the studio. "Ends in ten. Wanna wait?"

"If you don't mind."

"Fine by me. You positive you don't want a tour? Kill some time?"

"Sure, why not."

She came around the counter and flashed another smile. "I'm Alyssa."

"Callie."

We started with the circuit section of the gym. "These ten machines are the perfect place to start if you're deconditioned, new-to-exercise programs, or time conscious," she began. "There are no set up adjustments beyond pressing a button to select the intensity of your workout, making them user-friendly, and they provide both cardio and strength training for a full body workout. For example, our AB Cruncher targets the lower abdomen, our Chest Press works the biceps and latissimus dorsi muscles, and our Leg Extension works the quadriceps."

I hid a smile at the lingo. *Deconditioned. New-to-exercise. Time conscious.* I wondered what category Alyssa slotted me in. Probably not time conscious, since I'd been willing to wait, and I was too old to be considered new-to-exercise. That left deconditioned. I glanced at my image in the mirror. Did I look out of shape? Maybe a little. I vowed to get back to running, something I'd let slip these past few months.

"It sounds very efficient," I said, just as the studio door opened.

"That's Jamie in the red hoodie," Alyssa said, gesturing to two forty-something men deep in conversation. "They might be a few minutes. Hey, he's expecting you, right?" Her face clouded over, realizing her earlier omission. "I suppose I should have asked you that before."

"Tell him I'm here about Kelly Anne Acquolina."

Alyssa frowned, shrugged, then nodded. It was obvious that the name meant nothing to her, but then, why would it? She wouldn't have been born when Kelly had disappeared. I stood rooted to my spot, watching the sweat-stained faces trickle out of the studio, when Denim strutted out. She averted her eyes to avoid mine as Alyssa approached her.

"Well, what did you think?" Alyssa asked, approaching her, and beaming.

"Loved it," Denim said. "I think I might take you up on that two-week trial if I can afford it. I think you said it was fifty percent off?"

"That's right," Alyssa said. "Fifty percent off and no obligation to join if you decide it's not for you. Of course, almost everyone does. The classes are very popular, and it's a great way to meet people since you're new to the area."

Denim cast a surreptitious glance in my direction, then focused her attention on Alyssa, her expression serious, as if considering.

"That does sound like a good deal," I said, to let Denim know that I'd cover the expense, "I'd go for it myself, except I live in Marketville."

"That *is* too far to travel for a gym," Alyssa agreed. "Hey, it looks like Jamie's free. I'll go get him for you. Denim, if you'd like to take a seat at the table across from reception, we can take care of the paperwork. That is, if you're interested."

"Definitely interested," Denim said, and made her way to the front without so much as a backward glance. The girl was a natural.

34

To his credit, Jamie Gardiner managed to keep his expression neutral while Alyssa pointed in my direction. He looked good for his forty-some years, long, lean, and athletic, with sandy brown hair that curled at the nape of his neck, and gray eyes the color of polished pewter. A man who exuded charisma and sensuality in equal measure and knew it.

"I understand you're here to see me about Kelly," Gardiner said, the frost in his glance belying the warm smile put on for the benefit of others around us. "Let's go to my office, shall we?"

I followed him into a glass-partitioned cubicle not much larger than a closet and took a seat across from his desk. The walls were lined with a dizzying array of diplomas and certificates of completion in a variety of disciplines. Whatever success Gardiner had achieved, he'd worked hard for it.

"Who are you and what do you want?" he asked, once we were both seated.

"My name is Calamity Barnstable, I go by Callie. I'm the owner of Past & Present Investigations, based in Marketville. I've been hired to find out what happened to Veronica Celeste Goodman, an eighteen-year-old woman who disappeared from Miakoda Falls on Valentine's Day, 1995, two weeks after your girlfriend, Kelly Anne Acquolina, disappeared. I have reason to believe the cases may be related, along with another, that of Wanetta Georgina Bulmer. At present all three disappearances remain unsolved."

"I can't imagine what I could tell you that would be of any help. I didn't know Wanetta. Veronica was the girl Kelly Anne's pain-in-the-butt brother dated for a while. As for Kelly Anne, I'm not sure what you expect me to say."

"I was hoping—"

"Hoping what?" Gardiner asked. "That I'd be delighted to rehash the worst part of my life?"

I blushed, in spite of my resolve to be cool and professional. "Well, no, but…"

"But what? Did you think I'd share a secret I've been harboring from the police all these years? That I knew who she'd been talking to in that black car, possibly a Toyota Corolla, in front of Fiona's Fish and effing Chips? The car the police grilled me about, over, and over, and over again? Because I can assure you that I told them everything I remembered, which, frankly, was precious little. I drank at the time. A lot. Sometimes I supplemented alcohol with other stimulants. It wasn't unusual for me to wake up with no memory of what I'd done or how I'd gotten home, or if not home, to someone else's bed, couch, or floor. Frankly, I don't know why Kelly put up with me for as long as she did. I was unfaithful, abusive, and utterly lacking in motivation to look for a job, three qualities I emulated from my old man. He was a serial cheater who broke my mother's heart, spirit, and, on occasion, a bone or two, until she finally had the good sense to leave us when I was fifteen." Gardiner grimaced at the memory. "As you can imagine, that did nothing to improve my father's temperament. Or his drinking problem."

I hadn't been sure what to expect from Jamie Gardiner, but this raw reflection on his past wasn't it. "I'm sorry to dredge all of that up."

Gardiner lips skewed into a sad smile. "The truth is the day that Kelly pressed assault charges turned out to be the best day of my life. It made me see who and what I had become, and I didn't like the person staring back at me in the mirror. I entered rehab as soon as the charges were dropped, and I haven't had a drink or taken so much as an aspirin since. I know it sounds like a cliché, but these days I get high from exercise and helping others. Alyssa, for instance. She's put on twenty pounds since I hired her. Anorexic and bulimic, but she's getting better and stronger every day, gaining confidence and self-worth. In a year from now, give or take, she'll be ready to leave, maybe go back to school, or get a fresh start somewhere where no one knows her past. And I'll have done everything in my power to make that possible for her."

"But you didn't do that, did you? Move somewhere to start fresh. It would have made your life easier, wouldn't it?"

"In some ways, sure. But everyone loves a good comeback story, and I was lucky to have more people rooting for me than against me. Even the police came around, especially Detective Merryfield, though he wasn't a detective at the time. Small towns can be like that. I'm not sure I would have made it in a big city without that support, without knowing that if I slid back, I'd let everyone down who'd been willing to give me a second chance."

"What about your father? Did he follow your lead?"

"I cut all ties with my father when I entered rehab. He didn't believe in rehab, he would have had to admit that I—and maybe he—had a problem. He died of cirrhosis fifteen years ago, on January 31st, the anniversary of Kelly's disappearance, as if she was reaching out from the grave. Ironic, and oddly comforting."

"You believe Kelly is dead?"

"You don't?"

"I don't know. Her family believes she would have been in touch in some way if she was. But a former teacher claimed to see her in 2005 at Canada's Wonderland."

For the first time since I'd sat down, Gardiner grinned. "I think you'll find that Miss Dartmoor has a vivid imagination. Do you really think, if Kelly was still alive, that she'd risk going to Canada's Wonderland? It's in Maple, not much more than a ninety-minute drive down the 400 on a good traffic day. I don't see it. No, if Kelly is still alive, she's somewhere far, far away, living her own version of a fresh start. Now, if you'll excuse me, I have a Pilates class in ten minutes."

"Can I ask you one more question?"

"If you must."

"You were surprised that Kelly put up with you as long as she did. Why do you think she hung on? Was she a drinker too?"

"No, she never acquired the taste. But she was tired of being a server at Fiona's Fish & Chips, which is where I met her. She was seventeen, I was twenty-three. Things between her and her parents were strained, partly because she'd taken a gap year and never gone back to school and partly because she continued to see me, a guy five years older with a substance abuse problem and an old man everyone in town knew was a loser. Who could blame them? And her parents weren't exactly gems, either. But I guess if I could pinpoint it to one thing, I'd say it was that she wanted to save me from myself. And maybe because of the ring."

"The Claddagh ring?" I took note of his confusion. "It's mentioned on the Missing Adults Registry."

"It is? I had no idea. Is that an online thing?"

A Google search of Kelly Anne Acquolina would bring up a link to the Registry. Could it be true that he'd never once done a Google, never once visited the site? If so, what did that say about him? That he didn't care? Or that all he wanted to do was move on with his life? My gut feel told me it was the latter, but…

"Yes. The Ontario Registry of Missing and Unidentified Adults. The ring is referenced in Kelly's case listing."

Jamie considered that, then, "The Claddagh symbolizes friendship, loyalty, and love. I gave Kelly the ring when we first started dating. She took that ring, that message, as seriously as any vow. Maybe she thought that somewhere underneath all the booze and bad temper, that guy existed."

I waved my hands toward the busy gym, at Alyssa, chatting with a plus-sized woman pedaling a stationary bike. "From where I'm sitting, it looks like he did."

"I appreciate that." He stood up and extended his right hand. "I wish you success with your search,

Calamity Barnstable, goes by Callie. Just do me one favor, if you can."

"Name it."

"If you do find Kelly, let her know that I'm sorry for everything."

"I will. Anything else?"

"Yeah. Tell her not to come back. There are too many ghosts in this town."

"I'm not sure what you mean."

The sad smile returned. "There are skeletons in every closet, in every basement, in every attic."

"And the ghosts?"

"Lurk behind each and every one of them."

He slipped out of the office and into the studio before I had a chance to respond, but it didn't matter. I knew what he meant. We might be able to hide our skeletons, but the ghosts of our past, those never went away.

No matter how much we tried to store them in our spare bedroom.

35

I CHECKED my messages in the car. There was a thumbs up from Poppy and one from Denim asking if she could come by the next morning at nine to compare notes. I liked that she was being proactive and texted back, *SOUNDS GOOD*.

I went through my mental filing cabinet of everything I knew about Poppy Spencer. She'd been in real estate for ten years, originally working alongside another realtor, Bob Wilkes. They'd split, and she joined the Lount's Landing RealtyMaxx, where she quickly became the agency's top producer in Cedar County.

A few months ago, Poppy left RealtyMaxx and rejoined Wilkes to form Spencer & Wilkes Realty, with offices in Lount's Landing and Miakoda Falls. They'd gotten cozy at Luke and Emily's wedding, and I suspected their relationship had blossomed beyond the borders of business. Based on the number of listings, rentals, and solds the pair had already accumulated under the S & W banner, the partnership was going well.

THE MIAKODA FALLS office of Spencer & Wilkes was housed in U-shaped industrial strip mall that accommodated an assortment of medical and professional offices, with ample parking in the center of the U. Unit 28 was in the rear, right-hand corner, the window covered with photographs of homes, some marked Available, and others Sold. I opened the door. A young man, about thirty, looked up from his computer and smiled. "Can I help you?"

"I have an appointment with Poppy Spencer."

"You must be Ms. Barnstable. Hang up your coat. I'll buzz Poppy to let her know you've arrived."

The buzzer must have been somewhere on the desk because he didn't pick up a phone or touch his keyboard. I wondered if it was also a security measure. Did things get that tense when there were bidding wars?

Poppy Spencer arrived moments later, her red-soled Louboutins clicking on the tiled floor. An attractive woman in her mid-fifties, with steel gray eyes partially hidden behind dark designer frames and artfully highlighted short brown hair, she still resembled the photograph on the firm's website, though how much of her flawless complexion was due to clean living or Botox was anyone's guess.

"Good to see you, Callie. Ready to sell Edward Street?"

I shook my head. "It suits my life."

Poppy cast a quick glance at the young man at reception, then, "I knew it would. Come to my office and we'll talk."

Unlike the certificate-lined walls of Jamie Gardiner's office, the only thing adorning Poppy's wall was a large poster of a boat sailing under a bright yellow setting sun, the orange sky melting into rippling blue waters, the word OPPORTUNITY written underneath with the message: DON'T WAIT FOR YOUR SHIP TO COME IN... SWIM OUT TO IT.

"Thanks for taking the time to see me. I know the market's been hot."

"Sizzling, though the pundits are predicting a cool down. The good news is your house will have more than doubled in value since you purchased it in 2018. The bad news is upsizing would cost you every penny of your profit and more. Meanwhile, most first-time buyers are shut out of the market unless they've got parents to help them with the down payment. But you're not here to talk about real estate. I gather you're on a case?"

I nodded, then gave her a quick recap of the facts.

"I remember hearing about those women," Poppy said. "I was twenty-eight and staying at Miakoda House, a women's shelter in Miakoda Falls. Closed about a dozen years ago, government cutbacks and a lack of private funding."

I couldn't picture the impeccably dressed real estate icon sitting across from me working at a women's shelter. Did the staff live on site?

"As you can imagine, we were already living in fear. The thought of someone abducting young women intensified that. Kelly Anne Acquolina's story, especially, resonated with us. We were all there for the same reason, after all."

A victim, not staff. "You were in an abusive relationship?"

Poppy nodded, her lips pressed tight. "My ex-husband was abusive, both physically and verbally, and despite a restraining order, I was terrified that he'd come after me once I filed for divorce."

It went to show you never really knew someone. I was also doing a great job of digging up painful memories, first with Jamie Gardiner, and now with Poppy.

"I'm sorry. I had no idea."

"There's no reason you would have known, and there's no need to apologize. Thanks to the support I received at Miakoda House, I landed a job as a receptionist at a local brokerage, where I listened and learned what to do from the best agents, and what not to do from the worst." Poppy smiled. "After a while, I decided I could do as well or better than the best, took my real estate exams, and never looked back."

"And your ex?" The words were out before I could stop them. Fortunately, Poppy didn't seem to take offense.

"The last I heard he was living in Cambridge, married with two kids and a cat. I hope that's true. Has he changed? I don't know. I may never forgive him, but I stopped hating him long ago. That's the other thing I've learned through countless hours of therapy. Hate only hurts the hater, not the hated. But enough about me. You want to know if I know anything that might help you with your investigation."

"Do you?"

"I wish I did, but no, at least nothing you couldn't learn from a dozen other people. The Acquolinas sold their house a couple of years after Kelly disappeared, too many ghosts in this town."

Too many ghosts. The same expression Jamie had used. Except he'd used it when speaking about Kelly. I shivered, despite the warmth of the office. It was the sort of thing Misty Rivers would call a sign.

"There is one other thing," Poppy said, interrupting my thoughts.

"What's that?"

"Everyone at Miakoda House believed that

Kelly Anne Acquolina ran away. Maybe it was just wishful thinking on our part, but one of the girls claimed to have known her in high school, said Kelly was always going on about leaving Miakoda Falls for a fresh start."

A fresh start. Another echo of my conversation with Jamie.

"Do you remember the girl's name, the one who claimed to know her?"

"Diane."

Diane. Couldn't have been something exotic, easier to trace. "Any last name?"

"We only used first names at the house, a security thing, and Diane might not have even been her real first name. I called myself Penelope when I was there. But I'd like to think that Diane was right about Kelly, that she's still alive, that she's found her way out of the darkness."

"And the other two women? Veronica and Wanetta?"

Poppy shook her head. "I wouldn't want to take that bet."

36

IT WAS ALMOST two o'clock by the time I left Poppy's office, and while I knew Loretta Dartmoor's shift ended in an hour, my stomach was rumbling, the two oatmeal cookies I'd had for breakfast a distant memory. I stopped at a convenience store, grabbed a can of club soda and a pre-made tuna salad wrap with a Best Before date of three days from now—I didn't want to think about what preservatives were in that wrap to make it last that long—and ate and drank on the drive to the Miakoda Hills Sales Office.

I arrived at the gated entrance minutes later. The sales center was on my left. I pulled into the parking lot, checked my teeth in the rearview mirror for specks of food, popped in a breath mint, and got out of the car.

The sales office looked like a model home from

the outside, but resembled a hotel lobby inside. There was a reception desk in the middle and seating areas situated on either side. A couple in their early sixties was perched on one of the taupe suede sofas and were leafing through a brochure. Loretta was working at the reception desk and conveniently wore a name tag.

I'd half expected the woman who demanded to be called Miss—not Ms.— Dartmoor to resemble a caricature of a spinster schoolteacher, with heavily etched crow's-feet, starched collar, and iron gray hair tied into a tight bun. The woman who was sizing me up was both attractive and mirthful, with shoulder-length auburn hair streaked with silver. I couldn't imagine how she'd earned her nickname Miss Dark Mood and hoped I'd age half as well.

"How can I help you, Miss…"

"Barnstable. Callie."

"Miss Barnstable. You'll forgive my saying, but you seem a bit young for the Miakoda Hills crowd. Unless you're here for a relative?"

I shook my head. "Nothing like that. I'm the owner of Past & Present Investigations. We're based out of Marketville." I slid a business card across the counter. "I was hoping to speak to you about a cold case I'm working on."

That netted me a raised eyebrow from Loretta and furtive looks from the couple on the sofa.

"How cold?" Loretta asked.

"1995."

She flicked a glance at the couple, who had dropped all pretense of leafing through the brochure. "There's a coffee shop on the corner, Café Culture. You would have driven by it on your way in. I can meet you there after my shift ends at three. They won't mind if you wait, as long as you pay for refills and don't nurse the same cup of coffee for an hour. Try to get a booth in the corner if you can."

It would mean killing forty-five minutes when I'd hoped to do this here and now, but I also knew the offer might not be repeated.

I offered up a grateful smile. "I can do that."

FROM THE LOOK of the clientele, Café Culture was a popular spot among the Miakoda Hills fifty-five-plus crowd, and I could understand why. Everything about the café was comfortable and homey, with chocolate brown leather chairs and low-slung tables that had been placed, living room style, throughout the space, and one wall with an oversized electric fireplace that radiated warmth and ambience. The smell of cinnamon, cocoa, and sugar permeated the air, a combination that drew me to a glass case filled with a variety of cakes, cookies, and pastries. I salivated for a moment, my sweet tooth aching to be fed, and decided that today's efforts had earned me a reward. I opted for a slice of cream cheese iced carrot cake—could I count that as a serving of vegetables?—poured myself a mug of fair-trade Columbian coffee from one of a dozen black urns, each one offering a different blend or flavor, paid for my purchases at the cash register, including the extra charge for "free" refills, and found a table for two in the back corner.

My chair was every bit as comfortable as it appeared, the carrot cake worth every caloric bite, and the coffee full-bodied and brewed to perfection. Sometimes, you just had to give in to your urges.

My sagging strength restored by caffeine and sugar, I reread the Registry case listings one more time, then turned to my notes, specifically the parts that referred to Loretta Dartmoor, and added comments in the margins.

Detective Merryfield:
• Loretta Dartmoor, Miss, not Ms. *Reason? A feminist? Does it matter?*
• Students called her Miss Dark Mood. *Why?*
• Avid golfer. *Unlikely to factor in.*
• No reason to believe she knows more than what she told us in 1995, but… *But what? What wasn't Merryfield telling me?*
• The teacher who reported seeing Kelly Anne Acquolina at Canada's Wonderland. *Possibly also saw Wanetta Bulmer run across the school grounds. Ask for details.*

Jamie Gardiner:
• I think you'll find that Miss Dartmoor has a somewhat vivid imagination when it comes to her old students. *Was the "vivid imagination" a way to divert my attention? Any personal history with Dartmoor?*

My memory refreshed, I got up to pour myself a second cup of coffee and had just settled back in when Loretta Dartmoor arrived. She waved in my direction to indicate she'd seen me and joined me a couple of minutes later.

"Butterscotch pecan," she said, pointing to the muffin in front of her. "Probably the worst choice of all when it comes to muffins, but I'm addicted."

I smiled. "I think there are worse addictions."

"You're right about that. As a high school teacher, I've seen too many of them firsthand. Good kids losing their way because of drugs or alcohol, the impact it had on their families. No amount of intervention from the stern Miss Dartmoor could change that, though lord knows I'd stop at nothing when I saw the signs. Even acquired the nickname Miss Dark Mood for my trouble, though I doubt the students knew that I knew. I expect some of them called me worse."

"Did it ever do any good, the intervening?" I asked, genuinely curious.

"Not often enough, and certainly not after they'd left the confines of school. Sometimes I wonder if my interference did more harm than good, but I did my best. Now what's this about a cold case from 1995?"

"I've been hired to find out what happened to Veronica Celeste Goodman, which has led me to the case files for Wanetta Georgina Bulmer and Kelly Anne Acquolina. I believe all three cases may be related. That you came forward and reported seeing Kelly Anne at Canada's Wonderland and possibly Wanetta dashing across the front lawn."

Loretta smiled. "Yes, that was me. The young cop on the case, Danny Merryfield, always believed I knew more than I was saying. He's a Detective now, though I expect you know that. His boss, on the other hand, took everything I said at face value. Not one for digging deep, was Detective Marty Renner."

Danny, not Sheridan. Marty, not Martin. I leaned forward, intrigued. "Who was right? Merryfield or Renner?"

Loretta toyed with her uneaten muffin, studiously picking out the pecans and placing them around the perimeter of her white ironstone dessert plate until there was nothing left but a mound of butterscotch cake crumbs in the center. Finally looked up, her eyes glistening with tears.

"Does it matter?" she asked. "After all these years, does it actually matter?"

"If it didn't, neither one of us would be here. So, yes, it matters."

"Then I suppose in a way they were both right.

Renner, he was all about the facts. Merryfield, he might have listened, but at the end of the day, he's a cop. They're not big on conjecture. And that's all I've ever had. Conjecture. Theories. Call them what you will."

"But you believe them."

"I do, or at least I did."

"Did you talk with anyone else about your theories? Someone not with law enforcement?"

"I tried to tell someone what I thought, why I thought it, what…who…I'd seen. I trusted him, thought he would listen, tell me how to frame it so the police would listen." Loretta barked a short laugh. "Instead, he told me I had a vivid imagination."

A vivid imagination. The exact words Jamie Gardiner had used. But why would Loretta have gone to Kelly's ex-boyfriend with her theories? And why did I get the feeling she was still holding back?

"Did they have anything else to say beyond the fact that you had a vivid imagination?"

This time I thought I saw a flicker of fear cross her face. "Yeah. They warned me that nothing good ever came from dredging up the past. And now here we are, doing just that."

Tell Kelly not to come back, Gardiner had said. It seemed Loretta Dartmoor wasn't the only one keeping secrets. "My job is to dredge up the past, and I'm not guaranteeing a fairy tale ending. But the families of those three missing women deserve better than what they've been given."

"Closure," Loretta said.

I shook my head. "Not closure. A resolution. They're seldom the same thing."

Loretta pushed a couple of pecans around her plate, popped two in her mouth, chewed, and swallowed. "I need to sleep on it for a day or two, maybe longer. Before I decide if I should tell you what I suspect or let it go, once and for all."

It wasn't the response I was hoping for, but it was the one I expected. She had, after all, been sleeping on it—whatever *it* was—for a very long time. I also sensed that Miss Dark Mood was simmering under the surface. Pushing her before she was ready would be a mistake.

"You have my card," I said, getting up. "Call me anytime, day or night."

I left the café, never once looking back. I figured Loretta Dartmoor would take that as a sign of weakness. I needed her to believe I was strong.

Or at least, stronger than she was. The way I figured it, that was the only way she'd tell me her version of the truth.

37

———

I ARRIVED HOME tired but took a couple of hours to transcribe my notes into a Word document. I was rereading them when I spotted the niggle that had come to me when talking to Merryfield about Wanetta's case.

Merryfield: Miss Dartmoor was Kelly's high school teacher. Wanetta wasn't a student at Miakoda High, though her adult night classes were held there.

Then I reread the missing person's case listing and highlighted what I was looking for: Wanetta appeared to be a newcomer to Miakoda Falls and police were unable to locate any next-of-kin.

Which meant Wanetta had graduated from a different high school. But why would Merryfield choose not to disclose that information? Should it have been obvious to me? And did Miss Dartmoor know the answer?

I made a note to ask them, then checked my messages. There were two, one from Betsy Ehrlich and one from Levon. Both wanted to meet with me. I put off chilling out with a glass of wine and some mindless television and called them back.

I started with Levon, who answered on the first ring. Thankfully, Arabella had filled him in on the basics. He'd also been planning a trip to Marketville to meet with the owner of a used and rare bookstore that was going out of business. We set the time at 10:30 Sunday morning, coffee on me, scones on him. That settled, I called Betsy. From the clanging of what sounded like pots in the background, she was in the kitchen of The Hanged Man's Noose.

"Callie," she answered, breathless. "I'm in the middle of the dinner rush and trust me I'm not complaining. Folks are finally coming back to drink and dine, and I couldn't be happier. Arabella filled me in, wanted to know if I remembered the three young women who went missing in Miakoda Falls in 1995."

"And do you?"

"I can't help you with Kelly Anne Acquolina. I knew of her, but she was two years ahead of me. Might as well have been a decade at that time of my life. Nicki, on the other hand, was my best friend all through high school. At least she was until grade 12." I heard muffled voices in the background, then, "Look, Callie, it's a madhouse here. I'm closed Mondays. Can we talk then?"

Today was Friday. I felt my heart sink at the wait and understood it at the same time. Betsy was trying to survive, and weekends were her busiest time. Veronica Goodman's case was cold. It, I, could wait.

"Monday would be great," I said.

We agreed to ten o'clock Monday morning, my place, Betsy in "dire need of a change of venue." I hung up, knowing I had one more call I should make.

Ben.

Unless I sent Denim to see him. That might work. *Coward.*

I turned off my cell, put my landline ringtone on mute, poured myself a generous glass of Australian chardonnay, and turned on the TV, flipping through the channels until I found the repeat of a holiday baking show, the kind where teams make massive sculptures with moving parts. It wasn't the holidays, and I didn't bake anything more ambitious than the occasional muffin or cookie recipe, but that was okay. Right about now, all I wanted to do was turn off my brain.

38

———

MY SATURDAY MORNING meeting with Denim started off as more of a pep talk than a deep dive into what she'd learned, which, she reported, looking dejected, was virtually nothing outside of learning that Plank-It was the place to go for a good workout and better gossip.

The Miakoda Bar & Grille hadn't been replaced by another restaurant, as we'd both hoped, but by a florist shop that had opened five years earlier, replacing a blink-and-you'll-miss-it retailer of hot tubs and patio furniture.

Results for Fiona's Fish & Chips had proved equally disappointing. According to the server Denim had spoken with, Gloria Moroziuk was an absentee owner living "somewhere in Alberta" and hiring a succession of interim managers. Word on the street was the restaurant was one halibut and fries away from foreclosure.

That had left the Blue Goose Grocery, and while Nathaniel Spracklen was indeed the current owner, he hadn't been part of the day-to-day operations for the better part of a decade, and was a victim of early onset dementia. So much for Ben's dark web intel. It only went to confirm my belief that while online resources were a place to start, nothing beat boots on the ground. If I felt a sense of relief because there was now no urgent necessity to contact Ben, well, what of it?

After I reassured Denim that coming up empty was often part of the job, and a necessary part at that—ruling things out was every bit as important as ruling things in—I told her I'd be meeting with Levon and Betsy, then filled her in on what I'd learned from Detective Merryfield, swearing her to secrecy, followed by my meetings with Lindsay Doucette, Poppy Spencer, and Loretta Dartmoor. Recapping it all exhausted me, and I was just getting to my meeting with Jamie Gardiner.

"He seems like a good guy who's turned his life around and tries to help others who want to do the same," I said, summing things up. "Maybe that's all there is to it, but I can't shake the feeling that there's something he isn't telling me. That comment about telling Kelly to stay where she is if I find her, about there being too many ghosts in this town, there was a message there beyond the obvious. Can you find out more about his good deeds inside and outside of the gym?"

Denim bobbed her head, enthusiasm back. "I can do that. I plan to go every day at different times. I'll also let it drop that my ex left me for my former best friend, draining my bank account in the process. That I plan to find him and seek my revenge."

I nodded my approval. "That might appeal to Jamie's knight in shining armor. There is one more thing I'd like you to do, though I warn you it can be tedious."

"I'm okay with tedious. I'm here to learn."

"I hoped you'd say that. I've taken a cursory look at the Miakoda Falls Public Library website, and it offers some options for local history, including a historical society, which is unlikely to be of much use, but you never know. What might prove useful, however, is the town's newspaper, the *Miakoda Sentinel*. Everything pre-2008 has been transferred onto microfiche."

Denim was giving me an odd look. "What's a micro-fish?"

"*Microfiche*," I said and spelled it.

Denim tapped on her phone. "Oh, I see. Very analog. What's the deal?"

"It's a way of storing many documents in a small space. The film is an index-sized card, which you insert into a microfiche reader—it looks like an overhead projector. The reader blows up the image and displays it on a screen. Today, with scanning documents and photographs into PDFs and JPEGs, it can seem like an archaic technology, but it's still used by some libraries and medical facilities, and it was quite groundbreaking in its time. Without microfiche, many newspapers, by virtue of their ephemeral nature, would have been lost to the elements, yellowed and brittle with age."

"Is the reader easy to use?"

"Very, though it is a laborious process. I'd like you to visit the library, go through the microfiche archives, and print out any reference to the missing women. Check throughout 1995, and then move to 2005, when Loretta Dartmoor reported seeing Kelly Acquolina. That one will take longer, since we don't know exactly when that was in 2005, and Loretta didn't specify, but it *was* Canada's Wonderland. I'd start with May and work my way through the summer."

"I'll get started this afternoon," Denim said, looking keen. "Anything else?"

I thought about my father coming to pick me up after my shift at Sunnydale Food Market. "Check out the Cedar County Reference Library. They have the *Toronto Star* and *Toronto Sun*. It would be interesting to see if anything was reported in the city papers that wasn't just a reprint or recap of the *Miakoda Sentinel*."

"I can do that." She blushed. "You know, all this talk about newspapers reminded me that I was supposed to look for yearbooks for Miakoda High. I totally gapped that."

I'd forgotten as well, likely because I didn't want to be reminded of yearbooks right about now. "Don't beat yourself up. You've done a lot in one day, and this is your first investigation. You might find it helpful to write a massive to-do list, throw in everything you want to do, and then break it down into daily tasks. That way it won't seem so overwhelming."

"That's a great idea. Any other advice?"

"I always transcribe my notes into a Word document at the end of every day while everything is fresh in my mind, drilling down what I've learned and my initial impressions. I'd like you to do that, too."

"I'll get started as soon as I get home." Denim paused, then, "Callie?"

"Uh huh?"

"Thank you again for giving me this opportunity."

"Nothing's an opportunity until you take it," I said. "Good on you for doing that. Now scoot."

It was still morning in British Columbia, but not so early that I'd be rousting Misty out of bed. I decided to take a chance and called her.

She answered on the second ring, and after the usual pleasantries, I told her the reason for my call.

"I *do* remember Lindsay Doucette," Misty said, when I'd finished. "One of my regulars referred her, said I might be able to help, and it's not every day I'm consulted about a young woman, long missing. But a tarot reading couldn't give Lindsay what she wanted to know. Was her sister dead or alive? If alive, where was she? A charlatan might have filled her head with false hope, spun a good yarn, but I told her the truth."

"If it's any consolation, Lindsay told me how much she appreciated you not stringing her along."

"Did she? I'm glad, though I might have been able to tell her more if she'd been more forthcoming."

"I don't understand."

"I recall feeling she wasn't being entirely truthful."

"I had the same impression."

"Then maybe that's your angle, Callie. Find out what Lindsay is holding back and see where it leads."

Easier said than done, I thought, hanging up, though at least Misty's recollection mirrored mine. Her psychic powers might be questionable, but she could read people like a book.

I realized I had a bit of idle time. I could have taken the opportunity to read or binge watch something on TV, maybe cook up some pre-made meals to reheat through the week, but all I could think of was my mother's high school yearbooks, waiting for me on a bookshelf in the spare bedroom. I grabbed a fresh notebook and pen and headed upstairs.

39

THE YEARBOOKS COVERED the school terms 1974-75, 1975-76, 1976-77, 1977-78, and 1978-79. Except for the dates, the covers of each were identical and uninspired, lakeside high in uppercase, printed diagonally from the top left corner to the bottom right, the years numbered on either side, white lettering against a deep purple background.

I selected the yearbook dated 1974-75, sat down on the rose and cream floral sofa bed—not my taste but a freebie from Chantelle, given to me when she moved, and a freebie to her from some aunt or another—and turned to the first page.

Our School Song
Stand up for Lakeside High
Stand and cheer, cheer, cheer
For we are assembled here today

To sing our song out loud and clear
Purple and White forever, raise
   on high
Virtus, integritas, doctrina, our
   motto 'til we die.

Virtue, integrity, and learning. Latin had been an elective subject when I was in grade nine, though I expected that was unlikely today. Our teacher had worn a laurel wreath, sandals, and a toga on the Ides of March and liked to quote Julius Caesar. The latter came in handy since Shakespeare's *Julius Caesar* was required reading in second term English.

I turned the page to find acknowledgments to the faculty and Yearbook Committee, as well as a shoutout to the Camera Club for all photographs. There was no mention of Abigail Osgoode in any of the lists.

The third page included a Table of Contents. Classes were listed from graduating students first to grade nine students last, with an Athletics and Clubs section in the center. I skipped past all of it, focusing my attention on Grade 9.

There were two group photos, labeled as 9A-4 and 9B-5, signifying the four-year and five-year programs, Grade 13 still very much part of the Ontario School Board curriculum. I scanned the pictures, determined to identify my mother without reading the captions, and spotted her in the five-year class. *Just one more thing to disappoint my grandfather*, I thought. Graduating from Grade 12 gave you a high school diploma and the possibility of community college, but acceptance into university had required Grade 13. Getting married in December of her senior year had meant leaving school before completing her final year, and moving from Lakeside to Marketville. Had she tried to transfer to Marketville High? Or had she merely dropped out, believing that university with a newborn and no money or family support would be out of the question?

I studied the photograph with a critical eye. My mother's blonde hair framed a heart-shaped face, her blue eyes clear and without guile. She looked younger than most of her classmates, but she had a December birthday. She would have been just thirteen entering high school, almost a full year behind those born in January.

Only the graduating students had individual photos and bios, so unless my mother had joined a club or taken part in sports, this would be the only photo of her. I studied the faces in the four rows of students, read the names in the captions, did the same for the four-year grade nine class. Not a single name was familiar.

I shouldn't have been surprised, let alone disappointed, but I found myself feeling more than a little bit of both. The reality was my mother hadn't been part of my life since I was six and my father never uttered her name after she left. I had no idea how, when, or where my parents had met. I didn't even know where my father had gone to high school, only that he'd had a physical altercation with my grandfather on at least two occasions, one outside of Ben's Convenience.

I put the yearbook aside, paced the room, and suppressed the urge to throw it against the wall. How could I not know these simplest of facts? Weren't the "how I met your mother or father" the kind of stories parents loved to tell their children?

I turned my attention back to the yearbook, looking for Abigail Osgoode. Looking for Jimmy Barnstable. Looking for my parents, before they became parents.

Looking for the answers.

40

I spent the better part of the next two hours scouring every face, caption, and page in the yearbook. There was no sign of my father, though I did find my mother in a collage of photographs with the Volunteer Club, whose mandate was "to make a difference in the community." The club's projects included visiting seniors in long term care homes and organizing a Christmas toy, food, and clothing drive for families in need.

One photo showed her with another girl, taller than my mother by a good three inches, sorting toys and books into large plastic totes labeled by age and gender. I flipped back to the class photo of Grade 9B-5 and spotted her standing in the back row, counted the spaces, five from the left, and looked for her name. Bernadette Robertson. Not just taller than my mother, but taller than most of her classmates.

The photographs were black and white, but it appeared that Bernadette Robertson had medium length brown hair, poker straight and half-way down her back, blue or gray eyes, a thin build, and a wide smile with a noticeable gap between her two front teeth.

I turned to the last few pages, reserved for student comments. My mother's yearbook was filled with scrawled signatures, but beyond messages like "Love, luck, laughter," and "We made it!" the comments did nothing to shed light on who my mother was, or even if she'd been generally well liked. There were no last names, zero Bernadettes, and one Bern.

Was Bern Bernadette? More searching revealed that Bernadette Robertson also belonged to the run club. A blurred photograph of her in motion, her legs long and lean, feet barely touching the track beneath them, was captioned "Feel the Bern." Bern, then, was a safe bet. I wrote her name down in my notebook, then shelved yearbook 1974-75 and removed 1975-76 from the bookshelf.

The format of 1975-76 was identical to the prior year, right down to the School Song on page two. I flipped straight through to class 10B-5, found Bernadette Robertson, still at the back, my mother in the center of the middle row, her blonde hair longer now with feathery waves. Several other girls wore a version of the same style, the long shag cut Farrah Fawcett had first made famous in *Charlie's Angels*. I thought about the "Rachel" made famous by Jennifer Aniston, all the rage when I was in high school. Why were we so keen to channel celebrity instead of ourselves?

It was a rhetorical question, even if there'd been someone with me to answer it. I kept turning the pages. My mother had ramped up her school presence. Still a member of the Volunteer Club, Bernadette Robertson at her side once again, but now also a cheerleader, her short white pleated skirt showing shapely legs, the purple crop top, a large "L" for Lakeside stitched into the front, just short of revealing more than taut abs and toned arms.

I studied the football collage, but it wasn't my mother's smiling face at the top of a cheer pyramid, purple and white pompoms held high in a victory "V," that caught my attention. Rather it was a picture of the cheer squad, the football team behind them, one player's hand, resting ever so gently on my mother's tiny waist, the other holding his helmet. I counted his position in the lineup and checked the caption.

Joseph (Joey) Perella, QB.

Well, well, well. My mother had dated the team's quarterback in grade 10. What had I expected? That my father had been her one and only?

Yes, that was exactly what I'd expected. Instead, this dark-haired, dark-eyed athlete had been there first. Had they been intimate? Or was it more of heavy petting kind of thing? I flipped to the back pages, found his message scrawled in black ink:

"To Abigail, your love CHEERS me on.
Yours always, Joey, xxooxx."

I found his photo class of 11B-5, one year ahead of my mother, and wondered if Yvette and Corbin had caught wind of their relationship, or if she'd had to sneak around behind their backs. I made my second notation of the day: Joseph (Joey) Perella.

I closed the yearbook and replaced it on the shelf. Two down, three to go, but it had been an age since I'd eaten. Besides, it wasn't as if any of this was going to change the past, and it was just as unlikely to change my future.

41

LEVON ARRIVED right on schedule Sunday morning. He'd grown a beard since I'd seen him last and reminded me of Kris Kristofferson in *A Star Is Born*. I'd seen the remake with Lady Gaga and Bradley Cooper, and it had intrigued me enough to watch the 1978 movie. In my not-so-humble opinion, the Kristofferson-Streisand version won hands down, at least when it came to story development and character arcs. And while Cooper was no slouch, Kristofferson oozed sex appeal. So too, did Levon Larroquette, not that he ever seemed aware of it, which made him all the more charismatic. Arabella was one lucky lady.

We exchanged the usual niceties over coffee and lemon blueberry scones, then got down to business. I started by showing him the printouts from the

Ontario Registry of Missing and Unidentified Adults.

"Arabella tells me you were living in Miakoda Falls at the time. Did you know any of these women?"

Levon shook his head. "No, but I did know Travis Acquolina, Kelly's younger brother. We were in boot camp together."

"Boot camp?"

"It was an experimental initiative. Instead of juvie hall, some young offenders were sent to a place called Camp Miakoda. It was about ten miles outside of Miakoda Falls, on the Dutch River, locked in between two sets of waterfalls and surrounded by forest. Quite remote, but also very beautiful. The government of the day sank a fair bit of money into it, but it faced a lot of public and political opposition. It was only open for that one season. The land and buildings were sold off several years ago to a real estate developer, and it's been resold at least a couple of times since. Some say the land is cursed. I like to think it's just waiting for the right owner, someone who will treat it with the respect it deserves. The project might have been abandoned, but Camp Miakoda saved a few teenaged boys, me among them."

I didn't think it was my place to ask what Levon had done to wind up at a boot camp for young offenders, but I needed to know everything I could about Travis Acquolina. I was debating the best way to find out when Levon spoke again.

"You're too polite to ask, and it's a bit of a longer story than shoplifting, though that was the charge. Let's just say I had a cop who cared in my corner. So did Travis, though it was a different cop."

"Do you remember the cop's name? The one who cared about Travis?"

Levon nodded. "Sheridan Merryfield. Travis used to call him Danny Boy, though never to his face. It was all more bluster than muster. We boys blustered a lot at Camp Miakoda, always trying to prove how cool we were, how being there didn't matter."

"I'm guessing it mattered."

"More than you can imagine. Travis was there because he'd beaten up his older sister's ex-boyfriend, guy by the name of Jamieson Gardiner, went by Jamie. That would have been the spring of '95. Gardiner had been charged with assaulting Kelly Anne a few months before. Got away with it, too, once Kelly Anne went missing, but the justice system works in mysterious ways. That's what set Travis off, that Jamie got off without so much as probation. He never said as much directly, but I know he blamed Gardiner for her leaving."

"Blamed in what way? Did he think that Jamie had something to do with her disappearance?"

"As in, did he abduct her? No. Travis believed Kelly Anne had left on her own. According to Travis, she was terrified of going to court, tried to recant and that went nowhere. Like I said, the justice system works in mysterious ways."

"But surely if she was still alive, she'd have made contact with her parents, with Travis, eventually?"

Levon smiled. "Who's to say she hasn't? Travis did his time, the same as the rest of us. Took anger management classes, walked out of Camp Miakoda in August 1995, never to be heard from again."

I caught the nuance. Not never to be *seen* or heard from again. Just *heard*. "Are you implying that someone saw him?"

That netted me another smile. "You might want to talk to that high school teacher. The one who reported seeing Kelly Anne at Canada's Wonderland in 2005. The one mentioned on the Registry."

I thought of Loretta Dartmoor's reticence. "Are you saying the high school teacher saw Travis and Kelly Anne together?"

"I don't know what or who she saw. What I do know is that Travis Acquolina loved his sister and he loved Canada's Wonderland. They'd been going there as a family since it opened in 1981. He was a big fan of the Vortex."

I'm not much of an amusement park person,

and despite its proximity to Marketville, I'd never been to Canada's Wonderland. "The Vortex?"

"A suspended roller coaster that goes over the open water behind Wonder Mountain. If he was going to meet his sister, where better than a giant amusement park they were both familiar with?"

"So, you believe Kelly Anne is still alive. Or she was in 2005."

"I think it's worth keeping an open mind."

"And the other two cases? Wanetta Bulmer? Veronica Goodman?"

Levon shook his head. "In the four months I spent with Travis at Camp Miakoda, he never mentioned their names. Either he didn't believe they were related or—"

"Or," I said, finishing his thought, "he knew they weren't."

"Exactly." Levon looked at his watch, got up, stretched. "I've got to get to the bookstore."

"Thank you for coming, for sharing your story with me. For trying to help. I really appreciate it."

"I'm not sure how much help I've been, or if all I've done is muddy the waters. I'll let you decide."

I thought about that after Levon had left. Thought about it for a good long time. The waters seemed muddier than when he'd arrived, but there was one more thing to note: Kelly Anne had disappeared in January, Travis in August. Had Wanetta's disappearance given Kelly Anne, Travis, and Veronica an idea? Maybe.

But *if* Wanetta's disappearance had given Kelly Anne an idea…*if* I could take Kelly Anne out of the equation, then I could concentrate solely on the similarities between Wanetta and Veronica. But first, I would talk to Betsy Ehrlich and see what she could tell me. My phone chimed, a text from Denim: CHECK YOUR EMAIL.

There were a few others, but I zoned in on Denim's—the rest could wait.

Hi Callie, I found some interesting news articles and have scanned them as PDFs. I'm sending them as email attachments. Denim.

Both Miakoda papers published photos of the girls, identical to the ones in the missing persons' case listings. There were also interviews with the girls' friends, parents, teachers, and statements from police. People were worried there was a serial killer in the area. I glanced at the byline: G.G. Pietrangelo. Gloria Grace, writing for the *Miakoda Sentinel,* not the *Marketville Post.* She had reported on my mother's disappearance in the *Post* and been a key player in my investigation. We'd remained friends, though I hadn't seen her since her last wildlife photography show. I called, got voice mail, and left a message.

That was enough work for the day. It was Sunday, and even the self-employed deserved a day off.

Besides, there were always my mother's yearbooks.

I could almost hear them calling my name.

42

THE NEXT YEARBOOK WAS 1976-77. The first thing I did was check Grade 11B-5, and once again, Bernadette Robertson was in the back row, my mother now front and center, her Farrah Fawcett hair fluffed like a halo around an angelic face.

My gosh, she was beautiful. Did she know, then, how beautiful she was? Or was she filled with the same insecurities I'd had back in grade 11? The year I'd met Arabella Carpenter, a sassy, smart-mouthed transfer from another school, no reason given. I never did find out why Arabella had transferred in, a mystery sprinkled with fairy dust. I only knew she'd become my best friend. We hadn't stayed as close, post-graduation, Arabella heading to Lount's Landing while I stayed in Toronto, but we'd never lost touch completely. I decided to view my mother's yearbook through the same lens, that one or more of her classmates had remained in her life, if not forever, for the early years of her marriage.

I skipped ahead to the collage of photos of the Lakeside High football team and cheer squad. As could be expected, Joey, as quarterback, was in most, though this time his hands were wrapped firmly around the waist of a petite, ponytailed blonde.

So much for love always. I wondered who had initiated the break-up, Joey or my mother. People like to spin splits if they're a mutual decision, but in my experience one person is the dumper and the other is the dumpee, and amicable meant both parties had stopped caring enough to argue.

The blonde was Delphina Gunton, class 11B-5. Her blue eyes sparkled for the camera, her hair cascading in waves past her shoulders. Pert and pretty, with tiny teeth and delicate features, she reminded me of someone. Not Farrah Fawcett, though the hairstyle was similar. Meg Ryan, that was it, circa *When Harry Met Sally*, *Sleepless in Seattle*, and *You've Got Mail*. What can I say? I'm a huge Nora Ephron fan.

I added Delphina's name to my notebook, flipped through the pages—still no trace of my father and it appeared the Volunteer Club had disbanded—and made my way to the comments.

I wasn't expecting to find a message from Joey, and there wasn't one, but I was surprised to find

"Cheers! Delphina," the i dotted with a tiny heart, on the center of the page. The message, written in swirling black ballpoint, had been crossed out in bold, turquoise strokes. I grinned. I wasn't a handwriting expert, but the turquoise ink matched the "PROPERTY OF ABIGAIL DORIS OSGOODE" on the flyleaf. It seemed getting dumped ran in the family.

I was contemplating that when my phone rang, Gloria Grace returning my call, and told her about the cases and the newspaper clippings.

"I was a couple years out of journalism school at Ryerson, working at the *Miakoda Sentinel*," she said, when I'd finished. "Not much went on in Miakoda Falls and those girls were big news. Let me get my notes and call you right back."

She'd kept her notes all these years? Of course. She'd saved all her notes and photographs from my mother's disappearance too. I paced the floor while I waited, phone in hand.

"Found them," she said a few minutes later. "But first, tell me what you know."

I heard her rustling papers as I spoke, and I could envision her flipping the pages, her eyes narrowed in concentration.

"Here's what I can add," she said after my recap. "Veronica and Kelly had grown up in Miakoda Falls, well-known, etcetera, but Wanetta was an enigma. She had recently moved to town and was living in the dodgy end. Her landlady told the police she changed her hair color several times, she was a brunette when she first rented her room, then she had pink streaks, then red and blonde streaks, then platinum. The landlady didn't think much of that, it ruined the hair and so forth."

"Who was her landlady?"

"Henrietta St. Pierre. She isn't named in your notes?"

"No, although I'm sure Merryfield knows."

"Ah. She was in her late seventies. I'm sure she's long passed over into the next world. She had turned her place into a boarding house, all female renters. The girls called her Mrs. Henri. The house is gone, sat on the corner of Jarvis and McLaren."

I channeled Denim and googled the area—an empty lot, at least when the photo was taken. The high school was three blocks away.

"Okay, the next bit is all conjecture on my part," Gloria Grace said. "Mrs. Henri said Wanetta worked hard, never took any time off, except for one weekend at the resort on Little Moon Island."

"Little Moon Island?"

"It's a five-minute boat ride from Miakoda Island, which is a Chippewa Reserve. They used to run a four-season resort on Little Moon Island, though now it's all private cottages on Chippewa leased land. Back in 1995, a stay at Little Moon Island was pricey."

"Maybe a rich boyfriend?" I ventured. "Or a married guy trying to keep a low profile?"

"Both possible," Gloria Grace said. "There was also talk, at the time, of a guy with a camera hanging around the school grounds, claimed to be a talent scout. Marty Renner wasn't buying it, ran the guy out of town quick. Anyway, I remember thinking at the time, did Wanetta fall for that dude's story? My notes say she bought new clothes and boots just before she disappeared, the kind of thing I'd do if I was trying to impress someone."

I had to admit it would be something I'd do as well. I said as much to Gloria Grace.

"Hmm, yeah, though here's the thing. There was no record of Wanetta staying at the resort. Of course, she could have used a different name, or maybe they registered as Mr. and Mrs. Smith or what-have-you. But what if she knew someone who worked there? The private ferry stopped at Miakoda Island before going to Little Moon, still does. So, then I thought, could Wanetta be Indigenous? Her skin tone was listed as medium whereas the other missing women were fair, and her race was left blank. That always bothered me. And Mrs. Henri's maiden name was George, which is a common last name on Miakoda Island."

"And Wanetta's middle name is Georgina."

"Yes, and there you go—a whole of 'what-if' and loose ends, and takes us nowhere concrete, except back to Wanetta being an enigma."

We chatted a little longer, but Gloria Grace didn't have anything to add to what I already knew about Kelly Anne and Veronica. She promised to go back over her notes and call if she found anything interesting. I promised to come to her next wildlife photography show, which was going to be all about the birds of Prince Edward Island, where she'd spent the past summer playing golf and snapping photos.

And then it hit me. *Photos. The one photo of Wanetta.*

I hung up, tapped my pen on my notepad and thought, then called Lucy Daneluk and recapped my conversation with Gloria Grace, including the bit about the supposed talent scout.

"I was thinking, what if Mrs. Henri knew more than she let on? The photograph of Wanetta, the one on your website, it looked like a studio headshot to me, something a professional would take, or at least, a guy claiming to be a professional. I didn't think anything of it at the time, but now I'm not so sure, like maybe I should have questioned it. Do you know the source?"

"The source? I believe it was the Lakeside PD."

"Do you have any way of verifying that?"

"Doubtful. Wanetta's been missing almost twenty-five years. That photograph could have been taken anywhere."

Could have, I thought, though I'd swear on my last breath it was a studio pic. Graduation photo? Was it from one of those glamor shot places that used to be in shopping malls? If it was from a studio, the photographer's imprint might be on the photo. But the police would have looked for that.

And then another thought crossed my mind. What if Wanetta had changed her last name when she moved to Miakoda Falls? Could she be related to Mrs. Henri?

Okay, my imagination was running rampant. I ran the idea by Lucy anyway.

"A name change *would* explain why the police didn't find any next-of-kin," she said, "but Wanetta had a bank card and a credit card, right? I don't think you can get those with fake ID, but what do I know? I suppose with the right connections, anything is possible."

Would a young woman like Wanetta have the right connections? Unlikely, but something to consider. I was debating the possibilities when Lucy interrupted me mid-stream.

"I have an idea," she said. "It's a long shot but…I'll get back to you."

I could have returned to the yearbooks, but I didn't have it in me. It was time to call it a day, maybe binge watch some old movies. I settled on *Uncle Buck*, *Cool Runnings*, and *Planes, Trains & Automobiles*. You could never go wrong with John Candy. May he rest in peace.

43

———————

MY JOHN CANDY MOVIE MARATHON had done wonders to restore my flagging spirits. I woke up Monday morning, refreshed and ready to meet with Betsy Ehrlich at ten, the Veronica Goodman case once again my top priority, my mother's high school yearbooks safely on the back burner.

It had been several months since I'd seen Betsy but despite the challenges the past two years had brought, she remained much as I remembered her. Tall and lithe, with dark brown hair, diamond-studded earlobes, and a long, thin neck: Audrey Hepburn in *My Fair Lady*.

We made small talk, then got down to the reason for her visit.

"You said you were Veronica Goodman's best friend in high school, at least until grade 12," I began. "Tell me how you met and how you became friends."

Betsy's eyes took on a faraway for a moment, then, "It was the first day of grade nine, everyone was older than me. I'd accelerated from grade four to six, skipping grade five, a practice that thankfully has been abandoned. So, there I was, a full year younger than most. By the time you're twenty, a year or two on either side is nothing, but the difference between thirteen and fifteen is huge, emotionally and physically. The other girls looked like women to me, and I felt like a little kid playing dress up.

"I was in home room, hiding in the back row and feeling completely out of place, when Nicki took the seat next to me. The first thing I noticed was that she looked every bit as young and miserable as me. And then she caught my eye and smiled, and her whole face lit up, as if she recognized a kindred spirit. Turned out she'd skipped a grade, too, only instead of four to six, it was three to five."

I'd been an "accelerated kid," too, also skipping grade five, largely thanks to my book report on *In Cold Blood* by Truman Capote when my classmates were still into Nancy Drew and the Hardy Boys. I hadn't considered the challenges, all I wanted was to be the smartest kid on the block, and I was, at least when it came to English and reading. Math and science were another matter.

To my father's credit, he'd been anti-acceleration, but I'd begged him to let me do it, and in a rare show of acquiescence to my pre-adolescent whims, he'd succumbed to my pleading. I wish he'd stuck to his guns. Junior year of high school is tough enough without being the latest of the late bloomers.

"I expect the impact of acceleration is the same, regardless of the grade skipped," I said, deliberately excluding my own experience. This wasn't about me.

"I can't speak for other kids," Betsy said. "But Nicki and I formed a bond when we were at our most vulnerable and insecure. I believed that bond would last forever, and maybe, if Nicki hadn't disappeared, we would have found our way back to it. But she did, and so we didn't."

"But for a while, you did have that bond."

"I tried to blend in, you know? Nicki, though, it always seemed as if she was trying to be three different people. To her family, she was Roni, the good girl who helped with the chores and didn't make trouble. To our teachers, she was Veronica, an honors student who studied hard. To her friends, she was Nicki, loyal to a fault and full of fun, always up for a lark, though not exactly what you'd call spontaneous."

"Meaning?"

"Everything in her life was planned to the nth detail. I think that came from accelerating. Nicki didn't take kindly to anything spur of the moment, whether it was an ad hoc exam, a last-minute change of menu at the school cafeteria, or a party. She was careful, cautious, name your adjective. Is that important?"

I contemplated the implications. "It might be. Do you think the pregnancy was planned?"

"I can't imagine that anyone plans to get pregnant at seventeen."

And yet, I thought, *this girl who didn't respond well to change, who planned every step of her life, who was careful and cautious, did get pregnant.* "Do you have any idea who the baby's father might be?"

A lengthy pause, then, "She'd stopped confiding in me by that time."

"But you have your suspicions."

Betsy nodded. "A musician we'd met at the CNE the summer before grade 12. He'd been playing at the Bandshell for some group whose name I no longer remember. He was older than us by a good ten years, looked a bit like Eddie Vedder of Pearl Jam. It wasn't long after that she started pulling away. If she was seeing him, maybe she thought I wouldn't approve because of the age difference, or maybe he told her to keep their relationship a secret."

"Did you tell this to the police?"

"I dithered. What if I was wrong, gave the guy a world of hurt for no reason? I had no proof that they were seeing each other, it was just a gut feeling."

"And if you were right?"

"Then I wouldn't be the only person who suspected."

"Did you keep track of him? After Nicki went missing?"

Betsy shook her head "Until now, I'd all but forgotten about him, wasn't like he ever became famous."

"Do you remember his name?"

"Isaac something…Buckley, no…Buckman. Isaac Buckman."

Isaac Buckman. The nephew of Edith Buckman, Veronica's landlady. It went a long way to explaining why Edith Buckman had rented her basement apartment to Veronica, why she'd left Kate a trust for her post-secondary education.

But hadn't Lindsay Doucette said that Veronica had found out about the apartment while working at the Miakoda Bar & Grille? And that implied that Kate had already been born. But she hadn't said so, specifically, had she? I'd just assumed that was the case. What if Veronica Goodman had moved out of her sister's house *because* she was pregnant? Any number of scenarios popped into my head. Scenarios I should have thought about. Asked about.

Like asking Lindsay if she knew where Isaac Buckman was now, or if he'd stayed in touch with Kate.

So many questions, none of which were Betsy Ehrlich's to answer.

44

THE FIRST THING I did after Betsy left was to google Isaac Buckman. There was a brief blurb on Wikipedia, with a note requesting additional citation.

ISAAC ANDREW BUCKMAN
Born: September 5, 1964, Miakoda Falls, Ontario
Died: June 15, 2012 (age 47)
Occupation: Musician
Years active: 1984–2012

Isaac Buckman was a Canadian session musician often hired by bands playing at the CNE Bandshell and Greater Toronto Area taverns. Buckman was killed in a single vehicle crash in Toronto on June 15, 2012. There were no witnesses, and the cause of the crash remains unknown.

Even if Buckman had been Kate's father, there was no way of proving it ten years after his death, and a DNA test wouldn't help if no Buckman relatives could be found. But I wasn't giving up that easily. The CNE Bandshell and session musician had been hyperlinked. A photograph of Buckman, captioned "Buckman at the CNE Bandshell, 1999" was attributed to C. LaPorte.

Buckman was hunched over a guitar, eyes closed, his wavy brown hair parted in the center, the ends brushing against a faded denim shirt. I opened a new tab and entered "Eddie Vedder photos." Betsy was right. Isaac Buckman could have been Vedder's twin brother.

I wasn't entirely sure what a session musician was and clicked the link. There was a three-paragraph blurb that could be boiled down to three sentences:

Session musicians, studio musicians, or backing musicians are musicians hired to perform in recording sessions or live performances. Session musicians are used when musical skills are needed on a short-term basis. Session musicians are usually not permanent or official members of a musical ensemble or band. They work behind the scenes and rarely achieve individual fame in their own right as soloists or bandleaders.

I clicked on the CNE Bandshell link next. I knew, even without checking, that anything Wiki had on the Bandshell would be a time waster, but I went there anyway.

As expected, the CNE Bandshell entry on Wikipedia revealed nothing beyond confirming what I already knew:

> The CNE Bandshell is an open-air concert venue in Toronto, Ontario, Canada. Built in 1936, it is located at Exhibition Place on the shores of Lake Ontario. It hosts the annual music program of the Canadian National Exhibition (CNE) and is also used for festivals and picnic events, for which the "Bandshell Park" can be rented from the City of Toronto.

I closed the page and entered "C. LaPorte" into the search engine. The top hit was Christophe LaPorte, a French cyclist born in 1992. There was also Clément LaPorte, a French rugby player born in 1998, and a couple of PhD scholars based in Montreal, with work history that didn't begin until the 2000s.

Those dismissed, I tried "C. LaPorte obituary,"

albeit without success. Either C. Laporte had died without anyone caring enough to post an obit, they liked to keep a low profile, or the name was an alias.

It was time to call Lindsay Doucette.

45

"Apologies if I caught you at a bad time," I said when Lindsay answered. "I've just met with Betsy Ehrlich, and I have a couple more questions."

"I'm not doing anything that can't wait. And well done, you, for finding Betsy. I haven't thought of her in years. She and Roni were best friends in high school, though they drifted apart. How is Betsy?"

"She's doing well, owns a pub in Lount's Landing called The Hanged Man's Noose. Great atmosphere, good food."

"I'm glad. I always liked her. What is it you want to know?"

"I should have asked this before, and I don't know why I didn't, but was Veronica pregnant when she moved into Edith Buckman's basement apartment?"

"She was, but I think you're asking if she was pregnant when she left home, and the answer is no. Roni had moved out to share a flat with three other girls. When she learned that she was pregnant, it was clear that wouldn't work in the long term. I offered to have her move in with me, and I knew she'd need help if she planned to keep the baby, but she insisted on going it alone. I think she thought the baby's father would come through for her, though of course, he didn't."

"Betsy seemed to think the father was a musician they'd met at CNE."

"A musician. Did she have a name?"

"She thought it might be Isaac Buckman."

There was a prolonged silence, then, "Edith may have believed so. Maybe that's why she was so kind to Veronica, and why she left an education trust for Kate. But Isaac wasn't the kind of guy to walk away from responsibility. He was a musician who was away a lot, but he always made sure Edith was okay. He was kind to Roni, but it was never in a romantic way, and he never demonstrated any paternal feelings for Kate. Have you been able to find him and arrange a meeting?"

"I'm afraid that will be impossible." I filled her in on the Wikipedia entry for Buckman.

"How tragic for him, and if I'm being honest, for Kate. If he were her father, there's no way of finding out now." She paused for a moment, then, "There's one other factor to consider."

"What's that?"

"If Isaac was Kate's father, wouldn't he have provided for her in his will? We didn't even know he'd passed. In fact, we only saw him a couple of times after Edith died, when he came back to sell the house."

It was a fair point, and one I was embarrassed to admit hadn't crossed my mind. Even so, I wasn't prepared to drop the Buckman connection altogether, and I was all the more convinced that C. LaPorte held, if not *the* key, a key to Veronica's disappearance.

"There's still one more avenue I'm trying to explore. There's a photograph on Wikipedia dated from the summer of 1997 at the CNE Bandshell. The photo is attributed to a C. LaPorte. Unfortunately, I haven't been able find anything more, not even a first name. I wondered if you might have known him?"

"C. LaPorte? I'm sorry, but the truth is Roni had become increasingly secretive, even before she got pregnant, and I didn't want to pry. Maybe if I had…"

"You can't go down that road, Lindsay. It doesn't lead anywhere. If it's any consolation, Betsy noticed the same thing."

We chatted a few more minutes, mostly about Betsy's recollections, but it was clear that Lindsay had nothing more to add. I hung up, disheartened but not discouraged. I would follow up with Poppy,

Betsy, Levon, Loretta, and Gloria Grace on the off chance they'd heard the name. Maybe I'd get lucky.

Except I didn't. Five hours and five phone conversations later, I was no further ahead.

I tried Detective Merryfield next, got voice mail, and left a message asking him to call me back.

The only one left was Jamie Gardiner, but I didn't trust him to tell me the truth. Denim, on the other hand, might have a shot. Was it worth taking the chance, knowing that it would blow her cover?

I spent the next hour mulling that over. The pros, the cons, the what ifs. Made a list, checked it twice. Balled up the paper and tossed it in the blue bin.

Because I knew, in that spidery-sense way a woman knows she's going to get dumped, even when she wants to believe anything but, that whoever C. LaPorte was, he—and I was certain LaPorte was a man—had played an integral part in Veronica Goodman's life, if not her disappearance.

And it was up to me to find him.

46

———————

Denim answered on the first ring.

"How's it going?" I asked.

"Slow, but steady. I spent the morning at the gym, nothing new there and didn't get to speak to Jamie, grabbed a quick lunch, and headed to library. I've gone through the *Sentinel* archives to June 1995. I want to go through to March 1996 before going to Spring/Summer 2005 when Kelly Anne was apparently spotted. I figure there might be some one-year later type of articles. Then I'll go to the Cedar County Reference Library, check out the Toronto papers."

"Sounds like a plan. Tedious though, isn't it?"

Denim laughed. "It beats serving bacon and eggs. What about you? How did it go with Levon and Betsy?"

I wasn't sure if I should tell Denim about

Levon's time at boot camp. True, she was working on the case with me, but it seemed like a violation of his confidence, and the *why* of where he was at Camp Miakoda wasn't important. I opted for a version of the truth.

"He was at a camp in Miakoda Falls with Travis Acquolina in 1995. Got to know Travis a bit, said he never mentioned Veronica or Wanetta."

"Meaning Travis didn't think their cases were related to Kelly Anne's disappearance?"

"That was Levon's impression, though I've given that some thought. It's possible that Travis deliberately didn't mention them for some nefarious reason of his own."

"Do you want me to search for Travis Acquolina, see if his name turns up anywhere? I mean, not just newspapers, online."

"That would be great, but there's something else I want you to do." I filled her in on my meeting with Betsy and how that led to finding the Wikipedia entry for Isaac Buckman.

"Buckman died in 2012, but there's a photograph of him playing guitar at the CNE Bandshell in 1999, attributed to a C. LaPorte, that's La, no space, uppercase P-o-r-t-e. Unfortunately, I can't find any trace of a C. LaPorte that fits. I checked with almost everyone I've interviewed so far with no hits. I'm waiting to hear back from Merryfield."

"You said 'almost everyone.' Who did you miss?"

"Jamie Gardiner. I'm not convinced he'd tell me, even if he knew."

"You want me to do that." A statement, not a question.

"Yes, though I'm not sure how you'll go about it. Or if there are any other ways to find him."

"Leave it with me. Maybe I'll stumble across another photograph taken by him while I'm scouring the newspaper archives. When I get to the Toronto papers, I'll check for mentions of the CNE from 1995 to 2000. It's a long shot but..." Denim's voice trailed off.

"But?"

"Maybe C. LaPorte is or was a session musician, too. There must be associations for musicians."

"That's a good idea. I don't know why I didn't think of it."

"You would have. In the meantime, I've added C. LaPorte to my list."

"You're the best," I said, feeling the tension ease out of me. "Did you find out if the library had yearbooks from Miakoda High?"

"I was planning on getting to that. They don't, and neither does the Cedar County Reference Library. The librarian I spoke to thinks the high school might have copies. Did you want me to check?"

"No, I've dumped enough on you. Besides, if

the school has copies, I'll want to look at them. I won't know what I'm looking for until I find it, if that makes any sense."

"It does."

I hung up feeling a faint hint of something akin to optimism. Denim and I were a long way from finding out the truth, but at least we were working together. It felt good to have a partner again.

47

———————

NAVIGATING Miakoda High's automated phone system and endless prompts to press 1, 2, 3, 4, or Star to repeat the options proved to be a supreme test of my patience, but I endured, and I was eventually connected to the school library, only to listen to a recorded message informing me that the library was closed until 10 a.m. the next day. I left my name and number at the beep, asking for a callback, and tried to keep the frustration out of my voice. No one needs to start their workday with a cranky message.

Tracking down Isaac Buckman and C. LaPorte had made me forget about lunch. I nibbled on an oatmeal cookie and set about preparing dinner, a simple but nutritious meal of boneless breast of chicken, baked potato, and, to fancy things up a bit,

Green Beans Almondine, making a double portion of each to reheat tomorrow.

I'd just popped the chicken and potato in the oven when my phone rang. Merryfield.

"Detective, thank you for calling me back."

"I'm on dinner break. Not that I'm eating dinner."

"I'm sorry."

"No need. How are things going? Did you solve the case yet? Or should I say cases?"

I ignored the implied sarcasm. "I might be making progress. I wondered if I could run a name by you?"

"This isn't television, Callie."

"I'm well aware. It's just that I think this name might give us the break we need."

"Us."

"Yes."

"So, I'm in on this investigation with you. Is that what you're saying?"

"If you'd like."

"I don't like." Merryfield sighed. "I can't believe I'm going to ask, but what's the name?"

"C. LaPorte."

"How do you spell it?"

I spelled it for him and said, "I searched online but the only C. LaPortes I found were too young or too unlikely. Can you run a background check?"

A lengthy silence, then, "I can, but even if I find something, there's not much I can tell you beyond a full name, age, and possibly that the name came up in a routine traffic stop if there was one. But for me to share more than that would be illegal. Regardless, I'll have to weed through the hits. You need to give me some time."

I wanted to ask how much time, but I held my tongue. I was already pushing it with Merryfield. The last thing I needed was for him to shut me out altogether. "I appreciate whatever you can do, whenever you can do it."

"Can I ask how the name came up in your investigation?"

"I was looking for Isaac Buckman. The nephew of Edith Buckman, Veronica's landlady."

"Isaac Buckman. A musician, not overly successful but eking out a living. Renner and I interviewed him, separately and together. As I recall he had nothing to add and was on the road doing gigs at the time of the disappearances. We ruled him out as a suspect early on. Is he related to C. LaPorte in some way?"

"I think so, Detective. I just don't know how." I told him about the photo of Buckman attributed to C. LaPorte. I sent him the Wikipedia link, heard the ping as it landed in his e-mail.

"According to this, Buckman died in a traffic accident in 2012," Merryfield said. "There will be police reports on it in the PIP—Police Information Portal—of course. The photograph, however, does help, or at least the date of 1999 does. We can assume that our C. LaPorte was eighteen or older at the time, which means he was born in or before 1981. That will help narrow things down. I'll get back to you with what I can as soon as I'm able."

It wasn't ideal, but it was better than I'd hoped. Sometimes, that's all you could ask for, that and a little bit of luck. I thought about Merryfield's warm brown eyes. Maybe I could go for it.

"Detective Merryfield?"

"Uh huh?"

"Do you happen to like Green Beans Almondine?"

"Not so much. Allergic to tree nuts."

"Ah," I said, and hung up. So much for luck.

48

I'd finished dinner, cleaned up, and was binge watching season three of *The Marvelous Mrs. Maisel* when my cell rang.

Merryfield. I hadn't expected him to call back so soon and wondered if that was a good sign or if I was about to get the brush-off.

It turned out to be a bit of both.

"Your C. LaPorte has lived a clean life, apart from getting picked up at a rally in Queen's Park a few years back," Merryfield said. "It started off as a peaceful protest but, as is often the case, things heated up and the Toronto police were forced to get involved. According to the report, LaPorte was released a few hours later."

"A few years back" and "a rally" were vague enough that I'd be unlikely to find out more, and I suspected that vagueness was deliberate. I asked for details anyway.

"I'm afraid that would be crossing a line," Merryfield said, "though I can tell that the C stands for Cadel."

Cadel LaPorte. It was something. "Can you tell me anything else? Social media links I missed? His age? Where he lives?" I knew it was a long shot, but I had to ask.

A long pause, then, "Mr. LaPorte would be in his fifties. No social media presence that I could find, not common in these times, but less rare than you might think. As for where he lives, I'm not at liberty to say."

I was disappointed, but not surprised. "I understand, you have regulations to follow. At least I know LaPorte's first name and approximate age. That's more than I had before. I appreciate it."

"You're welcome. And Callie?"

"Yes?"

"If you're ever in the mood for a quiet drink, you might want to check out a bar in Marketville. A place called Unwired, no cell phones or electronics allowed. The owner is an ex-IT guy who seems to know things, though it might be better if you left my name out of it."

It looked like I was going to be paying a visit to Ben Benedetti after all. "Thank you, Detective. I know the place."

"I thought you might."

Was that a trace of amusement I heard in his voice? I hung up wondering just how much, if anything, Merryfield knew about my on-again, off-again relationship with Ben and whether it mattered. Fretted for the next hour on the best way to proceed until I couldn't think about it a minute longer. Then I turned my attention back to *Mrs. Maisel.*

Avoidance can be quite cathartic.

49

———

I TEXTED the name Cadel LaPorte to Denim first thing Tuesday morning, knowing it might assist her as she researched musician groups and had just finished breakfast when the librarian at the Miakoda Falls High School called me a couple of minutes after ten.

"Janis Choumont," she said, introducing herself. "I understand from your message that you're looking for old yearbooks?"

"I am. I'm the owner of Past & Present Investigations in Marketville, and we are working on three missing persons' cases dating back to 1995. I'm not sure if high school yearbooks hold any answers, but I like to be thorough."

"An admirable quality, especially for an investigator. The answer is yes, we do, but those yearbooks would be stored in our basement archives. I'd be happy to retrieve them if you can give me a day or two. Unfortunately, yearbooks are considered reference materials and so you wouldn't be permitted to remove them from school property. You would, however, be welcome to view them in the school library. Would that work for you?"

"It would, thank you. Do you think I could bring a team member with me? It would reduce the amount of time required and two sets of eyes are always better than one."

"I see no problem with that request. In fact, if you'd like, I'd be happy to assist."

"That's very generous of you."

"Not generous, intrigued. I wasn't here in 1995, but you've piqued my interest. What years are you looking for?"

I was ashamed to admit I hadn't thought that far ahead. "Two of the missing women were twenty at the time of their disappearance. The eighteen-year-old accelerated a grade in elementary school."

"The twenty-year-old girls would have been born in 1975, and would have started grade nine at fourteen, which would bring us to 1989. Your accelerated student would have started grade nine at thirteen, which would take us to 1990. I'm going to suggest starting with 1989 through 1993. If it turns out you need another year after you go through those, it can be arranged."

"That sounds perfect, thank you."

"I'll call you as soon I find them in archives."

Choumont laughed. "That may be easier said than done. The last time I was down there, there were boxes piled upon boxes, and not in any particular order. I'll be back to you."

The outcome was better than I'd expected, but the discussion also served as a reminder that I had more of my mother's yearbooks to face. I also had to face Ben, and while Unwired wouldn't open until six, I did have his cell number. Forced to choose between the lesser of two evils and knowing Veronica's case took precedence over my mother's past, I picked Ben. I'd have to face him sooner or later. It might as well be sooner.

50

THE COWARD in me hoped for Ben's voicemail. No such luck. He answered on the first ring.

"Callie. To what do I owe the pleasure?"

To what do I owe the pleasure? That's where we were now? It was the sort of greeting you'd say to a former colleague, not a former lover. Maybe I was overreacting. Yeah, probably overreacting.

"Callie? Are you still there?"

"Yes, sorry. I, um, I wondered if we could meet. Or talk on the phone if you'd rather. About a case. I'm working on a case."

"What sort of case?"

"A young woman who went missing in Miakoda Falls in 1995. Actually, there were three women who all disappeared within the period of a month. There's a strong possibility the cases are related."

"Sounds fascinating. Not sure how I can help, though."

"Word on the street is you know…things."

"What street might that be?"

Tongue-in-cheek or a purposeful dodging of the question?

"I can't reveal my sources."

"Ahh…sources, plural. Interesting. If, and I'm not saying I do know…things…what sort of things would you be looking for?"

"Information on a person."

"A missing person?"

"I don't think this person is missing. I think they just keep a low profile. I'm hoping to talk to them. I have reason to believe they may know something that could help with the investigation."

"I seem to remember that's how we met. You were working on a case. Then again, you are a detective."

"The term is investigator."

"I'm not seeing a distinction."

I wasn't sure Merryfield would agree. "Will you help me or not?"

"No promises, but I'll try. Can you come to Unwired around four? We open at six, but I'm always there a couple of hours early. There never seems to be an end to the paperwork."

"I'll see you at four."

I hung up, already planning my wardrobe. Skinny black jeans, a black camisole paired with an emerald and gold tweed jacket, the one that brought the green and gold flecks out in my hazel eyes. Black suede ankle boots. Diamond stud earrings. Professional but suitable for the casual atmosphere of a pub.

Who was I kidding? It was one of my best winter looks. And as much as I hated to admit it, I wanted to look good when I met with Ben.

51

———

WITH TIME TO kill before my meeting with Ben, and Denim on the task of searching library archives, I decided to tackle my mother's 1977-78 yearbook.

I opened it and found a small white envelope filled with newspaper clippings and a ticket stub for a Meat Loaf concert on Friday, April 28, 1978, 8 p.m. at Massey Hall in Toronto, presented by CHUM and CHUM FM. The ticket had been purchased on March 31 at a cost of $7.00 plus .70 tax—times had certainly changed—and row D Center Floor, seat 20. I did what I'd come to think of as "a Denim" and googled Massey Hall seating chart on my phone. Seat 20 was an aisle seat, and row D was the fourth row from the back. Why had my mother saved this ticket?

The five yellowed newspaper clippings were

from the *Lakeside Mirror* and arranged by date. The *Mirror* had shut down since I'd moved to Marketville, one more victim in the continuing demise of print media and ongoing budget cuts from the conglomerate that owned it, but in 1978 it would have been the lifeblood of a town on the verge of rapid expansion.

The first story was dated Thursday, March 2, 1978, and took up the top half of the front page. The headline read LAKESIDE HIGH STUDENT MISSING, byline Ramona Hobson. A large color photograph accompanied the article, and I didn't need to read the caption to know the missing student was Bernadette Robertson, the long-legged runner from the Volunteer Club. I jotted down the name Ramona Hobson in my notebook, then began reading the story.

> Seventeen-year-old Lakeside High student
> Bernadette Robertson has been missing
> since February 14, when she left home after
> a heated argument with her mother.
> According to her teachers, she has been
> absent from school without a permission slip
> since February 15.
> Mrs. Robertson, a recent widow, is pleading
> that anyone with information on her
> daughter's whereabouts to contact the
> police.

"I am very concerned for my daughter's wellbeing," said a tearful Mrs. Robertson. "Bernadette has threatened to run away from home before, but she always returned within a few hours, and never missed so much as a day of school."
Anyone with information regarding Bernadette's whereabouts is asked to contact Lakeside Police Services.

The Cedar County Tri-Community Policing Center now covered Lakeside as well as Miakoda Falls and Lount's Landing. I wondered briefly when the forces had amalgamated, then absorbed that Bernadette had gone missing on Valentine's Day and pondered that for a moment, then flipped the clipping over. Another Lakeside High headline caught my attention.

LAKESIDE HIGH STUDENTS CHARGED WITH JOYRIDING
Ramona Hobson

Brent Markham, a sixteen-year-old student from Lakeside High, has been charged with joyriding, a criminal offense that is punishable in court. Mike West, a passenger in the vehicle taken by Markham, has also been charged. While children under the age of sixteen are charged under the Juvenile

Detention Act, both Markham and West are considered adults, and will be tried as such. According to Canada's Criminal Code, Section 335, "Everyone who, without the consent of the owner, takes a motor vehicle or vessel with intent to drive, use, navigate or operate it or cause it to be driven, used, navigated or operated is guilty of an offence punishable on summary conviction." An occupant of a motor vehicle or vessel, who is aware that it was taken without the owner's consent, can also be charged under section 335.

Yet another sign of changing times. Under Ontario's current Youth Criminal Justice Act, Markham and West, both younger than eighteen at the time of committing the offence, would be considered young offenders. Not only did the Youth Criminal Justice Act emphasize rehabilitation and reintegration, the name of a young offender, or any information related to them that could lead to their identity, could not be published or broadcast in any format.

Instead, I had 1978 laws to thank for learning the identities of Brent Markham and Mike West. At sixteen, the boys would have been in grade 11, one year behind my mother. While it was unlikely that she'd kept this clipping for any reason other than the front-page article about Bernadette Robertson, my gut told me something about this story was important. I wrote down their names in my notebook—at the very least I could check out their student pics, see if either was in the 1978-79 yearbook.

I turned my attention to the next clipping, this one dated Thursday, March 9, byline Ramona Hobson. Still on the front page, but barely there in the bottom right corner, was a brief update on Bernadette Robertson.

LAKESIDE HIGH STUDENT COMES FORWARD

Bernadette Robertson, first reported missing by her mother on February 15, has come forward to police to say that she has been living with a friend since leaving home. "I'm fine and I apologize for wasting police resources," the teen said. "I have been in touch with my mother to assure her that I am well. I have some things to sort out, but I hope to return to school in the fall."

No name for the friend, which made me think Ramona Hobson didn't know, or had been asked or told to withhold their identity. I scoured the rest of the page and the reverse side, but there was nothing about the two teens who'd gone for a joyride.

Bernadette Robertson was back in the news on

Thursday, May 5, 1978, and once again the byline belonged to Ramona Hobson.

FORMER LAKESIDE HIGH STUDENT
REPORTED MISSING AGAIN

Seventeen-year-old Bernadette Robertson
has been reported missing once again.
Readers of the *Mirror* might remember that
Lakeside High student Robertson was
reported missing after leaving home on
Valentine's Day, following an argument with
her mother. Our coverage of the story led to
the troubled teen coming forward to state
that she was safe and staying with a friend.
According to police, Robertson left the
friend's house on April 21 to attend a rock
concert, but never returned.
Neither the friend's family, who have
requested anonymity, or Robertson's mother
have heard from Bernadette since. A
Missing Person's report was filed on
April 28.
Anyone with information about the
whereabouts of Bernadette Robertson is
asked to contact Lakeside Police Services.

The "troubled teen" reference was interesting, and I wondered if there was more to the story than was being reported. So, too, was the reference to the rock concert. Was that the reason my mother had saved the Meat Loaf ticket stub and the newspaper clippings? She'd been a classmate and a member of the Volunteer Club alongside Bernadette, but had they also been friends? I turned to the next clipping. Maybe it would provide a clue to the answer.

52

I'D EXPECTED the next two clippings to be more about Bernadette Robertson. What I wasn't expecting was an article about Joey Perella dated August 17, 1978.

LAKESIDE HIGH QB INVITED TO FOOTBALL TRAINING CAMP

Recent Lakeside High quarterback Joey
Perella has plenty to celebrate on and off
the field. His scholastic achievements earned
him an acceptance, and scholarship, into the
University of Toronto's Economics
program. Now he's been invited to attend
training camp for the university's football
team.
The Toronto Varsity Blues football program

has a rich history. Dating back to 1877, the Blues initially competed for the Canadian Dominion Football Championship and won six national titles, including the first Grey Cup game in 1909, as well as winning in 1895, 1905, 1910, 1911, and 1920. After intercollegiate teams no longer competed for the Dominion Championship, in 1965 the Blues won the first Vanier Cup, the championship of Canadian university football.
Perella was voted "Most Likely to be Drafted into the Canadian Football League" by his classmates.

The story was accompanied by a photograph of smiling Perella standing mid-field, arms held high overhead, a football in his arms. The caption read: JOEY PERELLA LEADS LAKESIDE HIGH BULLDOGS TO THIRD STRAIGHT CHAMPIONSHIP IN NOVEMBER 1977.

My first assumption, that my mother still had a crush on Perella, changed with the final clipping dated August 31, 1978.

RECENT LAKESIDE GRAD GOES MISSING
Ramona Hobson

Seventeen-year-old Delphina Gunton, a recent grade 12 graduate of Lakeside High, has been reported missing by her parents.

Last seen on August 17th, Gunton was a friend of Bernadette Robertson, who was reported missing in April. Police have reason to believe the two cases may be related. Any information about the whereabouts to Gunton or Robertson should be directed to Lakeside Police Services.

"Last seen on August 17th" had been circled in red ink. It was also the same date the article about Joey Perella ran in the *Mirror*. Was the date a coincidence, or was there a connection? Based on the red circle and the fact that Delphina had dated Perella—or at least had during the previous school year—it was a safe bet that my mother had believed there was a connection.

But why?

I studied the photograph that accompanied the article. My head ached and my stomach rumbled, reminding me that it was time for lunch. The mystery of Delphina Gunton would have to wait.

53

My interest piqued, but not expecting a positive result, I decided to search the Ontario Registry of Missing and Unidentified Adults for Bernadette Robertson and Delphina Gunton while grilling a cheddar cheese and tomato on rye. And yet, a positive result, or rather results, was exactly what I found.

BERNADETTE MARIE ROBERTSON

Summary
Date of Disappearance: April 21, 1978
Location of Disappearance: Lakeside,
Ontario
Age at Disappearance: 17 years
Height (estimate): 5'9"

Weight (estimate): 125 lbs.
Hair Color: Dark brown, shoulder length, straight
Eye Colour: Blue
Gender: Female
Race: Caucasian
Aliases: None known

DETAILS
Complexion: Fair
Build: Athletic
Dental: Noticeable gap between two front teeth.
Medical: Bernadette was four months pregnant at the time of her disappearance.
Clothing/Jewelry:
Clothing: Unknown
Jewelry: 10 ct. gold ring with center opal, sapphire chip on either side, worn on the left ring finger.

ADDITIONAL INFORMATION
Bernadette Robertson was a 17-year-old high school student when she ran away from her Lakeside home on Valentine's Day following an argument with her mother after discovering she was pregnant. One week later, after her disappearance was reported in a local newspaper, she called her mother

to say that she had moved in with her boyfriend and his parents.

Bernadette left her boyfriend's house on April 21 to attend a rock concert with two girlfriends. Her friends returned home. Bernadette did not.

On April 28, after a week of not hearing from her, the boyfriend's father filed a missing person report. Upon being interviewed, the girls from the rock concert stated that they had been separated from Bernadette at the Dundas Street subway station, which was busy after the concert. The police learned that the opal ring Bernadette had been wearing at the time of her disappearance had been pawned for cash in early May in Peterborough. Two weeks later, Bernadette made a collect call to her mother from a payphone in Minden, saying she was doing fine and would call again. She did not.

There was a confirmed sighting of Bernadette in late 1979, working as a waitress in downtown Toronto, as well as one unconfirmed sighting in the summer of 1981, in the Haliburton area with Delphina Gunton. Her mother grew increasingly concerned when Bernadette did not collect thousands of dollars left to her in a trust when she turned 21.

Five months after Bernadette vanished, another student, <u>Delphina Gunton</u>, who was also pregnant, ran away. Because Bernadette and Delphina were friends, the police believe the cases may be related.
In 1995, an anonymous tip was received indicating Bernadette and Delphina might be alive and well in Ontario but using different names.

SOURCE FILE: Lakeside Police Services, Case LPS03281978.

The case listing was accompanied by five photographs. I recognized two from my mother's yearbooks. The other three were age progressed sketches, one with Bernadette's hair bleached an unbecoming shade of straw blonde. Was that how she'd looked when sighted? Or a leap by the police artist? Either way, the gap between the two front teeth remained, and I couldn't help but think that if I had run away, not wanting to be found, that the gap would be the first thing I'd want eliminated. And I suspected a good dentist could do just that. Even in the 1980s.

Once again, there was a reference to Lakeside Police Services contact information, versus the Cedar County Tri-Community Policing Center. I wondered whether the files would now fall under Merryfield's jurisdiction. It would be something to ask him if I was planning to dig into this case. *Which*, I told myself, *I was not.* But that didn't stop me from wanting to know more.

54

———

I WAS JUST ABOUT to click on link under Delphina's name when the smell of burning bread reminded me that I had a grilled cheese and tomato sandwich on the stove. I managed to salvage it before it was too charred—a little scraping on the outer edges needed but nothing too serious. I added a sliced dill pickle, celery and carrot sticks, and a dollop of ranch dressing for dipping on the side, and plunked myself down, reading while I ate.

DELPHINA MARGARET GUNTON

SUMMARY
Date of Disappearance: August 17, 1978
Location of Disappearance: Lakeside,
Ontario
Age at Disappearance: 17 years

Height (estimate): 5'6"
Weight (estimate): 120 lbs.
Hair Color: Blonde, wavy, shoulder length
Eye Colour: Blue
Gender: Female
Race: Caucasian
Aliases: None known

DETAILS
Dental Information: Left back molar extracted
Medical Information: Pregnant at time of disappearance
Notable Identifiers: None
Complexion: Fair
Build: Slender
Clothing/Jewelry:
Clothing: Blue jeans, Meat Loaf *Bat Out of Hell* concert T-shirt, gold with red "Bat Out of Hell" logo, Adidas sneakers
Jewelry: Sterling silver mood ring, worn on the right-hand ring finger. Sterling silver filigree link bracelet with a floral pattern.

ADDITIONAL INFORMATION
Delphina Gunton left her parents' house in Lakeside, Ontario on August 17, 1978. She may have left home because she was pregnant. Five months before Gunton vanished, another student, Bernadette

<u>Robertson</u>, who was also pregnant, ran away. Because Bernadette and Delphina were friends, the police believe the cases may be related.

There has been one unconfirmed sighting of Gunton in the summer of 1981 in the Peterborough area with Bernadette Robertson. In 1995, an anonymous tip was received indicating Bernadette and Delphina may be alive and well in Ontario but using different names.

Source File: Lakeside Police Services, Case LPS04171978.

Unlike Bernadette's report, there were no age progressed photos of Delphina, and the two on the site were clearly school photos, probably from the 1977-78 yearbook.

But it was the Meat Loaf *Bat Out of Hell* concert T-shirt that caught my attention. Gone was any doubt that my mother had gone to Massey Hall with Bernadette and Delphina or that she'd been one of the friends the police had interviewed.

I could imagine Meat Loaf's song, "Paradise by the Dashboard Light," a huge hit in 1978, would have resonated with all three young women. Had they really gotten separated at the subway? Or had Bernadette told her friends, in confidence, that she was running away for good to start a new life?

Whatever the answer, my mother had almost certainly known it. So, too, it would seem, had Delphina. And yet, I couldn't help but think I was overlooking something obvious.

And then one more thought occurred to me. I was born May 8, 1979, which, by my calculations many times in the past, meant I would have been conceived in August 1978. Three friends. Three teen pregnancies. Was this some sort of BFF baby club? Or merely coincidence?

The plot was indeed thickening. For the first time since my grandmother had given me the yearbooks, I was anxious to get back to them.

But first, a quick google of Joey Perella, because Delphina's disappearance on August 17 fell on the exact same day the *Mirror* had written about him attending football training camp for the Varsity Blues.

Another possible coincidence? I wasn't sure, but the coincidences were starting to pile up.

55

AN ONLINE SEARCH revealed that Joey Perella had done well for himself. Graduated U of T with an Honors degree in Economics. Drafted into the CFL by the Hamilton Tiger-Cats where he played for two years before being traded to the Ottawa Rough Riders. Played an additional two years before getting injured, injury undisclosed, though it appeared to have ended his career. Went on to get an MBA from Harvard. CEO of a major bank, served on a staggering number of finance-and union-related Boards of Directors, and supported several diversity-based and Italian-Canadian charitable initiatives. Married since 1989 with two sons and twin daughters, though his wife and children were unnamed. No social media beyond his Linked In profile.

I tried googling "Joey Perella, wife," "Joey Perella children," only to come up empty. Despite his success on and off the football field, Joey Perella had lived a very private life, and while what I'd gleaned from a collection of online press releases and accolades were interesting, none of it shed any light onto Delphina Gunton's pregnancy or disappearance. It had, however, managed to eat up the better part of the afternoon.

My mother's yearbooks would have to wait. It was time to get ready for my meeting with Ben.

I HADN'T BEEN INSIDE UNWIRED for months—even when I was dating Ben, I didn't go often. Sitting alone in a bar while my boyfriend worked had lost its luster early on in our relationship. Even so, the décor was exactly as I remembered it: mid-century modern with a distinctly Scandinavian flair, round glass-topped coffee tables, and slung-back swivel lounge chairs in vibrant shades of teal, emerald green, and violet. A brass starburst clock was the focal point behind a well-stocked teak bar, the bartender not yet on duty. Too bad. I could have used a drink.

Ben greeted me with a smile and led me to a table underneath a woodblock poster of stacked navy-blue circles and half-moons. He'd grown a beard since I'd seen him, one of those close-cropped ones that were more like a scruffy five o'clock shadow. It suited him.

"You look good, Callie," he said after we'd sat.

"As do you. Thanks for taking the time to see me." *Could I be any more stiff and formal?*

If my manner bothered Ben, he didn't show it. "I'll always have time for you, you know that. Just because we didn't work out, doesn't mean we can't be friends. How can I help?"

I gave him a recap of Veronica's case and finished with my search for Isaac Buckman. "Unfortunately, Buckman died in a car accident a few years back. But I did come across a photograph of him, taken at the CNE Bandshell in 1999 by a C. LaPorte, who I have since learned is Cadel LaPorte. Beyond that, there's nothing, no social media, no hits on Google."

"And you believe Cadel LaPorte might have stayed in touch with Buckman? Or have some information to share as it relates to Veronica Goodman or the father of her child?"

"I know it's a long shot, and it wouldn't solve the mystery of why Veronica disappeared, but knowing who her father was might bring Kate some comfort. She's tried the DNA route on Ancestry without results. She just wants some answers.

"And you came to me because…?"

"You've helped me before. And I was told that if

I was ever in the mood for a quiet drink, to check out bar called Unwired, that the owner is an ex-IT guy who knows a thing or two."

Ben laughed. "And just how is Danny Merryfield doing these days?"

56

DANNY. Loretta Dartmoor had also called Merryfield Danny, but the man I'd met looked far more like a Sheridan than a Danny. I hadn't questioned her on it, but I did question Ben.

"You call Detective Merryfield Danny?"

Ben smiled. "He's not nearly as bureaucratic as you might think. Out of his police uniform, he's quite human. He's also one heck of a golfer. We've enjoyed many a round together, and he's always up to participating in a tournament for charity."

Now the "Danny" made sense. Ben and Loretta were avid golfers. It stood to reason that they all had played in the same tournaments. But talking about golf wasn't getting me any closer to Cadel LaPorte. Unless, of course, he was a golfer too.

"Now that I know *how* you know Merryfield, perhaps you can tell me why he sent me your way."

"I've helped him out on a few occasions. Quietly, of course. I expect he thinks I might be able to do the same for you."

"And can you? Or should I say, will you?"

Ben studied me for a long moment, then, "Yes, I will, if not for you, for Kate Goodman. She deserves the truth. But you'll have to give me a day or two."

A day or two. By then, Denim might have found out something from Jamieson Gardiner, or from delving into the musician associations route. In which case, I wouldn't have needed to come to Ben, asking for a favor, putting myself in the position of owing him. Well, too sad, too bad, Callie. That's where you're at. And I expected Merryfield's barely suppressed amusement earlier was in knowing just that.

I managed a smile. "A day or two will be fine, Ben, and thank you. Now, I better get going, let you get back to your never-ending paperwork."

I was halfway home before it struck me that Ben's paperwork might have had nothing to do with Unwired. Or that, perhaps, Unwired, for all its no WIFI, no electronics policy was nothing more than an elaborate front for his return to white hat hacking. Maybe that wasn't his plan pre-Covid, but with the lockdowns and mounting bills to pay, it was possible.

More than possible, probable.

Dare I think it? It might even have been the

reason I'd been dumped. If Ben didn't want me to know, was trying to shield me in some way…

The more I thought about it, the more it seemed likely. I just didn't think it would change anything.

57

I ARRIVED home wired from my visit to Unwired, too keyed up to even think about dinner, and decided to get through the rest of my mother's 1977-78 and 1978-79 yearbooks.

I remembered something Lucy Daneluk had told me when I was investigating the Brandon Colbeck case, that some missing adults fall under the category of "deliberate disappearances," the decision to disappear sometimes a way to escape a difficult situation. Like an unplanned teen pregnancy?

I also knew that there was no law preventing an adult from voluntarily picking up and starting a new life somewhere else, though I was reminded of something else Lucy had told me.

"There is a tendency to assume that adult disappearances are voluntary, when in fact this assumption is wrong. Adults go missing for many reasons. Until the individual is located and the true reason for the disappearance is learned, our assumptions are just speculations. It's a delicate balance between respecting the adult's privacy while trying to determine exactly what has happened to them. At the same time, family and friends are left to grapple with feelings for which there is no guidebook."

I tried to put things into perspective. In 1978 anyone over sixteen would have been considered an adult, no Amber Alerts for Bernadette or Delphina, even if such a system existed back then.

I could understand how Bernadette's trust, not claimed in 1982, when she turned 21, would have worried her family. But people did walk away from money. My mother had done just that and never looked back. My father had done the same, refusing to take a penny for my care from either set of grandparents.

What about the anonymous tip in 1995 stating both women were alive, well, and living under different names? Had Bernadette or Delphina been the tipster? If so, why? They would have been thirty-four by that time, their children thirteen.

Children.

I took another look at Delphina's photograph. Finally realized who she reminded me of, and it wasn't Meg Ryan.

It was Veronica Goodman. The hair, the eyes,

the shape of her face, her body type. It all fit. But hadn't Kate told me her mom had been a menopause baby?

I ran the stairs, taking two at a time. Placed the photos of Veronica and Delphina side-by-side. There was no question about it. They could be sisters.

Or mother and daughter.

Was that why Lindsay Doucette had been unwilling to dredge up the past? Because Veronica had been adopted, and not a late-in-life baby? But if so, why lie to Kate about it?

If I was wrong, it changed nothing. But if I was right…

It was time to call Lindsay.

58

Once I assured Lindsay there was something we needed to discuss in person, she agreed to meet with me the following afternoon. That done, I heated up a tin of minestrone soup for dinner, went upstairs for the remaining two yearbooks, and brought them back down with me to flip through while I ate.

I started with 1977-78, the stashed envelope set aside for the moment. In a time when the only option would have been printed photos, it was a safe assumption that any photos would have been taken during the first semester. As such, I was unsurprised to find Bernadette Robertson standing tall behind my mother in their grade 12 class. I studied the boys in the group, wondering if any of them could be the father of her baby.

The photo of the cheerleading squad showed a couple of new faces replacing graduate students from last year's squad. My mother and Delphina were mugging for the camera, their arms wrapped around one another's waists, and I guessed Delphina had dumped Joey or vice versa. My hunch was confirmed in the football highlights section, where one of the new cheerleaders, a petite redhead with a smattering of freckles and sturdy legs posed in front of him, his hands resting on her shoulders in a way that was both intimate and possessive.

Nothing can bring two girls together faster than being spurned by the same guy. It also explained why they'd become friends after being rivals, though not who had gotten Delphina pregnant. I flipped back to the graduating classes, where each student had their own photo, tagline, and blurb. Joseph (Joey) Perella was listed in 13B-5 as "Most Likely to Make the CFL." Underneath was his statement, "No matter how far I go in my life, I will never forget where I came from, or the people who got me there. TOUCHDOWN!" I had no way of knowing if Perella had kept his commitment to remember his roots, but he'd certainly lived up to his potential and then some.

I turned my attention to the back page of signatures and comments. Nothing from Joey, no surprise there, and nothing from Bernadette, she would have already left Lakeside. There was, however, a message that read, "Friends forever, luv, Delphina." I wondered if that had remained true, if my mother had known where Delphina and Bernadette went. Had they visited our house on Snapdragon Circle? I had no recollection of meeting either of them, but then again, the memories of a six-year-old are far from reliable.

I scanned the rest of the comments and came up empty, then went back to the laborious process of looking at every class photo and reading every name from Grade 9 onward. I got lucky, if you could call it that, in the class of 10B-5 when the name Mike West caught my eye.

Wasn't he the passenger charged with joyriding? What was the driver's name? Something Markham. Brent, that was it. There he was, in the back row, a burly kid with a mass of dark, curly hair and an improbable five o'clock shadow for someone his age. He didn't look familiar.

Mike West, on the other hand, I knew. Brandon Colbeck's stepfather had aged over the past forty-plus years, had grown from a skinny kid into a slender adult, his shaggy, sandy brown hair now close-cropped and steel gray, but I'd recognize that chiseled chin and those pale blue eyes anywhere. Eyes so pale they were almost translucent.

No wonder Chantelle hadn't been able to find a record of him prior to 1986. She'd stopped digging once the Colbeck case had been solved—a legal demand versus a request—but the loose end had never stopped bothering me.

And now it all made sense, might even have

explained why he'd never adopted his stepson. Why he'd been such a firm disciplinarian. He hadn't wanted Brandon to repeat his mistake.

Mike West of Lakeside had transformed himself into Michael Westlake of Marketville. I snapped a pic of the class photo and sent it to Chantelle, with a short text. She replied almost immediately with *!!!!!!!!* and a smiley face emoji.

I could have left it at that, but curiosity got the better of me, not just for Mike West, but for Brent Markham, Bernadette Robertson, and Delphina Gunton.

I picked up the phone and called my grandmother.

I SHOULD HAVE KNOWN Yvette wouldn't make it easy. I hadn't gotten beyond a mention of the yearbooks when she interrupted.

"I don't discuss personal matters on the phone. You never know who might be listening. If you have questions to ask, you'll have to do it in person."

"I really don't think anyone has tapped our pho—"

"Be that as it may, that's my position. I can see you tomorrow morning at ten. You needn't worry about your grandfather. He'll be back in Toronto on business."

I wanted to tell her to sod off, that it wasn't that

important. But if she knew anything, however remote, the investigator in me needed to know what it was. I found myself acquiescing and despising myself for doing it. I hung up and turned my attention to the final yearbook, feeling every bit like a high school student cramming for an exam. And hated it, every bit as much.

BERNADETTE, Delphina, Mike West, and Brent Markham nowhere to be found. My mother, on the other hand, was pictured with the cheerleaders, as well as under the Grade 13 Graduates page. She would have been barely pregnant at the time the photo was taken, still thinking her future lay unaltered.

Her hair still had remnants of Farrah's iconic blowout, but there was a harder edge to it now, and it looked as if she'd lightened the blonde a few shades. Since my yearbook journey had begun, I'd found an online article in *Harper's Bazaar*—there's no rabbit hole I won't go down in the name of research—and recalled that in 1978 Debbie Harry's platinum blonde scissored layers had been trending. This style, then, was my mother's interpretation of that look.

The blurb was titled, "Abigail Osgoode: Most Likely to Take a Flyer." A what? A quick search revealed a flyer was a cheerleading move, clever.

Underneath, her statement read, "Looking forward to all life has to offer. Bring on the chances and the challenges."

Chances, maybe not so much. Bring on the challenges, on the other hand, was an ironic example of "Be careful what you wish for," if there ever was one.

For the first time in a very long while I cried myself to sleep.

59

I took the new highway extension to Lakeside this time, getting there fast taking precedence over a trip down memory lane. There'd be more than enough of that once I sat down with Yvette. I just hoped she would be forthcoming.

I arrived promptly at ten and noted the addition of a Coming Soon sign in the front window. The brokerage was one that specialized in high end real estate, and I wondered when the property would be listed. I wasn't close to my grandparents, but I did feel a tinge of empathy for Yvette, who seemed reluctant to sell. My guess was moving was Corbin's idea, and he was a master at bulldozing any opposition, in and out of the construction business.

I'd no sooner rung the bell when she opened the door and invited me in. I shrugged off my coat and boots and followed her into the kitchen.

"I see you've got a sign in the window," I said. "I'm used to seeing them on the front lawn."

"We're not permitted to do that. Moore Gate Manor bylaws. Ridiculous but there you have it. We go live in three days and not a moment too soon. The stagers have been hard at work. This is the only room in the house that still feels as if it belongs to me."

"Moving is stressful."

"It is, but you're not here to talk about my impending move. Would you like a cup of tea or coffee?"

I didn't, but now that I was here, I wasn't sure how to begin. "Tea would be nice. Earl Grey if you have it."

"I do."

As Yvette set about making the tea, I found myself second guessing my reason for coming. I was supposed to be finding out what happed to Veronica Goodman, not chasing down ghosts from my mother's past.

"A penny for your thoughts," Yvette said, setting down a tray with two blue and gold pottery mugs, a matching teapot, and a glass plate of chocolate-coated digestive cookies.

I'm not sure why, but the fact that my grandmother drank her tea from a hand thrown mug instead of a bone china cup warmed me to her somewhat. I poured tea for both of us and took a cookie to be polite.

"They were your mother's favorite." She smiled, pointing to my cookie. "She liked to dunk them in her tea, probably got that from me, though Corbin finds it an appalling habit."

"I've been known to dunk a time or two. Let's go for it, shall we, seeing he's not here?"

We sat in companionable silence, sipping and dunking, and for a moment I'd almost forgotten why I was here, or how much hurt she had caused. *Almost* being the operative word. "I have another meeting in Marketville this afternoon. Would you mind if we got started?"

A flicker of some emotion crossed my grandmother's face, though I couldn't tell if it was relief, disappointment, or a combination thereof.

"I gather the yearbooks yielded some questions for you?"

"Yes, though not about the cases I was working on. There was a newspaper clipping inside one of the yearbooks, a story about a boy named Mike West being charged with joyriding, even though he was the passenger. The driver was a Brent Markham. I wondered if you knew what became of them, or why my mother would have kept that clipping."

Not entirely true, of course. The joyriding story just so happened to be on the flip side of the missing person article on Bernadette Robertson. I had no way of knowing if my mother had known or cared about them.

"I can't imagine why Abigail would have saved that, it's not as if she was friendly with either boy. I do know the story behind the story because both families lived in Moore Gate Manor, and it created a terrible scandal. The car Brent stole was his father's. He was always getting into trouble, that child. Rumors of drinking and drugs and what-not. From what I gather, Gabe—Mr. Markham—believed pressing charges might straighten Brent out."

"And did it?"

"I doubt it. Jail seldom rehabilitates. He did, however, later confess that West believed he'd had permission to take his father's car. As if Gabe would have entrusted a brand-new Cadillac Seville to his son. But the judge seemed to buy it."

"So, Mike West…"

"Started over in a new town, is my guess, maybe with a new identity." Yvette studied me through narrowed eyes. "You seem very interested in this Mike West. Is there something you're not telling me?"

I blushed. "It's my investigative instinct, I'm afraid. I believe he's connected to another case I worked on."

"But that's not why you're here."

I decided to come clean. "The joyriding story was on page two. On the front page was a story about the disappearance of one of my mother's classmates. Bernadette Robertson. And later, Delphina Gunton."

Yvette's face was inscrutable. "Go on."

"From what I can piece out from the yearbooks, Bernadette and my mother were in the same class, in the Volunteer Club, while it existed, and later the cheer squad. Delphina and my mother were on the cheer squad together. I believe they also dated the same football player, the quarterback, though not at the same time. Joey Perella."

Yvette's smile didn't quite reach her eyes, whatever imagined warmth we'd shared over tea and chocolate-dipped digestive cookies gone. "Corbin had a talk with Joey Perella one evening when he came to take Abigail to the movies. *Rocky*, as I recall. I remember thinking the title ironic at the time. Corbin encouraged Perella to understand that a girl like our daughter needed a stable future, not some high school jock with an impossible dream. To the boy's credit, he moved on without so much as a fight. Abigail took it badly at first, but she recovered."

Had she? Or had it been the first step towards alienation between her and her parents? I suspected the latter. "I've googled him. He made the CFL, went on to get an MBA from Harvard, and became the CEO of a major bank, among other prestigious honors." I paused. "So much more suitable than a sheet metal worker."

"Don't be tiresome, it doesn't become you."

The barb irked me. "Would anyone have been good enough for my mother?"

Yvette flinched, ever-so-slightly.

"Did you know Bernadette or Delphina?"

"Delphina, yes. Always polite, well-mannered. Bernadette only by reputation, which was less than stellar. But after Joey, Abigail didn't make it a habit to bring friends home. When Bernadette went missing, the police came here to interview Abigail."

A wry smile crossed Yvette's face. "She'd begged Corbin and I to let her go to that concert. Meat Loaf, what kind of name is that? But she told us she was going with two girlfriends, and she'd been to a concert in the city a few months before without incident. We knew Delphina was one of the girls, and Abigail implied that the other was on the cheer squad. We didn't know the other girl was Bernadette. If we had, I doubt we would have allowed Abigail to go."

"Did she know that Bernadette planned to disappear that night?"

"She claimed not, and the police didn't seem to doubt her. But when Delphina disappeared a few months later, the police returned, and that time they were far less trusting. Despite that, Abigail's story never changed. She didn't know where either girl was, though she believed they had left voluntarily, that they were together, and that they were safe."

"Did she have a reason for feeling that way?"

"The police asked the same question in a dozen

different ways. She said that even before their pregnancies, Bernadette and Delphina often talked about starting a new life where no one would judge them."

"What about the boys who got the girls pregnant? What did they have to say?"

"No idea. I assume the police knew their identities, though I couldn't say with any certainty. If Abigail knew who they were, she never admitted it."

"Do you think she knew where the girls went?"

"No. If she had known their whereabouts, she might have joined them, instead of running off with your father. I'm grateful to him for that, at least. We may not have stayed in her life, but at least we knew where she was. The Robertsons and the Guntons had no such answers."

Faint praise, indeed. But at least it opened the door.

"About my father…"

60

———

"I wondered when you'd get to your father," Yvette said. "Ask your questions, and I'll answer them if I can."

I wasn't sure what I expected, but my grandmother's resigned acquiescence wasn't it, "Begin at the beginning."

Yvette smiled. "The beginning is always a good place to start." Her eyes took on a faraway look, as if remembering, then snapped back into focus. "July 1, 1978. Osgoode Construction was a much smaller company back then and Corbin thought it would be nice to host a Canada Day barbecue for his employees. Abigail helped with the decorations and the food and for the first time since the Joey Perella incident, she seemed truly happy. Little did we know she'd already set her sights on Jimmy Barnstable."

"My father was working for Osgoode

Construction? How long had he been working there?"

"A little over a year. He started as a general laborer the summer before. The Barnstables had an RV at Winding Lake Trailer Park."

I almost laughed out loud at the way she said "trailer park," as if it were some sort of infectious disease, but I managed to keep a straight face. "My father never told me any of that."

"Then I expect Jimmy never told you that the only way he could afford the house on Snapdragon Circle was because of Osgoode Construction." She must have sensed my surprise because she clarified the statement. "The site supervisor, Dwayne Shuter, for whatever reason, he had a soft spot for Jimmy. Encouraged him to apprentice, helped him with the down payment, not that Corbin ever found out about the latter."

I knew from my parents' marriage certificate that Dwayne Shuter had witnessed their wedding. I also knew the address listed for my father was the house in Marketville. But it had never occurred to me to wonder at how someone his age could afford the down payment, let alone qualify for a mortgage. It's funny, the things we take for granted. It also served as a reminder of how little I knew about my father's past.

"When and how did my parents meet?"

"It was the summer before Grade 13. Abigail was working in the office, a trailer that moved from site to site, in this case a new strip mall on Lester Street. Dwayne had set up picnic tables for the workers to use at lunch and breaks. I expect that's where she and Jimmy first met, though I can't be sure. I do know that on the day of the barbecue she was flirting with him to beat the band. To be honest, I couldn't blame her. Jimmy was a handsome lad who seemed comfortable in his own skin, something you didn't often see in someone so young, and by all accounts he was a hard worker. Even so, if Corbin had caught wind of their relationship, it would have spelled the end of Jimmy's job at Osgoode Construction and Abigail and Jimmy both knew it."

"But you could have told him. Why didn't you?"

"I thought it would be a summer fling, that it would fizzle out when school started. Of course, Abigail was about three weeks pregnant by then."

"When did you find out?"

"Mid-November. She kept it from us until it became all too apparent—there's only so much baggy clothes can conceal—and by then it was too late to do anything about it, not that Abigail ever considered abortion. I suggested sending her to a private school in Toronto, where she could have the baby and give it up for adoption, but she wouldn't hear of it, and neither would Jimmy."

I felt a weight lift off my shoulders. I may not have been planned, but I had been wanted. "What happened next?"

"I'm afraid Corbin handled the whole thing badly. He followed Abigail one night when she went out, saw her meet up with Jimmy in front of Ben's Convenience. There was an…altercation." Yvette pursed her lips. "Corbin was the instigator, the police were called, it was all very sordid. Two weeks later, Abigail left us a note saying she was getting married and that we weren't invited. I never heard from her again though I had an investigator on retainer who kept tabs on her. On you. I thought she was happy. And then I guess she wasn't. You know the rest."

"What about the Barnstables? I've never met them, and my father refused to speak of them."

"I can't blame him there. I tried to reach out to them. They suggested that Abigail had gotten pregnant on purpose. 'Entrapment,' they called it." Yvette sniffed. "As if a girl with Abigail's looks and brains would resort to that. A girl from Moore Gate Manor chasing after a trailer park boy." She sniffed again. "They told Jimmy if he married Abigail, he was dead to them. I expect he took them at their word. They left Lakeside shortly after you were born. I have no idea where they went, nor do I care. And now you know what I know. I hope you're happy."

Yvette leaned back, her shoulders slumped, the lines in her face etched deeper than before. This confession, if that's what you could call it, had cost her dearly. A small part of me even felt sorry for her. But she should have stood up for her only child. Stood up to her husband.

She could have tried harder.

I wanted to tell her that and more. Instead, I thanked her for the tea and cookies and left, never looking back.

It was time to let go of the ghosts in my past.

61

I STOPPED at a diner in Lakeside before heading back to Marketville. I didn't think I'd be returning to Lakeside any time soon and a farewell lunch seemed appropriate. I ordered a BLT and fries. When it comes to comfort food, bacon is on the top of my list. Fries come a close second. It might be time to forget the past and move forward, but I needed to decompress before I met with Lindsay.

I was midway through my sandwich when a gaggle of teenage girls plunked themselves down at the table next to me, their voices animated as they oohed and awed over a new bracelet dangling off the wrist of a pretty brunette. I snuck a surreptitious glance as she blushed and pulled back her hand, embarrassed by the attention.

And that's when I realized what the "something

obvious" was, the thing I'd missed when reading Delphina Gunton's case listing. I pushed my half-eaten food aside, dropped three fives on the table, more than enough to cover the meal with a generous tip, texted Lindsay to tell her I'd be late, and charged out the door. I needed to go home, snap a couple of photos, and send them to Arabella.

I ARRIVED at Lindsay's house shortly before three, declined the offer of tea or coffee, and got right to the point.

"I've been going through some old high school yearbooks relating to another case dating back to 1978. I found a possible connection to Veronica." I'd brought a photocopy of every picture I had of Delphina. I removed them from my bag and placed them on the coffee table between us.

"Her name is Delphina Gunton. She was a cheerleader at Lakeside High. Left home in August 1978. Her family never heard from her again, though there was an unconfirmed sighting in 1981 of her with a friend, Bernadette Robertson, who had disappeared in April 1978. In 1995, the police received an anonymous tip that the girls were alive and well and living under different names."

"What does this have to do with Roni?" Lindsay

asked, though I couldn't help but notice a faint tic in the corner of her left eye, and that her face had paled.

"I'm getting to that. Both girls were pregnant at the time they left home. When I first saw the picture of Delphina, she reminded me of someone."

I took out the photograph of Veronica and set it beside the largest one of Delphina Gunton. "They could be sisters, don't you think? Sisters, or mother and daughter. Kate believes her mother was a menopause baby, something she'd been told by you and your parents, and she has no reason to doubt it. True, she doesn't resemble you physically, but that happens. Then, earlier today, I was sitting in a diner in Lakeside and a young girl was showing off her bracelet to her friends, a gift from a boy, most likely. And I remembered how much Kate treasured her grandmother's antique bracelet. Except it's not antique, though by now I suppose it might qualify as vintage."

"How can you be certain? You're not a jewelry expert, are you?"

"No, but my friend Arabella Carpenter *is* an expert when it comes to antiques, and her partner, Caitie Meadows, specializes in antique and vintage jewelry. I sent them photographs of Kate's bracelet." I pulled a copy of Caitie's email out of my bag and began reading.

"This bracelet has openwork silver panels decorated with

an intricately detailed flower and foliage ornamental pattern. The stamped number 835 is the purity hallmark of European silver, which is 83.5% silver and 16.5% copper. The bracelet is what we call '1900s Dutch heritage jewelry in the Biedermeier style,' meaning it wasn't made in the 1900s, but as a nod to the period. I can't be sure of when this bracelet was crafted, but I have seen similar examples that were made in the mid-to-late 1970s. I hope that helps. Caitie."

I placed the email on the table, alongside the rest. Lindsay's tic had become much more pronounced. "Here's what I think. Delphina Gunton gave up her child in a private adoption. I believe the adoptive parents were your mother and father, and that Delphina gave them her bracelet and requested that they give it to the child when she turned sixteen. What I don't understand is why they wouldn't tell Veronica she was adopted, or why you, who would have been fifteen at the time and old enough to know the truth, perpetuated the deception, especially after she disappeared. Unless you were keeping more than one secret."

I had to hand it to her, she tried to hold it together, but in the end the lies were too much to bear.

"I'll tell you what you want to know," she said, her eyes brimming with unshed tears, "but you must promise not to tell Kate."

"I can't make that promise. Kate deserves to learn the truth."

"She does," Lindsay said, "but she deserves to learn it from me."

"In that case, I'm listening."

62

———————

"YOU HAVE to understand that being an unwed mother in 1978 carried more stigma that it does today," Lindsay began. "Maybe not as much as ten or twenty years before, but Delphina Gunton was the only child of affluent parents, and their expectations for her were astronomical. As such, she had every advantage, and some might say, disadvantage. Music lessons—piano, guitar, violin. Dance classes—modern jazz, tap, ballet. Extra tutoring in math and science to ensure her grades never dipped below an A, with A+ being the goal."

I expect my mother's upbringing had been much the same. I nodded my understanding.

"We were living in Lakeside, and Leo Gunton owned the law firm where my father was employed as an accountant. He became a confidante of Leo's, and my mother and Mrs. Gunton were on friendly terms. Both our families had daughters close in age, and that likely solidified their relationship."

"I didn't realize that you lived in Lakeside. I've been going through my mother's yearbooks recently. I didn't spot you in any of them."

"I expect your mother, like Delphina, attended Lakeside High."

"Yes."

"There's your answer. I attended St. Jude's Secondary. My parents believed the Catholic school system was superior to the public school system, or perhaps they thought a daily dose of religion would keep me on the straight and narrow."

I grinned. "Did it?"

"The daily dose of religion, not so much. The nuns who taught us, absolutely. But Delphina was a year ahead of me, and her pregnancy did more to scare me into being a good Catholic girl than anything else. As you can imagine, the Guntons were far from pleased. They came up with a plan. I wasn't aware of its full extent for many years."

"And the plan was?"

"Delphina would go away to have the baby. My parents would adopt her child privately and move to Miakoda Falls, where no one knew them. Leo Gunton would help my father establish his own accounting firm."

"But you knew the truth."

"I knew Roni was adopted, yes, and while I didn't understand the subterfuge of pretending otherwise, I accepted it. But I didn't know she was Delphina's daughter until Roni's sixteenth birthday."

"The bracelet."

Lindsay nodded. "I recognized it as Delphina's right away. And that's when the pieces started to come together. If anyone knew that Delphina was Roni's mother, then they'd know that the missing person report had been fabricated. I'm not sure what the penalty is for filing a false police report, but I expect it's significant and Leo Gunton would almost certainly have been disgraced."

I frowned. "Why is the case listing on the Registry still showing as active?"

"That's the irony. After Delphina had the baby, she really did run away. To the best of my knowledge, the Guntons never saw or heard from her again, but what could they do? They could hardly file another missing person report."

"The anonymous tip that both Bernadette and Delphina were alive, well, and living under new names, did that come from you?"

"No, but I have reason to believe Delphina made the call."

"What reason?"

"Delphina phoned me the day before Roni disappeared."

"And you were positive it was her?"

"I was. Because every word of what I just told

you came from that telephone conversation. I asked her if she was going to tell Roni."

"What did she say?"

"She hung up without answering."

"Did you tell the police?"

"No. I thought if I did, they'd think that Roni left voluntarily, that she ran off to meet with her birth mother. But she would never have left Kate. Never. I'll go to my grave believing that."

"There's just one more thing that I need to understand."

Lindsay pressed her lips into a thin line. "The heart-shaped pendant?"

I nodded.

"I figured you'd catch the contradiction once you had a chance to think about it."

"Did you give it to Veronica?"

"No, but the truth isn't what you think, that a boy gave it to her."

"Then what is the truth?"

"It was my locket, a Valentine's Day gift to myself. I tossed it in the parking lot behind the bar early the next morning. I thought it would prove she'd been abducted and tried to leave a message. In hindsight, it was ridiculous—"

"It's a lot more serious than ridiculous," I said, biting back my anger. "If the police had known the truth about the adoption, the phone call from Delphina, the pendant, their investigation would have taken a different direction. Veronica may have been found. She may have been around to raise Kate. Did you ever stop to think about that?"

"I've never stopped thinking about it," Lindsay said, "but that's the thing about lies. They pile up on top of one another until you can't find your way out of them."

They did indeed. The question was, what could we do about them now?

63

Lindsay resisted at first, despite her earlier promise to come clean to Kate, but it wasn't much of a debate. I pride myself on being a good investigator, but the reality is I don't have the same resources as the police. We agreed that I would update Detective Merryfield with everything I'd learned to date, including Lindsay's "confession," if you could call it that. I would have preferred she go with me when I met with Merryfield, but she argued that she needed time to tell Kate before speaking to the police, and I didn't want to delay things any longer. Too many years had already passed.

"I'll finalize my report and billing for Kate and return the bracelet and necklace at the same time," I said, donning my "all business" hat. "I should be able to have everything ready by tomorrow. I need to talk to my partner, Denim, first. She's been working Veronica's case in tandem with me."

"Please bring everything to me, including your invoice. The least I can do is pay you for your time."

The skeptic in me wondered if it was Lindsay's way of delaying her conversation with Kate, but I would have to take her at her word. "Is there anything you haven't told me?"

Lindsay shook her head. "I'm fresh out of secrets."

If only she had been fresh out of them in 1995. I wondered how Kate was going to take the news.

I CALLED Denim and recapped what I'd learned from Lindsay. "The bottom line is our investigation —at least into Veronica's case—is over. I'll contact Detective Merryfield and turn things over to him. But I need to know what you've found out, if anything, before I do that."

"No luck on locating Cadel LaPorte if that's what you're asking, though my focus has been going through the archives at the library. You were right, it's tedious work, but dragging it out for days isn't going to make it any less tedious."

"A fair point. Any hits?"

"Not really. Beyond the standard news articles, which are retreads of what we already know, there's nothing, though I've made copies of all relevant clippings for our client. I'll scan them and send those off to you tonight."

"Thank you. I'm sure Kate will appreciate that." *Maybe even more so after she has a sit down with her aunt.* "Is there anything else?"

"Jamie Gardiner pegged me as an investigator working with you as soon as I asked him about Cadel LaPorte, but it's not all bad. I'm convinced he knows more than he told you when it comes to Kelly Anne Acquolina, and I've almost got him talking. But if we're off the Goodman case…" Denim paused, and I could hear the disappointment in her voice.

What can I say? I like closure, even when such a concept isn't possible. I gave her the go-ahead to keep at Jamie Gardiner and knew that I'd be calling on Loretta Dartmoor once again.

It wasn't until after we hung up that I realized I hadn't updated Denim on the latest theory—if you could call it a theory—regarding Wanetta Bulmer. Perhaps it was just as well. Better to wait until I heard back from Lucy, had a chance to run the idea by Merryfield. There'd be time enough to catch her up, if there was any catching up to be done.

64

Perhaps Detective Merryfield thought I wanted to get more information rather than to give it, though it could just as easily have been the end of his shift. Whatever the reason, he put me off until nine o'clock the next morning. I wasn't sure whether to be irritated or grateful. I opted for the latter, arranged to meet Sam Sanchez for pizza and wine without any talk of business, and slept a dreamless sleep for the first time since taking on the Veronica Goodman case.

There's something to be said for secrets uncovered.

Especially when they aren't your own.

I ARRIVED at the Cedar County Police Department promptly at nine a.m. Thursday morning, where I was greeted at the door by Detective Merryfield. We settled into the icy shoebox he called an office and chatted about the weather, currently bitter cold, but dry, with March looming in the not-so-distant future and spring around the corner. That's the one thing you can always count on in Ontario, conversation about the weather. Maybe it's because our temperatures are so distinctly varied, from frigid cold and snow to hot, humid, and muggy. My former running group used to joke that Ontario had two seasons, Winter and July.

"What can I do for you, Callie?" Merryfield asked, once we'd discussed our predications for spring, early or otherwise. You can't always trust the groundhog to get it right.

"I've decided to stop investigating the Veronica Goodman case."

Merryfield's eyebrows shot up in surprise. "Now, *that* I was not expecting. How come? You don't strike me as the sort of person who quits or gives up easily."

"I'm not, but what I learned yesterday requires far more resources than I have at my disposal."

"You have my attention."

Where to begin? Perhaps, instead of hanging out with Sam last night, I should have planned what I was going to say. Or how I was going to say it.

Well, too late now. "I'm going to go a bit out of order, if that's okay with you."

"Go in whatever order you wish."

Was it inappropriate that I still found him attractive? Maybe. Probably.

Seriously, Callie, stop it.

"My mother was a student at Lakeside High in the 1970s. I was going through her old yearbooks, and there were some newspaper clippings about two teenaged girls who left home in 1978. Both were pregnant at the time of their disappearance. Both are, to the best of my knowledge, still missing, though there were two confirmed sightings some years back. The police contact listed on the Ontario Registry of Missing and Unidentified Adults is the Lakeside Police Services. I expect Cedar County amalgamated the individual departments sometime between then and now."

"That's correct. The tri-community towns of Lakeside, Miakoda Falls, and Lount's Landing combined forces in the 1990s. Government efficiencies."

"Right. Which means the cold cases of those two girls would fall directly under your jurisdiction."

"They would. Are you going to explain how two pregnant teens leaving home in 1978 would factor into the disappearance of Veronica Goodman in 1995?"

"I'm getting to that," I said, and proceeded to fill him in.

I'LL GIVE Merryfield one thing. Beyond being attractive, he was a meticulous note taker and an attentive listener, never once interrupting as I repeated Lindsay Doucette's confession.

"I appreciate you bringing this to me," he said, after I'd finished. "And you're right, if we'd known about this in 1995, our investigation would have taken a different approach. Of course, I'll be interviewing Ms. Doucette. In your experience as an investigator, do you believe she's holding anything back?"

I took a moment to bask in the fact that Merryfield had acknowledged me as an investigator, and not a meddling amateur. "I don't, but anything's possible. She's kept her secrets for a very long time."

"That she has," Merryfield said. "What about Kelly Anne Acquolina and Wanetta Bulmer? As I recall, you thought the cases were connected. Do see still believe that?"

I shook my head. "No. A friend of mine was in an experimental boot camp with Travis Acquolina. Camp Miakoda. He tells me that you were instrumental in placing Travis there after the Jamie Gardiner incident."

Not so much as a nod from Merryfield. *Fine, be that way.* "According to my friend, during all his time at Camp Miakoda, Travis never once mentioned

Veronica Goodman or Wanetta Bulmer, likely because he knew his sister was alive and that the cases weren't connected. He also believes that Loretta Dartmoor spotted Kelly Anne that day at Canada's Wonderland, and that Kelly was with Travis at the time. I suspect you believe that, too, which is why you've kept unofficial tabs on Loretta all these years."

Merryfield's expression, or rather, lack thereof, never changed. I soldiered on. "The piece of the puzzle that doesn't make sense is why Loretta would have reported seeing Kelly Anne, but not Travis. Travis had served his time and was free to go wherever he wanted. But I think she did tell someone—Jamie Gardiner—and he told her she had an overactive imagination, convinced her not to tell the police about Travis."

My last statement finally netted me a raised eyebrow. "That's rather a leap, wouldn't you say?"

"No. I believe Kelly Anne left because the police wouldn't or couldn't drop the charges against Jamie Gardiner. Furthermore, I think Jamie knew she left because of him, and it's haunted him ever since."

"And what would lead you to that conclusion?" Merryfield asked.

"When I spoke to Jamie he said, and I quote, '*If you do find Kelly, let her know that I'm sorry for everything and tell her not to come back. There are too many ghosts in this town.*' And later, when I had coffee with Loretta, she used the exact same phrase, 'Too many ghosts in this town,' and it was obvious that she was holding something back."

I told Merryfield about the way Loretta had shredded her butterscotch pecan muffin, how she'd promised to sleep on it, but that I hadn't heard from her and didn't expect to. "She's either scared or protecting someone, maybe both, and no amount of prodding her is going to change that."

"It's an interesting theory," Merryfield said, and I couldn't tell if he planned to follow it up or if he thought I was the one with an overactive imagination. I was about to ask when he switched the subject.

"What about Wanetta? Do you have any theories there?"

"As a matter of fact, I do."

65

———————

"BEFORE I START, the photograph of Wanetta. Do you know where it was found?"

Merryfield nodded. "On the table next to her bed, in her room at the boarding house. Why do you ask?"

"Didn't that strike anyone as odd? Who keeps an 8 x 10 photo of themselves next to their bed?"

"The table was more like a desk, not a nightstand, and a catch-all for a lot of things, books, magazines, and the photo. And how do you know it was an 8 x 10? Maybe it was a 5 x 7."

I knew he was teasing me and rolled my eyes. "Whatever the size, it looks like a professional headshot, the pose, the way the background is blurred. Gloria Grace mentioned a guy with a camera who was hanging around the school, claimed to be a talent scout. I've read about modeling scams, wondered if that could be why Wanetta bailed on her shift at the Blue Goose, missed her exam, ran off without her purse. Got the call she'd been waiting for and bolted. Excited, eager, a chance of a lifetime."

"You really do have an overactive imagination, don't you?"

Well, that answered my earlier question as to whether Merryfield bought my theory about Kelly Anne Acquolina. "Okay, yes, maybe I do, but it's possible, right?"

"It is," Merryfield conceded. "And yes, that September a 'talent agent' was on school grounds, approaching some of the students." He put air quotes around talent agent. "He was enrolling a few 'very special girls' in a modeling course that cost quite a bit, paid up front. The parents of one of the students reported him and he was encouraged to leave. He took the advice."

"You didn't try to question him?"

Merryfield's eyes narrowed at the memory. "Renner tended to prefer expedience over investigation. But something tells me there's more you aren't telling me when it comes to Wanetta. What is it?"

I recounted the rest of my conversation with Gloria Grace, how she'd talked to Henrietta St. Pierre, how we both thought that maybe Bulmer wasn't Wanetta's last name though we didn't know how she'd managed to get a bank or credit card.

Merryfield considered that for a moment, then,

"There was no evidence to point us in that direction, though that doesn't mean she didn't change her name, and with the right connections, anything is possible. I also remember Henrietta St. Pierre, the girls in the house called her Mrs. Henri. She sold the boarding house and moved back to Miakoda Island a year or two after Wanetta went missing. I always thought she was holding something back, but I figured she was trying to protect Wanetta's reputation. There were hints from some of the housemates that Wanetta might have been involved with a married man, maybe spent an illicit weekend at Little Moon Island, but we were never able to substantiate it."

"The ferry to Miakoda Island stops at Little Moon first. Wanetta could have gotten off there, and then had a friend pick her up for the short boat ride over, covered her tracks that way, though why she'd feel the need to do that...that part we haven't figured out. But Gloria Grace thinks Wanetta might have been from the Island, which is how she ended up at Mrs. Henri's boardinghouse when she moved to Miakoda Falls."

"Have you spoken with Lucy Daneluk about that?"

"I have. She said she had an idea, but I haven't heard back from her yet."

"Keep me apprised," he said, without promising to do the same.

I took it as my cue to leave and boogied out of

there before he could ask me what I was going to do next. Something told me Merryfield wouldn't approve of my continued search into the disappearances of Kelly Anne Acquolina and Wanetta Bulmer.

It's amazing how easy it is to convince yourself you're doing the right thing.

66

———

I CHECKED my voicemail in the police parking lot to find two messages, one from Janis Choumont, the librarian at Miakoda Falls High, telling me she'd located the yearbooks I was looking for, and one from Ben asking me to stop by Unwired at seven, no other explanation given. It annoyed me that it felt more like a summons than an invitation, but I set aside my annoyance and texted Ben back, telling him I'd be there.

That done, I called Janis Choumont to tell her I'd be at the school within the half-hour, then messaged Denim, asking her to join me if she could. A quick stop at the Timmy's drive-through for a cream cheese bagel and coffee and I was on my way.

From the outside, Miakoda Falls High had the industrial look of a school built in the 1960s, with rows of rectangular windows set prison-like against a brown brick façade. The inside wasn't much better, with taupe floor tiles in dire need of an update, and beige walls that cried out for a splash of color. Only the trophy case that lined the entry showed any sign of pride.

There was, however, plenty of life in the locker-lined halls. I'd arrived between class periods and a cacophony of student voices and footsteps echoed. A few minutes later a bell rang and a cloak of silence shrouded the corridors. I stood in the vestibule, waiting for Denim, and was just about to text Janis Choumont to tell her I'd arrived when an officious-looking man, who identified himself Mr. Goldring, the school's Vice Principal, asked me what my business was. I was about to respond when Denim breezed in and introduced herself as my business associate. After a brief explanation on my part, Goldring asked us to stand aside while he made a call. I presumed the call was to Janis Choumont, and Choumont, if that's who Goldring called, must have given us the all-clear, because he escorted us to the library, though maybe he didn't trust us to wander about on our own.

The library was a refreshing change from the rest of the school, with brightly painted walls in reds, blues, and greens serving as a backdrop to the bookshelves, tables, and computer stations. There were about a dozen students inside, all wearing ear buds, a few tapping their toes to the music while they studied.

A short, brown-skinned woman with glossy black hair and a wide smile greeted us at the door, allowing Goldring to get on with his day. "I'm Janis Choumont," she said, "and you must be Callie."

"Guilty as charged, and this is Denim, my associate. Thanks so much for digging out the yearbooks."

"It's nice to think they might be of some help, instead of collecting dust in the basement. I've set up a workstation with a computer for you in the reading nook at the back. You'll have a modicum of privacy there." She handed me a booklet of tab-sized post-it notes. "If you need anything photocopied, put a stickie on the page and I'll take care of it."

As promised, the reading nook had been kitted out to accommodate us, the yearbooks dating from 1989-90 through 1993-94 neatly stacked on the table. There were also three chairs, and I remembered her offer to assist if required.

"Would you have the time to help us, Ms. Choumont?"

"It's Janis, and I thought you'd never ask. I'll get one of the student volunteers to man the front desk."

"I'm guessing not much exciting happens in the school library," Denim said, her voice low as Janis sprinted off, "but is it…I don't know…proper procedure to get her involved?"

"I've just spent hours going through my mother's old high school yearbooks, and trust me, it's about as exciting as pouring over microfiche. Not to mention that we're doing this investigation on our own time, and my dime. If there's any way to streamline the process, I'm all for it."

"You had me at microfiche," Denim said with a grin. "Let the streamlining begin."

67

Janis Choumont was back within minutes, and I had to admit the librarian's wide-eyed enthusiasm was infectious. I was lucky that way. Every time I risked feeling jaded, someone would come along and remind me how fortunate I was to be in this line of work. I could tell that Denim felt the same sense of rejuvenation.

"The students we are looking for are Veronica Goodman, Kelly Anne Acquolina, and Jamieson "Jamie" Gardiner. We are also looking for a former teacher, Miss Loretta Dartmoor, who should be in all the yearbooks, as she has only recently retired. If my math is correct, 1989-90 will include Kelly and Jamie. Veronica is two years younger than the other students, but she skipped a grade in elementary school. That means all three students should be in 1990-91, 1991-92, and 1992-93, with only 1993-94 for Veronica and Loretta. Are you with me so far?"

Janis and Denim nodded in unison.

"Perfect. Now there are five yearbooks and three of us, but if we tackle them in order, it shouldn't be too overwhelming. Remember we are looking for class photos, clubs or sports teams they might have belonged to, anything that might stand out as a connection between one or more. If you find anything, put one of the stickie tabs on the page—try to keep them color-coded based on whatever system you come up with—and keep going. We'll compare notes when we're done."

I slid a yearbook in front of each of us, knowing as I did so that the odds of us finding anything of value were slim. Even so, I felt my pulse quicken at the prospect of "the dig."

We worked in silence for the better part of three hours, with Janis taking occasional breaks to ensure everything in the library was running smoothly and closing and locking the doors when the school day ended. It meant that Denim and I were able to go through two yearbooks to her one, but that was to be expected.

I pushed my chair back from the table to survey the collection of five colorfully tabbed yearbooks and the two bleary-eyed women in front of me. I suspected I looked every bit as tired. "I have a meeting tonight I can't get out of, and we're already here past regular library hours. Is it possible to meet here again tomorrow to review what we've found?"

"Why not let me take these home tonight and make notes, compile everything into some sense of order?" Janis asked. "It's what we librarians are trained to do. Then we could meet first thing tomorrow, say eight a.m. That would give us two hours before the library opens."

I felt a sense of relief flood over me, and based on Denim's perked up expression, I wasn't the only one, but... "I thought you weren't supposed to remove them from school property."

"That's for you regular folk," she said, grinning. "I have privileges."

"In that case, I'd be happy to take you up on your offer, and eight a.m. works for me."

"Me too," Denim said.

And with that, the three of us agreed to call it a day. Except I still had to meet Ben at Unwired.

I TOOK extra care with my makeup and tamed my hair into some semblance of submission, then selected my wardrobe. Jeans tonight, I decided, with a free-flowing turquoise patchwork tunic and matching low-heeled turquoise suede ankle boots. Both had been an impulse buy at a trendy boutique in Yorkville a couple of years back, and while I'd paid far too much for either, I seldom found an opportunity to wear them.

Ben greeted me at the door and took my coat, ushering me into small table in a dark corner.

"Cadel LaPorte is here," Ben said.

"Here?" I looked around the bar.

"He's in the private party room."

It felt like a lifetime ago since I'd last been in that room, drinking champagne on the house with

Chantelle and celebrating the end of the Brandon Colbeck case.

"How did you find him and how did you get him to come to Unwired?"

Ben ignored the first question and answered the second, "I told Cadel the truth, that Kate Goodman hired you to find her mother and you weren't the type to give up on an investigation. That you'd come up with his name impressed him, but he only agreed to come on the condition that he speak only to you, no bystanders, and no police. I can't say I like it."

"I don't need a babysitter."

"Promise me that you'll tell Merryfield whatever you learn."

Now was *not* the time to tell Ben I was officially off the Veronica Goodman case. "I promise."

Ben handed me a black coaster-shaped object. "Put this in your purse. It's what we use to let our servers know their drinks order is ready. Press on it if you feel as if you're in danger."

"Seriously?"

"Just take it."

I took it, partly to placate Ben, and partly because I was feeling the first hint of jangled nerves.

The room was exactly as I remembered it, with a gas fireplace set along one wall, and a variety of options for seating, from low-slung upholstered love seats to conventional tables and chairs. A man was sitting at a table in the corner. Cadel, I assumed. He rose as I approached.

"Cadel LaPorte, and you must be Calamity Barnstable."

He was tall and lean, with the long, slender fingers of a pianist, silver hair as thin as his moustache, blue-gray eyes, and a narrow nose in a winter-pale face.

"Thank you for agreeing to meet with me."

"Mr. Benedetti's request piqued my interest. Please, sit down."

"I'm curious," he said, after I'd done so. "How did your search for Veronica Goodman lead you to me?"

"I was trying to locate Isaac Buckman, the nephew of Edith Buckman, Veronica's landlady. There's a Wikipedia page about him. He died in a car accident in 2012."

Cadel shook his head. "I wasn't aware. We parted ways many years ago. Why are you trying to find Isaac?"

"There was a photograph on the Wiki page of Isaac playing at the CNE Bandstand in 1999. It was attributed to a C. LaPorte. It took some time and resources, but I was able to learn that the C stood for Cadel. Ben did the rest."

Cadel nodded. "You're an impressive pair, Calamity, you and Ben Benedetti, I'll give you that. If I ever need the services of an investigator, you'll be at the top of my list."

Ben and I weren't a pair, and I wasn't sure that was a list I wanted to be on, but I kept that opinion to myself. "That's very kind of you."

"How can I help you?"

I looked Cadel straight in the eye. "I thought Isaac might be Kate's father. But I believe that honor belongs to you."

A pause, then, "Why me?"

"A high school friend of Veronica's told me that she'd 'changed' after meeting a musician at the CNE Bandshell. I think it's safe to assume that 'changed' meant she realized she was pregnant. The musician looked like Eddie Vedder, which described Isaac Buckman. But Veronica's sister, Lindsay, was absolutely certain he wasn't Kate's father. But if not Isaac, who? Kate looks like her mother in almost every way. But she has your nose. A feminized version of it, to be sure, but it's a definite tell. What I want to know now is why you didn't stand by her."

A flicker of emotion crossed Cadel's face, though I didn't know him well enough to read it.

"I was on the road, playing at every dive bar in Ontario," he said after a few moments. "There were lots of girls, a different one every night. I didn't know Nicki was pregnant. Judge me harshly if you want."

Nicki. Not Veronica. Did that mean she was more to him than he was saying? Or that she wanted to be more to him than she was?

"I'm not here to judge you. All I want is the truth, for Kate's sake."

We looked at each other for a long time before he said, "I'd like to arrange another meeting, but it will have to be like this one. Just you, no police, no partners."

I slid my card across the table, Cadel slid it back. "I'll contact you through Ben. One request, please don't talk about this conversation to anybody, at least not yet."

The man knew how to captivate an audience.

69

─────────

JANIS CHOUMONT WAS a woman after my own heart. She opened her laptop and pulled up an Excel worksheet sorting everything we'd noted in the yearbooks about Veronica Goodman, Kelly Anne Acquolina, Jamieson "Jamie" Gardiner, and Loretta Dartmoor. I cast a quick glance at Denim and saw she was equally impressed. This, then, was a good learning opportunity.

"The one thing they all had in common was Drama Club," Janis said. "Miss Dartmoor was one of the club advisors, along with the drama teacher, Teresa Locke."

Janis pointed out Veronica, Kelly Anne, and Jamie were in productions of *A Midsummer's Night Dream, H.M.S. Pinafore,* and Agatha Christie's *The Mousetrap.* They were never in the lead or supporting roles but members of the ensemble. All three were also members of the Ecology Club.

And Travis Acquolina was there, though younger than the others, a member of the *Mousetrap* stage crew. "His name popped out," Janis said. "It's an unusual one, at least in these parts. It's clear that they knew each other well, and if either Loretta or Jamie said otherwise, they're lying."

I flashed back to my conversation with Jamie. He'd never claimed *not* to know Veronica or Kelly Anne. Conversely, Loretta had been upfront about Kelly Anne, evasive about Jamie, and had made no mention of Veronica, even after I'd told her that I'd been hired to solve Veronica's case.

How had I missed that?

I thanked Janis for her help and promised to keep her posted on our progress. As Denim rushed off to meet her stepbrother Levi—some sort of diner emergency—I went back to the Miakoda Hills sales office to confront Loretta Dartmoor, my earlier statement to Merryfield all but forgotten.

It was time to let the prodding begin.

I WAS twenty dollars the richer having finally gotten around to scratching the Crossword ticket I'd bought at Lakeside Convenience. I'd probably end up reinvesting the windfall back into the Ontario Lottery Gaming Association's well-fed coffers, but for the moment I felt flush with cash and hey, you can't win without a ticket, right? I splurged on a chai latte at Café Culture and once again waited for Loretta to finish her shift. Today she looked resigned rather than nervous, a large black coffee and a butterscotch pecan muffin in front of her.

"Thanks for coming," I said. "Since we were here last, I've learned a few more things."

Loretta nodded. "I thought you would. You seemed determined. In my experience as a teacher, determination can take a student farther than any natural born ability."

Was that a backhanded compliment or a dig at my skillset? Whatever it was, I could understand how Loretta had earned her Miss Dark Mood moniker. Time to get to the point.

"I've just returned from Miakoda High. We've been going through old yearbooks and noted that you headed the drama club. The same drama club that Veronica, Kelly Anne, Jamie, and Travis were members of. Which means they knew each other well, as did you."

"All true. What of it?"

"The thing is, when we spoke last, I told you that I was hired to investigate Veronica's disappearance. I suspected that Jamie Gardiner was the person you'd gone to after spotting Kelly Anne at Canada's Wonderland, you both used the same phrase, 'ghosts of the past,' but it was only after the yearbooks that I realized you never mentioned

Veronica. The question is, why not? And then I remembered something else you'd told me. How you'd seen so many kids lose their way because of drugs and alcohol, how it had impacted their families."

I leaned back and looked Loretta in the eye. "*Families.* And when I asked you if intervening helped, you replied, 'Not often enough, and certainly not after they'd left the confines of school. Sometimes I wonder if my interference did more harm than good, but I did my best.'"

Loretta folded her arms across her chest, "Your recall is impressive, but I'm not sure what you're getting at."

I leaned forward. "I think you do. Veronica was a server at the Miakoda Bar & Grille. It was close to the school, and according to her case listing on the Ontario Registry for Missing and Unidentified Adults, a popular hangout for teachers and staff. You were bound to see her there, even after she'd graduated. You suspected she'd gotten mixed up with something, drugs maybe, and tried to get her help. Instead, she disappeared. What I don't understand is why you wouldn't have shared your suspicions with the police."

"But I did. I told Marty Renner. He wouldn't hear of it. Said if Veronica had been on drugs, her sister would have known, that no one at the diner had suggested such a thing." Loretta's lower lip trembled. "He accused me of meddling in the investigation, making things up. *Dramatizing by the drama coach* is how he put it. Maybe he was right. I've been known to muckrake on occasion. And to be honest, Veronica never admitted to any drug use, it was just that she'd gotten so thin, so jittery. Renner attributed that to being a teenaged, sleep-deprived single mom, and he could have been right. I let it go."

"And Kelly Anne? My guess is you saw her with Travis and told Jamie. What happened?"

"Jamie told me I had a vivid imagination, that there was no way Kelly Anne and Travis would take a chance and go to Canada's Wonderland. But he was agitated about it, that much I could tell. Maybe he thought they'd come back and make his life difficult, maybe there was another reason. I don't know."

"But you couldn't let it go that time, could you? At least, not altogether, so you told the police you'd spotted Kelly Anne, but never mentioned her brother."

Loretta nodded. "In the end, it didn't matter. They couldn't confirm the sighting. Without another witness, it was just another lead gone cold. But Kelly Anne recognized me, I know she did. The guy she was with had his back to me, focused on the lineup for the ride, but I'm positive it was Travis. I'd watched him grow up, knew the way he stood, the way he'd shuffle his feet when he was getting impatient."

Loretta bit her lower lip, shook her head, then, "I'll never forget Kelly Anne's look, as if she was pleading with me. I thought, at the time, she wanted me to report seeing her. But now I think she was pleading with me to stay silent, that all she and Travis wanted was a fresh start. At least, that's the version I choose to believe." She paused, then, "I do know Jamie was right about one thing."

"What's that?"

"There really are too many ghosts in this town."

Loretta left without touching her muffin. I watched her go, knowing she had nothing more to tell me, recalling Lucy Daneluk's words again, that there was no law that prevented an adult from voluntarily picking up and starting a new life somewhere else.

I hoped that was the case for Kelly Anne and Travis Acquolina. I was rooting for them, wherever they might be. I had a feeling Loretta Dartmoor was, too.

70

Once again, Ben met me at the door of Unwired and pressed the coaster-shaped disc into my hand. And once again, Cadel was waiting for me in the private banquet room, only this time, a woman was with him. A few years older than Cadel, though not by a lot, I'd guess early sixties. Average height with a slim build and a wavy bob, more silver than blonde. No jewelry.

She looked at me and smiled. "You look like your grandmother, or at least how Yvette looked in 1978."

"And you are?" I asked, though I knew. I wondered when she'd ditched the mood ring, knew the thought was ridiculous.

"Delphina Gunton," she said, "though I've been Kristine Paris for many years. Paris always sounded so exotic to me, not that I've ever been. Cadel thought it best if we talk. I wasn't sure. Some secrets are better left in the past."

"And yet, you came."

"Cadel can be very convincing."

"And on that note, I'm going to leave the two of you to talk," he said, leaving the room.

Delphina—Kristine—got straight to the point. "As you may have surmised, Bernadette and I planned to run off together. Your mother might have suspected, but we didn't tell her anything, not before and not after, though that reporter, Ramona Hobson, stayed on our trail for months. It wasn't easy, trying to stay one step ahead of her, but we managed."

Ramona Hobson. I'd jotted her name down in my notebook and beyond a quick google that led nowhere, never dug any deeper. Maybe if I had… but I couldn't go there now. I focused my full attention on Kristine.

"We went from the concert to the Union Station bus terminal," she was saying, "and then to…to the place where I had the baby. The nurse put drapes across my knees so I couldn't see a thing, then I heard a cry, and they took the baby away. I overheard the doctor saying it was a girl, I'm pretty sure I wasn't supposed to know that. But if I'd seen her, held her for even a moment, I never would have been able to give her up. I guess they knew that."

"It must have been difficult."

"It was the hardest thing I've ever done, and I struggled with guilt and postpartum depression for months afterward. I'm not sure I would have survived it, without Amber—Bernadette—by my side."

"And her baby?"

Kristine shook her head. "Amber had a miscarriage at five months, and she hit a very rough patch after that. But she never stopped being a good friend."

"Where is she now?"

"She used to run in high school. Feel the Bern, as in b-e-r-n, that's what she used to call it when she'd had a good run. She got back into it, joined a run club. She met a nice guy there, and what with personal baggage, and…let's just say it took time, but a few years back they moved to Tiny Township and built a house together. We still talk, see each other on occasion, but she finally got her fresh start. I'm glad. She deserved a happily ever after."

"And Bernadette's mother? Didn't she deserve the same?"

"Don't let the weeping widow portrayed in the newspaper fool you. The minute Mrs. Robertson found out her daughter was pregnant, she turfed her out of the house. Bern called her mom after Hobson's first newspaper article was published. If she was expecting a warm welcome, she didn't get it."

"And the boyfriend?"

"Dumped her. Imagine, at seventeen, being abandoned by everyone you thought you could trust."

I couldn't, but my mother would have, and I understood, now, why she'd kept the newspaper clippings. "What about you?"

"There's not much to tell. After five years of transient living and a dozen aliases, I had my name legally changed to Kristine Paris. I moved to Toronto, went back to school, and became a paralegal."

"Weren't you concerned that your name change would pop up in a police search?"

"I figured if anyone was still looking, I was ready to be found. Turned out, no one was looking, least of all my parents." Kristine shrugged, but I could tell the admission still hurt.

"I'm sorry."

Another shrug. "Any other questions?"

I had a hundred. "Is Joey Perella Veronica's biological father?"

Kristine blinked, as if surprised I'd figured it out, then nodded. "I didn't want Joey to give up university or his dreams of a CFL career. When he got invited to U of T's training camp, I knew I couldn't tell him, at least not then. He was a player, in more ways than one, but he would have quit everything to do what he considered the right thing. Except it wouldn't have been the right thing, not for him and not for me. I contacted him after he was injured. We became friends again, and after a while, I told him about Veronica. He was the one who suggested that I take paralegal training, offered to pay for my tuition. We've kept in touch sporadically. His family thinks we're just old high school friends, and that's the way we're going to keep it. Anything else?"

"Did you call Lindsay Doucette the day before Veronica disappeared?"

"Yes. I thought it was time Veronica learned the truth."

The door swung open, and Cadel walked back into the room. "I believe that's my cue."

Had Cadel been waiting outside to hear what I had to say? He must have been. I pushed my chair back and waited to hear what he had to say.

71

"I MET NICKI—VERONICA— at the CNE Bandshell in the summer of 1993," Cadel began. "She'd come down to Toronto with her friend, Betsy, to watch Isaac play, and I was in the band. I was twenty-six, and if I'd known she was only sixteen, I would have run the other way. But she looked and acted older. Isaac and Betsy seemed oblivious to our mutual attraction, and neither one of us did anything to set them straight. Besides, we were just flirting."

"And then it morphed into more."

"Yes, and I wish I could tell you I was madly in love with her, but it wasn't like that. I didn't lie before. There were other women, and I never promised Veronica we were exclusive. By the time she found out she was pregnant, I was back on the road. Nicki was out of sight and out of mind."

Cadel grimaced at the memory. "I wasn't the nicest guy back then."

"That's when I entered the picture," Kristine said. "I knew Veronica was trying to file for support payments from Cadel LaPorte, if she could find him."

"How?"

Kristine shook her head. "Fate? I don't know how else to explain it. I was working at a firm in Toronto that specialized in family law. I recognized Veronica the minute she walked into the office. Even without the physical similarities, she was wearing the bracelet I'd left for her. I'll admit I didn't know what to do, the whole thing made me nervous. I arranged to have another paralegal meet with her in a conference room and watched through the two-way mirror. If the other paralegal noticed the resemblance between us, he didn't say anything, bless him. And then we started looking for Cadel LaPorte."

Cadel picked up the story. "They found me. I asked for a paternity test, and learned that, yes, I am Kate's biological father. I might not have been the nicest guy, but I was never one to walk away from my financial obligations. We were trying to determine the amount of child support when I realized Veronica didn't care about the money. What she wanted was a husband and a full-time dad for Kate, and she'd convinced herself it was going to happen. She'd even signed a new lease, paid first and last month's rent."

Cadel shook his head, regret etched on his face. "The guy I am today, I would have tried, not marriage, that wouldn't have worked out for either of us, but some sort of custody or visitation agreement. The guy I was then, not a chance. I paid the legal bills, and I gave Veronica $850 cash, which was pretty much every penny I had. Then I took off like a thief in the night."

It explained the cash found in her apartment. Not hard-earned savings by a single mom, but payoff by the baby's father. How long did it take for Veronica to realize Cadel wasn't coming back? And what, if anything, did that knowledge have to do with her disappearance?

72

Kristine picked up the conversation. "Cadel is being hard on himself. He was under no obligation to pay Veronica's legal bill. He left her a letter explaining that he would help to support Kate. But that's not what Veronica wanted. As time ticked by, and the longer Cadel stayed away, Veronica got more agitated. She was constantly in our office, begging us to find him, alternating between white hot anger and desperate denial. She talked about finding Cadel to anyone who'd listen. Two days before she disappeared, she mentioned meeting another musician who claimed to know where Cadel was, that he could take her to him."

Kristine bit her bottom lip. "I was worried. I thought if I called Lindsay and told her the truth about Veronica's adoption, she would tell Veronica, that if Veronica knew the truth, she would stay in Miakoda Falls, get over her unhealthy obsession with finding Cadel. That we could form a bond, and I could help her with Kate."

It all sounded good but… "Why wouldn't you have told Veronica yourself, if you were so concerned?"

"The laws surrounding adoption at the time would have prohibited it. Even talking to Lindsay crossed a line, and I was already beyond nervous. What was I going to tell Veronica, don't make the mistakes I did? What if she rejected me?"

What if, indeed. "Do you know if Lindsay told Veronica?"

"I don't." She twisted her hands on the table. "When I read in the paper that Veronica had disappeared, I should have come forward, told them about the musician who supposedly knew where Cadel was. But she'd never named the musician, and honestly, I thought she'd turn up in a week or two."

"And what about you, Cadel?"

He cleared his throat. "I was in Northern Ontario when she disappeared and if she was trying to get to me, she didn't. I was prime suspect number one, questioned, or should I say grilled, multiple times, but I truly did not know where she was, believe me. I had plenty of second thoughts. What if I'd stuck around? Would there have been a happily ever after? Or would we have been bickering within a couple of weeks and I would have taken off anyway? Every gig I played I looked for her. I did what I could, kept sending money for Kate's support, through her landlady, Isaac's mother, Edith."

Questioned/grilled multiple times. By Renner and Merryfield? Had Merryfield known who C. LaPorte was all along?

"Fast forward a year," Cadel continued. "I was back in Toronto and found an ad in the *Sun*, 'Looking for Veronica Goodman, a.k.a. Roni or Nicki, last seen in Miakoda Falls, February 14, 1995...' I called the number in the ad and got Kristine, told her the everything I knew."

"We searched high and low for Veronica," Kristine said. "On the street, in women's shelters, hospitals, rehab. We tried to get her case on a missing persons TV show, but the story wasn't 'compelling' enough. We've worked with a dozen different groups specializing in missing persons. It was early days for online stuff, but we even tried a website on Angelfire. Nothing."

Kristine glanced at Cadel. "Over time, we became friends, decided to purchase a ten-acre property outside of Sault Ste. Marie and start fresh. We fish, have a few chickens for eggs, grow our own fruit and vegetables. Cadel takes on handyman work, splits firewood. I take in sewing, alterations mainly. We tap maple trees in the spring, sell the syrup at the local outdoor market, along with some of our canning and preserves. It's a simple life, but it suits us. Neither one of us is looking for a lover, not at this point in our lives. We're just looking for peace."

I processed that for a moment, imagined them working together as partners, friends with a shared secret, and wondered what Kate would think about the arrangement. I was also getting a strange vibe from Cadel, though I couldn't put my finger on it, but maybe Ben got it too, thus the panic button in my pocket. Or did Ben know more than he was saying?

I put my feelings aside and said, "The police have just received new information, enough to reopen the investigation. I know you said earlier, no police, but you could help by telling them everything you've just told me. Will you do that?"

They looked at each other, then nodded in unison. "Yes."

"In that case, I'll contact the Miakoda Falls PD." I paused a moment, then, "That leaves one final question. Are you ready to meet Kate? To tell her your stories?"

"We thought you'd never ask," Kristine said and began to cry while Cadel took her hand, clumsy, but caring.

I left with their contact information stored on my phone. Ben patted me on the arm on my way out, the way you might pat a favorite niece.

I also knew he'd been listening, though how he'd managed it, I wasn't sure. Hidden video camera? Ear to the door? I decided it didn't matter. Without him and his mysterious resources, I would never have met Cadel or Delphina Gunton, the woman who would become Kristine Paris.

73

My first instinct after arriving home was to call Kate. But the right thing to do would be to call Merryfield and let him orchestrate how events unfolded from here. I waffled for a moment between what I wanted to do and what I should do. In the end, should do won, and I arranged to meet him at his office in an hour.

I took too much time getting ready for our meeting. The tweed jacket I'd worn to Unwired, but with a silk blouse instead of the camisole. Black jeans and ankle boots. A little extra mascara, some lip gloss. Then I raced out the door and drove well over the speed limit the entire way.

Merryfield was waiting for me. If he appreciated the care I'd taken with my appearance, it wasn't evident, and I chided myself for being ridiculous. I had to stop imagining things that didn't exist.

"Lucy Daneluk will be calling you," he said as I followed him into his office and took a seat. "We've been sharing what we know about Wanetta Bulmer, and we have some theories. That said, it would be best if she was the one to update you."

The fact that there was anything to update me on was more than I'd expected, and it filled me with hope. "Thank you for letting me know."

"You're welcome. Now, I gather you have news for me?"

"I do," I said, and proceeded to fill him in, ending with, "And you knew who C. LaPorte was, so why didn't you tell me?"

"I knew who he *was*, but I didn't know where he was *now*, though we kept track of him immediately after Veronica's disappearance. We thought—and Cadel thought—that Veronica would find him."

"Except she didn't."

"Cadel said she didn't."

I pondered what Merryfield had said and how he'd said it. Had Veronica found Cadel? And then what? A host of scenarios raced through my mind, linking all the disappearances to Cadel, ending with Cadel playing Kristine for a fool. I shook my head. I was trying to create a tidy, tied-up-with-a-bow ending to everything we'd been investigating. I knew all too well that not every missing person could be located, that not every family found the answers they were looking for. Cadel might have been cagey—that, I'd decided, was the vibe I'd gotten from him versus anything more sinister—but he'd come forward despite any personal reservations.

Merryfield was looking at me thoughtfully. "I suspect that on learning what you did, you wanted to run off and tell Kate. Instead, you came to me. Thank you for that."

"I appreciate your…appreciation, but technically Kate is no longer my client and I felt there might be legal complexities involved that I might not be unaware of. Can I ask what you will do next?"

Merryfield nodded. "I'll talk to Cadel and Kristine, determine the best way to facilitate a meeting with Kate Goodman and Lindsay Doucette. After that, it's up to them."

"What about Veronica? I told them you have enough new information to reopen her case, though I didn't tell them what that information was."

"I'll give Lindsay the opportunity to tell her side of the story, and hopefully there will be forgiveness all around." Merryfield smiled. "You would have made a fine police officer. Have you ever considered applying? There's no upper age limit and the department could use someone with your determination and work ethic."

"I'm flattered, but I like the flexibility of being my own boss, taking the cases that interest me and turning down the ones that don't. Besides, I think I'm making a difference."

"You are definitely doing that." He stood, and I took it as my cue to leave.

I was halfway out the door when he called out to me.

"Nice jacket, by the way. You should wear those colors more often."

I turned around and I could feel my cheeks turning pink, and managed to mumble, "Um…thanks."

I thought of all the witty, charming things I could have said on the drive back to Marketville. *Um, thanks,* didn't make the list.

74

I ARRIVED HOME, invited Denim over, updated her on my meetings with Cadel LaPorte and Delphina Gunton, now Kristine Paris, then arranged a Zoom call for the two of us with Lucy to talk about Wanetta Bulmer, knowing Denim would want to be involved.

It was good to see Lucy versus just talk to her, and after the introductions and a bit of small talk, she proceeded to tell us what she'd learned.

"As you know, I suspected that Wanetta Bulmer might have been from Miakoda Island. After speaking to someone on the Island, I was able to connect with the Chief. He was interested in the case and very willing to listen, though he told me right off the hop there were and are no Bulmers living on the Island. Despite that, he agreed to take everything to the Elders, who in turn would consult with the community."

"That's something," Denim said, pigtails bobbing.

"Unfortunately, no one recognized the girl in the photograph," Lucy said, "though a woman who worked at Little Moon Island Resort as a maid for the resort remembered a guy who came every weekend for months, would have been in 1994 because it was the last year the resort was open. He was never with the same young woman, and she thought he might have been a professional photographer because he brought a black camera bag and a lighting kit. He snapped pictures of the women in different outfits, and no matter what time of year, in swimsuits and bikinis. She couldn't say whether Wanetta was one of the women, though Wanetta would have been his type—petite, bottle blonde, and attractive."

The professional photographer angle fit with my theory Wanetta might have been the victim of a modeling scam. "Could the maid provide a description of the guy?" I asked.

Lucy shook her head. "Not much, it was almost thirty years ago. She recalled he was tall and slender with dark hair and eyes, maybe in his mid-thirties, and respectful to the staff, but beyond that, nothing."

I glanced at Denim and knew the

disappointment in her eyes mirrored mine. "Meaning we're no further ahead."

"You always say it's as important to rule things out as to rule things in," Lucy said.

"That's right," Denim piped up, an impish grin on her face. "It's one of the first things Callie told me."

"Well, there you go. Ruling out Wanetta being from Miakoda Island and knowing she might have been Photographer Boy's type allowed me to go to Plan B. Okay, maybe Plan C."

"And what exactly was Plan B, or maybe Plan C?" I asked.

"The unidentified," Lucy said.

75

"I'VE BEEN WORKING on trying to cross reference missing persons on my registry with unidentified adults listed on registries across Canada," Lucy began. "It seemed impossible at first, but then an IT guy approached me, gave Detective Merryfield as a reference, said he wanted to help solve cold cases if he could remain anonymous."

"Anonymous," I said, thinking of Ben and his newly acquired burden of never-ending paperwork.

"He's much smarter than I am," Lucy continued. "Mr. A.—that's what I call him, A for anonymous—developed a system where I can enter key information from online reports and do a data sort, not just by column or row, but by key words or characteristics, which then realigns the columns and rows into sub-sections, which Mr. A. then uses to tap into other databases. He says there are many people willing to share their information for the greater good, often outside of regular channels."

"It sounds…unconventional," I said, not sure of how else to put it.

"Maybe it is," Denim said, "but not everyone trusts the police. Besides, if it helps to identify the unidentified, then doesn't the end justify the means?"

I wasn't sure, but I also wasn't ready to debate the issue. "Was he able to find Wanetta Bulmer?"

Lucy shook her head. "Not yet. Going solely by the mole on her upper lip, her age, petite stature, and the approximate timeline, she might be a woman whose body was discovered in Vancouver's Eastside in the spring of 1995. But DNA testing is a long shot, with nothing of Wanetta's beyond a well-handled photograph. Even so, Merryfield is convinced we're on the right track, and so am I. Miracles happen every day. Look what happened to John Doe of Regina. His case was solved after 26 years."

Twenty-six years. I hoped it wouldn't be that long for Wanetta Georgina Bulmer.

I LIT a candle and poured a glass of wine after Denim left and typed up my notes. Despite our best efforts, we knew little more about Wanetta Bulmer than when we started. Kelly Anne and Travis

Acquolina were perhaps alive and maybe using different names. On the plus side, Jamie Gardiner had turned his life around and sidebar to that, so had Levon. As for the actual case, we hadn't found Veronica, but we had found Kate's father and grandmother, and the two had become friends.

I thought about my mother's yearbooks, knowing it was possible—no probable—that I would have discovered none of it if Yvette hadn't given them to me. Karma? Or some other mystical or spiritual force?

As for Denim, she had proved to be a worthy partner, and the "emergency diner business" with her stepbrother Levi turned out to be a lead that allowed her to nail down her ex and her former best friend's whereabouts. I hoped she—and they—got what was coming to them. In the meantime, Lindsay Doucette had e-transferred twice the amount of my invoice into my bank account and I paid that forward by doubling Denim's earnings. It would allow her a bit of time in the event a new case didn't come up right away.

I sent a quick text to Misty, Gloria Grace, and Chantelle, promising to update them on Veronica's case. It hadn't been solved yet, and maybe it never would be, but I knew that Merryfield would go to his grave trying.

Merryfield. I took a sip of wine and thought about him. Maybe I should take a chance, call him, only this time it wouldn't be about business. Nothing ventured, nothing gained, right?

And then fate and his text intervened. I glanced at the clock, 5:55.

Smiled at his message, then laughed.

GREEN BEANS, NO ALMONDS?

THE END

AUTHOR'S NOTE

The character of Lucy Daneluk, founder of the fictional Ontario Registry of Missing and Unidentified Adults, was first introduced in *A Fool's Journey*. While the character of Brandon Colbeck was a compilation of several missing persons, the character of John Doe of Regina was based upon the actual case of an unidentified man listed on Missingadults.ca.

Two years after publishing *A Fool's Journey*, and 26 years after his death, John Doe of Regina was identified by Jerry Bell of the Saskatchewan Coroner's Office using DNA evidence, though at the family's request, John Doe's name has not been made public.

Like *Skeletons in the Attic*, *Past & Present*, and *A Fool's Journey*—the previous titles in the Marketville Mysteries—*Before There Were Skeletons* is a work of fiction and the missing persons cases referenced in this novel are fabrications based on several unsolved case files.

Unfortunately, there is no shortage of missing and unidentified adults. At the time of this writing, there are more than 1,200 cases of long-term missing adults and some 270 sets of human remains in Ontario alone. According to the Royal Canadian Mounted Police (RCMP), in any given year, between 70,000 and 80,000 people are reported missing to police in Canada.

While most missing persons are found within seven days, these disappearances can be extremely stressful for family and loved ones, and the harsh reality is that many cases remain unsolved years, even decades, later. While the police often make public appeals for information about cold cases, sites like Ontario Missing Adults, Canada's Missing, and the Doe Network provide a permanent plea for assistance, a portal for families who are looking for information about police processes, or who may be hesitant to make first contact with police.

It is my hope that this novel leads to the awareness of compiled websites, and possibly, information on, or the resolution of, a cold case.

Judy Penz Sheluk
October 2022

ACKNOWLEDGMENTS

If you follow me on social media, you know that I'm the owner of a Golden Retriever named Leroy Jethro "Gibbs," after the Mark Harmon character on *NCIS*. What you might not know is that Gibbs is my fourth purebred golden, though I owned a Golden-who-knows-what-mix, Sandy, as a kid. My love of Goldens led me to goldenrescue.ca several years ago. Since then, I've logged a few volunteer hours, made purchases from their online store, and donated copies of my books to their online silent auctions, the latter brilliantly organized by Wanetta Doucette-Goodman.

Now, if you've read the book and are following the clues, you'll have already put together that *Before There Were Skeletons* includes the following characters: Wanetta Georgina Bulmer, Lindsay Doucette, and Kathleen "Kate" Goodman. But there's more to this story. At a past Golden Rescue silent auction, I donated a "Name the Character" for the next instalment of the Marketville Mysteries. Wanetta placed the winning bid and requested the character be named after her daughter-in-law, Kathleen

"Kate" Goodman. I subsequently learned that Kate has two sisters, Kelly and Kristine. Hence, Kelly Anne Acquolina and Kristine Paris. (Acquolina and Bulmer are the last names of two men I worked with decades ago and they just seemed to fit.) Paris? It's just as Kristine says in the book: I thought Kristine Paris sounded exotic.

There are also nods to Running Room and Running Free run club members from my marathoning past: thanks to Bernadette LaPorte, Sid Cadel, Ramona Choumont, Glenis McLaren, and Janis Jarvis for the inspiration behind the names of Bernadette Robertson, Cadel LaPorte, Ramona Hobson, baby Glenis, and Janis Choumont, and the street names Jarvis and McLaren. Your ongoing support of my writing journey from afar is truly appreciated.

But writing a book is a lot more than conjuring up names. I would be remiss if I didn't mention Janet Bell Crawford, another former running connection, who introduced me to her husband, André Crawford. A former University of Waterloo football player and a retired Deputy Chief of Police for York Region (the basis for the much-fictionalized Cedar County), André's knowledge of police procedures assisted in writing the scenes with Detective Sheridan Merryfield and university football training camp protocols. Any mistakes are mine, and mine alone.

Many thanks, as well, to Steve Daniel,

Canadian Football League (CFL) Record Book Editor, and Larry Irish, former coach of the Burlington Braves, who took the time to explain the ins and outs of the CFL draft process. Without their sage advice I would have created a world for 1970s high school quarterback Joey Perella that could not have existed.

A huge debt of gratitude also goes to Lusia Dion for suggesting several missing persons cases that got my creative juices flowing, and for her ongoing commitment to Ontario's missing and unidentified adults. Lucy Daneluk would be proud, and the world, and this book, are better off because of Lusia.

This book is also better because of the insights and efforts of my phenomenal editor, Ti Locke. Fate was indeed smiling upon me the day she entered my life, and I am blessed and humbled by her dedication and talent. Thanks, too, to my beta readers, Kathleen Costa, Lusia Dion (again), Mary Persch, and Petra Schmelzeisen, and to my proofreader, Catherine Bianco, for your commitment to making Marketville 4 the best it could be.

Last, but never least, to the readers who have followed Callie's journey, and to my husband, Mike, for his enduring belief in me, and my stories.

Judy Penz Sheluk

ABOUT THE AUTHOR

A former journalist and magazine editor, Judy Penz Sheluk is the bestselling author of the Glass Dolphin Mysteries and the Marketville Mysteries. Her short crime fiction appears in several collections, including the acclaimed Superior Shores anthologies, which she also edited.

Judy is a member of Sisters in Crime, International Thriller Writers, the Short Mystery Fiction Society, and Crime Writers of Canada, where she served as Chair on the Board of Directors. Find her at judypenzsheluk.com.

www.ingramcontent.com/pod-product-compliance
Lightning Source LLC
Chambersburg PA
CBHW072006190726
48293CB00001B/177